Paolo Dorsa was born in Naples, Italy, from a Brazilian father and an Italian mother. He spent much of his childhood in Brazil. Since 1995 he lives in Surrey. His wife is English and he has two children.

His job as a manager of an Italian bank lead him to live in Naples, Rome, Paris, Zurich, Los Angeles, New York, Hong Kong and finally England. He retired in 1997.

His first novel "Il Mercante", written in Italian, partially autobiographical, has been published in Italy in 2006 and now has been translated into English. He now spends his time between England and the island of Corsica where he is writing his second novel.

The Merchant
A Novel by Paolo Dorsa

Translated by
Denis V. Reidy

Paolo Dorsa

The Merchant

Translated by
Denis V. Reidy

To Ian.

24/11/2008

Vanguard Press

VANGUARD PAPERBACK

A CIP catalogue record for this title is
available from the British Library.

ISBN: 978 1 84386 442 4

Vanguard Press is an imprint of
Pegasus Elliot MacKenzie Publishers Ltd.
www.pegasuspublishers.com

First Published in 2008

Vanguard Press
Sheraton House Castle Park
Cambridge England

Printed & Bound in Great Britain

Dedication

To my wonderful, patient wife Jenny and to my children Valentina and Royston. Without their support this book wouldn't have been born…

Acknowledgements

I would like to thank Ben and Margaret Miller-Smith, my best friends in England and my personal proof-readers, for their advice and all the giggles while working on the English version of this book.

1

Tonio had reluctantly agreed to get in his car and to drive all the way to Saint Malo. The weather was not at all promising and he would willingly have remained at home all afternoon, and perhaps in the evening he would have gone to see one of those black and white films he enjoyed so much. He had not been able to say no to Irene's phone call. Those two nights spent with her, having only just met her the week before in the Post Office in Rue de Rennes, returned overwhelmingly to his memory. He had never met such an inexperienced and at the same time such a desirable girl, keen to learn what she called the 'prohibited frenzies' of sex. But then he had never before met such a spontaneous and open girl.

He had met her for the first time late one cold grey Saturday afternoon. She had been accompanied by Nunzia her elderly nanny and maid, who was also her companion, who was trying to telephone her family at Caltanisetta. Tonio had witnessed with considerable amusement the squabble between the elderly woman and the post office clerk, who was trying to inform her in a rather ill-mannered way that the telephone was working perfectly well, but that she had to wait for the correct dialling tone, after the operator's voice, before dialling the number for Italy. Speaking in Italian with a very pronounced Sicilian accent, Nunzia kept on insisting that the telephone was not working and that the operator was ignoring her requests. The angrier she got the stronger her accent became, so much so that at a certain point even Tonio was unable to understand her any more.

Then the girl who was with the woman, and who was trying to calm her down in a subdued voice, turned round almost as if she was trying to excuse herself to the other people behind them in the queue. Tonio was presented with the vision of a very beautiful face framed by long, black, raven hair and fleshy sensual lips. But what struck him most were the eyes: large, tender and a colour he was not able to determine because of the florescent lighting in the post office. Not black he decided, perhaps green. Tonio intended to look at them more closely if he had an opportunity. She was wearing a fox fur, a little on the sophisticated side for such a young woman, which however she carried off nonchalantly.

"May I? May I be of assistance?" said Tonio moving closer to the two women.

"Ah, you are Italian? Yes of course, by all means," the woman replied. And, dealing the clerk a further deadly glance, "He seems to me to be a *citrulo*[*] who doesn't understand anything, or who pretends he doesn't understand."

Deliberately ignoring the girl, Tonio concentrated on the woman and explained to her calmly that you had to be patient with these state employees who were poorly paid and ill-mannered. He took her to the telephone booth and helped her to dial the correct number for Sicily. After two attempts a male voice answered at the other end. Tonio was quick to hand over the mouthpiece to the woman who, almost as if in the presence of a miracle, began to shout that they were well; that the train journey had been long and tiring; that the hotel was perfect, but that the girl hadn't slept much. Then with frenetic movements she gestured to the young woman to come closer and to 'say hello to *babbone*'.

While the girl was talking to her father, the woman introduced herself to Tonio as Nunzia Fitelli, the nanny and lady

---

[*] Cucumber

companion to donna Irene Consalvo, the daughter of the celebrated don Calogero Consalvo. He was the owner of alimentary establishments known throughout the world, producers (among other things) of the famous Pasta Consalvo, and of the even more famous digestive liqueur Amaro Consalvo which had been the favourite drink of King Vittorio Emanuele. Donna Irene was due to marry don Peppino Cantera, who had inherited from his father, God rest his soul, the extremely rich sulphur mines *Cantera Mines* in the Province of Catania.

Nunzia was able to impart this information and further details in less than two minutes flat, the time that it took donna Irene to greet and reassure *babbone*.

"Irene, how can we thank our saviour?" the woman said to the girl who was leaving the telephone booth, and to Tonio, "What did you say your name was?" and without waiting for the reply, "Isn't my girl a real beauty?" Irene's eyes met Tonio's for an instant, and for Tonio it was like an electrical discharge along his spine. They were green as he suspected. A very intense green with light golden streaks which gave them an aura of incredible depth and sincerity but at the same time a great luminosity as if they wished to communicate to the world an uncontrollable joy for life. Tonio found it difficult to take his eyes off those of the girl. Irene bore no trace of make-up, but the natural pink colour of her lips seemed almost the result of a hint of an extremely expensive lipstick. For a thousandth of a second Tonio imagined he was nibbling that mouth…

"Nunzia! Don't embarrass me," the girl said in an imperious manner, and turning to Tonio with a faltering voice said in a delightful and light Sicilian intonation, "You have been really kind to help us. At home they have been waiting for news of us since yesterday. Now, however, we have to go and do some shopping. In fact do you happen to know where this shop is?" she asked him showing him the page of a *'Roche Bobois'* catalogue.

"Certainly, in Boulevard Saint Germain, not far from here. We can walk there. I'll come with you."

"Good Lord, don't trouble yourself," said Irene, "you have already helped us too much; I'm sure that you have other things to do."

"No trouble; anyway I have to go that way," Tonio lied.

On the way Nunzia explained to him, with a certain amount of embarrassment on Irene's part, that they were in Paris to finalise the dowry which donna Irene was bringing to her marriage, making any changes which she deemed necessary. In this Don Calogero had been quite clear. 'If there's something which you don't like, then by all means change it my girl, provided it's sensible of course. And if there is something which you really like, buy it by all means, within the bounds of reasonableness.' They were going to Roche Bobois to inspect all the household items such as, curtains, fabrics, furniture and other things bought by Irene's father during one of his last business trips to Paris.

The manager of the shop, Monsieur Picard, was very pleased to make Mademoiselle Consalvo's acquaintance, as the daughter of Monsieur Consalvo, one of their best clients of many years standing.

Tonio remained at a discreet distance admiring some *art deco* ornaments of good quality. At a certain point, however, he was called upon to help resolve a problem of language given that the manager's knowledge of Italian was rather limited. Taking advantage of the moment, Nunzia proudly showed him the items of furniture which were destined for donna Irene's bedroom suite.

"Look, aren't they fit for a queen?"

Tonio admired the shape of the bed and the bedside tables, but he was somewhat bewildered by the festoons of gilded leaves which covered most of the woodcarvings.

"You don't like them, do you?" It was Irene's voice behind his shoulders. "I saw your face in that mirror down there; tell the truth."

"Well...to tell the truth I like the furniture a lot, only that...all that gold, at least for my taste, seems a bit too...but it depends on how the rest of the room is furnished..."

Irene sat on the bed, and ran her hand over the gilded leaves of the headboard and then on those of the bedside tables; she got up again and said, "Could you ask this gentleman if I can have this furniture without the gilding?"

"But are you sure? I wouldn't want to have influenced you with my ideas. And then what would your father say?"

"*Babbone?* No, don't worry; *babbone* has given me free rein to change things if I want to."

"Within the bounds of reasonableness, of course."

"Within the bounds of reasonableness, of course," she repeated, laughing.

Tonio explained to the manager the changes Irene wanted. Naturally there weren't any problems, even if he was informed that the design was an exact reproduction of the decoration on a certain bedroom suite which could be admired in the Chateau of Chambord in the Loire Valley.

Before leaving Irene was asked to sign a document for final confirmation of the order. She was about to do so when Tonio stopped her and told Monsieur Picard that in his view the price of the furniture should be reduced since all the valuable and handmade gold ornamentation had been removed. After a brief discussion in French, the manager agreed to a reduction of five per cent on the original price, promising to send a new invoice to Irene's hotel the following day. Once out of the shop, Tonio explained what had happened. The two women looked at him with admiration and when Nunzia discovered that they had saved more than two million lire she grabbed him by the hand

and kissed it saying, "You are an angel come down from heaven!" once more provoking Irene's silvery laughter.

"Really," said the girl, "how can we repay you? Can you imagine *babbone*'s reaction when I tell him? I feel that I should repay you in some way…"

"Good Lord," said Tonio. "Listen, don't even talk about repayment – but I do have an idea. What do you think about having dinner with me this evening? I will allow you to pay for the aperitifs so that we are all square. What do you say? If you haven't got any other plans of course."

"Certainly…we haven't got other plans…but...I don't know…Nunzia, what do you think?"

"Donna Irene, I think that's all right. Signor Tonio seems a decent type. I'm sure that Don Calogero would approve. I will always remain with you, without offence, Signor Tonio."

"All right then," said Irene. "On one condition though: that the dinner is on us."

"Donna Irene!" said Tonio in a mock-offended tone. "That remains to be seen. But I can tell you straight away that from where I come from no one has ever seen or heard of a gentleman being the guest of two beautiful women, especially when they are visiting the country in which he lives."

They arranged that Tonio would pick up the two women from the lobby of the Meurice Hotel, where they were staying, at eight o'clock that same evening.

At eight, Tonio met the two women in the lobby as agreed, and he took them to La Coupole Restaurant in Montparnasse in his soft-top Triumph sports car, which fortunately had space for an extra passenger to sit, albeit not very comfortably, on the rear seat.

The women were amazed at the size of the restaurant and at the great number of diners already present at eight o' clock.

"Did you know," said Irene, "that at eight, restaurants in Sicily are still empty? In my country we only begin dining at around ten."

"Well," replied Tonio, "here you have to get used to eating a little earlier even if this particular restaurant is open all night. But let's see what we can order. I can recommend the onion soup. It's very good; it is a typical French dish. I'm sure that you'll like it. And for a main course, possibly a fine *filet au poivre,* which is a slice of beef cooked in a pepper sauce with French fried potatoes as an accompaniment, as only the French know how to cook it."

"Onions?" said Nunzia, "where we come from onions are for poor people: they eat them raw with bread…no…do you think that I could order a fine plate of pasta: perhaps *ziti* with aubergines?"

"But Nunzia, what are you saying?" interjected Irene. "Here we are in France, in Paris, and I really don't think that we'll be able to find something typical from home. Moreover, I want to try everything which isn't Sicilian. Do you know what I'll do? I'm going to follow Signor Tonio's advice and seeing that I'm really hungry, I'm having the onion soup and the fillet."

Saying this, she looked Tonio straight in the eye with such an intensity as to make him giddy.

"And the wine? Will you have a drop of wine? What would you say to a good French wine?"

"Why not. We like a drop of wine don't we Nunzia? We are used to the wine we drink at home; the one which *babbone* produces at Mazara del Vallo is really good, even if you have to be a bit careful as it's a bit on the strong side, and can go to your head. And our dear Nunzia knows something about that eh?"

"Donna Irene, I beseech you, don't show me up and make me out as a poor figure…"

"No, certainly not, you know how much I love you. Now, Signor Tonio, tell us what are you doing here in Paris? What kind of work do you do? You know everything about us whereas we don't know anything about you yet. It doesn't seem fair!" Saying this she rested her chin on the back of her crossed hands, assuming the air of a person who is interested and at the same time amused, and with her enormous eyes fixed on Tonio.

"Nothing particularly interesting really. For the last two years I've been the Branch Manager of an Italian bank here in Paris and…"

"What do you mean?" Irene interrupted, "you are the manager of a bank here in Paris and you say so as if it were nothing. But do you know that from where we come from a bank manager is an important person, who everybody listens to and respects…just think, one of *babbone*'s closest friends is the manager of the Banco di Sicilia…"

"But he's old," interrupted Nunzia, "and also a bit soft in the head!"

"Nunzia, please. Don Gaetano is such a good person, and then…"

Irene was interrupted by the waiter who came to take their orders. Tonio ordered dinner and a bottle of Bordeaux, speaking in French.

"How well you speak French!" Irene complimented him with another admiring glance. This time Tonio was not able to resist and exchanged her glance with one of equal intensity making her blush slightly. Irene continued to tell him how Don Gaetano, although over seventy years old, kept courting her discreetly without the knowledge of his very ugly wife. Tonio could hardly listen to her, by now completely bewitched by her eyes and by her mouth. Irene was speaking in a gentle but firm voice, with deep tones when she wanted to stress something. At the same time she looked straight into the eyes of whoever was in front of her and a couple of times Tonio felt uncomfortable when confronting such a limpid and direct gaze.

When the waiter arrived with the wine Tonio poured it into the glasses of the two women and proposed a toast. "Permit me to toast donna Irene's happiness. I wish you every blessing and many male children. And I also toast don Peppino Cantera: the luckiest man in the world." Tonio drank the wine without taking his eyes off the girl. Irene returned his glance without blushing this time. "You are really very courteous Signor Tonio; I appreciate this toast very much indeed. I detected so much sincerity in your voice. Thank you," said Irene, putting a hand on his arm.

"Donna Irene, I don't know you well, but I'm certain you deserve my toast," Tonio replied, in turn resting his hand for an instant on hers.

Nunzia, who wasn't aware of these minor manoeuvres, was intent on tasting the Bordeaux and seemed to be really enjoying it; so much so that her glass was soon empty and Tonio naturally was quick to top it up again.

When the onion soup arrived, there was a moment of perplexity for the two women; but as soon as they tasted it they were surprised by its special, intense taste. "I didn't expect anything like this *Signor* Tonio, you have really got it right with your suggestion, and this fine wine goes really well with the soup," Nunzia said, downing another glass of wine.

Before the arrival of the fillet, Tonio ordered another bottle despite the protests of Irene and the more restrained ones of Nunzia.

During the rest of dinner Tonio narrated to Irene the period of his youth spent in Brazil; how he had returned to Italy at the age of twelve; his studies in Naples; the beginnings of his career in banking and his travels in Europe and Africa. The girl was fascinated by these stories and when they had reached the stage when the fruit was served, said, "Do you know Signor Tonio, I on the other hand have travelled very little. I went skiing in Switzerland last year with *babbone*, but I didn't like it very much, and three years ago we took a trip to the main cities in Italy: Milan, Venice, Florence, Rome and Naples. And the one I liked the most was Naples. I'm telling you this not because you are from Naples, Signor Tonio, but because it is a bright, vibrant place…by the way, do you mind if I call you Tonio, and we address each other with the 'tu' form? I can't explain it but I have the impression that I have known you for many years and not just a few hours…and you…call me Irene please…"

"But of course certainly, donna Irene…sorry, Irene." They burst out laughing.

"I too have the feeling that I have known you a long time," said Tonio, and after a quick glance at Nunzia, took her by the hand.

Irene did not withdraw her hand, quite the contrary, she held Tonio's fingers in her fingers and in a very low voice said to him, "I think that our little Nunzia has had her fill. I have a feeling that when we come to leave we will have to help her. Her liking for wine is her only fault. She is such a good woman and she really loves me very much. She has almost been for me the mother I never had. My mother died when I was only two years old…that's why *babbone* and I are so attached to each other…he really suffered a great deal…in fact, he never got over it, and he tends to spoil me. I try not to upset him and to make him happy. *Babbone* is a marvellous person and only wants my happiness, even if recently there has been a bit of a squabble between us, precisely over this marriage…but let's forget it."

"But no, go on, please."

"No, forget it," and then, "Nunzia! What are you doing, are you asleep with your eyes open? Oh Mother of Mercy, she's had too much wine. What are we going to do now?"

"Irene, don't worry. I'll sort things out. I'll go and get the car and bring it to the front of the building, and I'll help her to get in. Would you mind too much if you were to rough it a bit in the back?"

" Of course not."

Tonio paid the bill quickly, went and got the car and parked right in front of the entrance to the restaurant. Amid the bemused glances of the other clients, Tonio and Irene helped Nunzia get into the car. The young woman settled down in the back and Tonio, who did not wish to leave Irene so soon, said, "Look Irene, would you like to go for a trip round Paris in the car by night? It's a very beautiful city. After all Nunzia is asleep here at the front."

"Um, I don't know. Perhaps it's best not to. I'm afraid that Nunzia might not feel well…and I wouldn't want her to get your car dirty. No, let's take her to the hotel please."

"Your wish is my command donna Irene."

"Thank you Signor Tonio," and they burst out laughing.

Having arrived at the hotel it was not easy to wake Nunzia and to get her to walk in a straight line. With Irene on one side and Tonio on the other, they propped her up as far as the lifts. In the few moments they were waiting, Nunzia abandoned herself completely into Tonio's arms, and once in the lift, she even began to snore.

"The shame of it! I'm really embarrassed."

"Don't worry. I think the whole thing's very funny. I've never seen a person asleep standing upright like this before, and snoring into the bargain!"

Having arrived at the right floor, Irene opened the door to the room, switched on the light and walked towards another half open door.

"Here, this is Nunzia's room," she said, "let's get her up on the bed. Perhaps later on I'll undress her and I'll make her put her nightdress on."

Tonio moved closer to the woman on the bed and said to her in a rather loud voice, "Good night Nunzia. Sweet dreams!"

"Even cannon fire won't wake this one!" said Irene, closing the door gently.

There was an embarrassed silence between the two of them as soon as they realised that they were alone together in a hotel bedroom.

2

“Tonio, I don’t know how to thank you. I don’t know what I would have done without you.”

“Well for one, if it wasn’t for me, our little Nunzia wouldn’t have got drunk. And it’s been really amusing, I’ve spent a fantastic evening in your company. But there’s something I’d like to ask you. Could I trouble you for a glass of water? All this movement has made me thirsty.” He was lying. He only wanted to delay his departure from her by a few minutes.

“But of course Tonio, there’s some mineral water in this mini bar. I’m going to have some too.”

They drank, looking into each other’s eyes, smiling at each other. Tonio rested the glass on a piece of furniture and said, “There’s something else I’d like to ask you, but I don’t want you to get angry.”

“What is this something else?” she asked, unexpectedly serious all of a sudden.

“Well, I’d like…you promise me you won’t get angry?”

“My God how you are dragging it out. Come on then out with it. In the first place I don’t think that you can make me angry when we hardly know each other…well then?”

“Well…I’d like to give you a kiss. May I give you a good night kiss?”

“Yes!”

“What do you mean ‘yes’? But…?”

“Yes,” Irene repeated, drawing near to Tonio. He took her in his arms and gave her an innocent kiss on the cheek.

Irene did not draw back when he continued embracing her. Slowly she turned her face towards his, half closing her eyes. Tonio accepted her invitation and kissed her on the lips. It was a long and tender kiss. At first it was delicate then, little by little, Irene slightly parted her lips and their tongues began to explore each other. Tonio embraced her even more closely and when his hands began to caress her back, Irene began to breathe heavily, abandoning herself even more to his embrace.

All of a sudden she drew back from Tonio and said, "Holy Mother, what am I doing? Now you'll think I'm a slut."

"Irene," Tonio said, clasping her more closely to him. "You could never be a slut. I feel it's as if I have known you a lifetime. You're...pure. I can see it...you're too beautiful for the dirt of this world to touch you."

The girl did not say anything. She knitted her eyebrows for an instant and then clasped his face in her hands, and kissed him with an impetuosity, which took Tonio by surprise.

With Irene clasped to him, Tonio approached the bed.

All of a sudden Irene must have felt his erection because she stopped abruptly and with her eyes wide open, said, "Tonio you're...you're...how do you say? Excited?"

"Well, you know...I can't help it...you're so beautiful...I'm sorry."

"You mustn't say you're sorry. I know that it's perfectly natural when two people like each other. And I do like you...but we have to stop here..."

"You're right, perhaps it's better if..."

Irene, however, did not allow him to finish. She embraced him so strongly that they fell on the bed kissing each other once again.

Tonio began kissing her on the neck while Irene's breath became increasingly heavy. He began to unbutton her blouse giving her gentle little kisses on her breasts which were still covered. After a while he helped her take it off, he turned her to one side and undid her bra.

Tonio had never seen anything so beautiful. The extreme whiteness of her breasts contrasted with the darker areas of her small nipples. He looked at her and noticed that the girl was blushing profusely while keeping her eyes tightly closed.

"Irene" he whispered in her ear. "I would never do anything against your will. If you don't want to, tell me."

"I understand…come here, kiss me again."

Tonio obliged her, caressing her breasts at the same time. Then he began unbuttoning his shirt while she looked on.

"Tonio, do you know that I've never seen…well, in a word…a man naked. Apart from my cousins when we were little…"

Tonio got up from the bed and took off his trousers and remained there in his boxer shorts. Then he undid her skirt, removed it and helped her to take off her stockings. When he began to take off her silk panties Irene closed her eyes once more and blushed.

"Irene," he said to her. "You have a fantastic body. It's really beautiful."

"And you are the first to see it…like this."

"Really? Then in that case, I'm the luckiest man in the world."

Tonio took off his shorts revealing his completely erect and throbbing penis.

Irene looked at it for a few moments and stretching her hand out to touch it, said, "How big it is…I didn't think that it could become so. It's…it's lovely."

"Come here, *piccolina,*[*]" Tonio told her, "hold me tightly and kiss me."

---

[*] Little one

Tonio's hands gradually began touching her in her most sensitive areas, and after a while Irene responded to his caresses, and started moving slowly.

When Tonio began touching her between her legs, parting them gently, Irene moved more decisively, her eyes closed, emitting a gently subdued moan. Tonio began to slide down the length of the girl's body, kissing and running his tongue first over her breasts, then gently and gradually lower until he reached the black triangle of her pubic area.

By this stage the girl's legs were completely open, and Tonio began passing his tongue first over the surface and then on both sides, and then he inserted it inside as far as he could. Irene abandoned herself to a pleasure she was experiencing for the first time and was savouring every moment.

After a while, Tonio reaching the limit of his endurance, said, "Irene, *amore mio*, I want you. I want to make love!"

"Me too," she said, short of breath.

"Are you sure?"

"Yes, I'm sure. But you have to show me. I don't know…be gentle…"

"I realise that it's the first time for you…I wouldn't want…"

"Yes, it's the first time. And I want to do it with you."

Tonio was amazed at the force and the determination with which she spoke these words. He perceived the repressed desire for something the girl perhaps knew she would no longer have afterwards. For an instant he asked himself what had moved Irene to speak in this fashion. He was disconcerted by the spontaneity and the innocence with which she had offered herself to him.

Slowly and gently, keeping the girl's legs open with his, he slowly entered her. At first he found some resistance in the narrow passage, then he began to push and to move backwards and forwards slowly until he felt something which was slowly yielding and he penetrated her completely. Irene uttered a gentle cry. Tonio stopped for an instant to look, and he saw that the girl had a tear rolling down the side of her eye, and that she was biting her lip.

"*Amore mio,*" he whispered to her, "have I hurt you? Forgive me."

"No, no, don't worry. Don't stop…I like it…I like it when you call me *amore mio.*"

"*Amore mio, amore mio, amore mio,*" Tonio repeated in her ear.

He moved inside her in a slow and regular rhythm, kissing her on her lips, her eyes and her neck. After many minutes, he realised that Irene was nearing the height of her pleasure, as she was moving increasingly quickly. When the girl finally reached it, she emitted a deep raucous scream, digging her nails into his back.

Tonio held back for a few seconds and then let himself go, savouring every moment of that extremely intense pleasure. He moved in an ever increasing rhythm and at the last moment, in a pang of conscience, the instant before the explosion, he withdrew spreading his seminal fluid over her stomach.

Then they stretched out panting for a few minutes, in each other's arms, without speaking.

It had been a completely new experience for Tonio. Even though he had known many women with whom he had made love in a hundred different ways, this time he experienced a new and very deep sensation. Confused, he asked himself what was the cause of this gratification which was so complete and at the same time so different. The fact that Irene had abandoned herself to him in such a complete way caused him to be euphoric, but at the same time, raised his curiosity. He could not believe it possible that he should be the receiver of such good fortune. An immense tenderness towards the girl pervaded his being. While he was still lying on top of her, he opened his eyes, he looked at her and he caressed her face.

Irene opened her eyes and smiled at him.

After a little while when the panting of the two young people had settled down, Tonio rolled over and raising himself on his elbows, asked her, "How do you feel *piccolina*?" Irene did not reply. Her eyes were closed and she seemed to be asleep.

"Irene…"

The girl slowly opened her eyes, turned towards him and said, "Tonio…it was fantastic! I had no idea it could be like this. It's been like going to heaven for an instant and then coming back…I've seen new colours, I've heard new sounds…I don't know how to explain it…it was fantastic!" She knitted her eyebrows as if to concentrate her mind and continued, "This burning sensation between my legs…I wish it could remain for ages to remind me that I haven't been dreaming."

Irene became silent and closed her eyes once more. After a while she asked him, "And for you Tonio, how was it for you? With all the women that you've certainly known…"

He did not reply straight away. After a while he said to her, "Irene for me it was…I don't know how to describe it…different. Yes, different. In a certain sense, you might not even believe me, but it was as if it had been 'a first time' for me too. It's true I've been with many women. You know it's easy in a city like Paris, being a bachelor and without a care in the world, to find female companionship. But with you…I don't know…I felt as if I were infected by your spontaneity, by your…by your…that's it, by your purity. At this very moment I'm really very happy indeed. And proud to have been offered this gift by you."

"Good Lord, how many big words, *Tunuzzu,*" said Irene, passing her fingers through his hair. "And do you know something?" she continued, "I don't know how I'll feel tomorrow. Perhaps I'll hate myself for what I've done, but I too feel very happy now." After a while she added, "And what's this story of a gift? What gift? I haven't made you a gift of anything whatsoever. If anything, it's you who have given me something. You've introduced me to a new world. New sensations…really beautiful ones. It's me who should be thanking you."

They remained in silence for quite a long time, naked, stretched out on the bed, lost in their own thoughts.

The room was in semi darkness lit only by reflections from the lampposts on the street. At a certain point Tonio said, "Irene, I wish you a happy life with all my heart. Really!"

The girl remained silent so that Tonio thought that she had fallen asleep. However, after a while, he heard her voice which whispered, "I believe you."

Then she turned towards him and embraced him closely, kissing him once more.

They made love again. Tonio moved inside her with a slow, constant rhythm bringing the girl to orgasm several times. At the end Tonio reached his climax, experiencing the same emotions as before, but this time perhaps even more intensely.

By now it was dawn. Tonio gathered his things and dressed.

"I don't like leaving," he said to her. "I'd like to fall asleep next to you. But could you imagine Nunzia's face if she found us in bed together, later on?"

"Poor little Nunzia. She really loves me, you know," she said, putting on her nightdress. "After mummy's death, I was only two years old, she has been my nanny, sister, confidante, but above all, a friend to me. I tell Nunzia everything. Well, nearly everything. She is a woman who has suffered a lot in life. You may see her now as a bit of a figure of fun, a bit of a country bumpkin, but she's full of wisdom."

"I can see that she worships you. But, there again, who couldn't love you. Listen, can I ask you…how did your mother die?"

"In a car accident. My father was driving. A lorry drove into him from a side road. His car went off the road and hit a rock. *Babbone* lost a leg and my mother died instantly."

"Irene, that's awful. And you were only two?"

"Yes."

"But how could it have happened? Was the lorry driver drunk?"

"They told me that the lorry didn't even bother to stop. They found it the day after in a field. Burnt out. It had been stolen the week before. They never found the driver."

"Jesus!"

Tonio approached her and clasped her to his chest.

"I'm sorry," he told her.

Before leaving, he gave her his business card on which he wrote his address, and told her to call him the following day as soon as she was awake.

The roads were deserted. Driving home he thought about the evening and the night he had spent with Irene. He smiled to himself, and once more felt a strong feeling of tenderness for that young woman who had entered so dramatically into his life.

"Entered into my life?" he asked himself. He could not think of Irene as an affair of a few hours' duration, on a par with many others. He knew only too well that the following day she would have gone and he might never see her again.

This thought saddened him.

Having arrived in Rue Blériot he saw the baker's shop in front already open, he bought a freshly baked *baguette* and went home.

He had been in bed a few minutes when the telephone rang. Guessing who it might be, he answered it, saying, "I can't sleep either. I'm thinking of you."

"I only wanted to wish you good night once more. I'm thinking of you too."

There was a long silence and then Irene asked, "Tonio are you still there?"

"Yes."

"What's up? What are you thinking?"

After a pause, Tonio replied, "I don't know…you see, I've had a great time with you. I've been happy and I'm still very happy now…but…at the same time I get the feeling that I have taken advantage of you in a certain sense. I can't get it out of my mind that in a few days you're getting married. I get the feeling that I have stolen something which belongs to someone else…"

"I know what you mean," said Irene, "but you can imagine how I feel then? But no, at least tonight I don't regret what I've done. Tomorrow…that's another matter. Do you think I'm a whore?"

"No darling, absolutely not. Let's try and get some sleep now. Let's speak to each other tomorrow. Give me a ring as soon as you wake up."

"Good night. But I prefer it when you call me *amore mio*. Ciao."

3

By now he had been driving for almost two hours, and the weather had progressively worsened. Rain mixed with sleet made driving slower and more difficult than usual. Tonio had left early with the intention of getting to Saint Malo in four or five hours, in time to have lunch with Irene. At the start of his journey there had not been much traffic on the motorway for Rennes but now, about ten kilometres after the turn off for Le Mans, he was moving at a walking pace. Probably due to an accident, he thought.

The sound of the rain on the soft-top of the car, the rhythmic movement of the windscreen wipers and the slow speed made him feel drowsy causing him to open his side window every now and then to let some cold air into the car.

Irene had called him at noon the next day. Tonio had been awake for a while, he had slept little and not at all well, but without knowing the reason why he was in such a bad mood.

"Ciao," she said to him, "did I wake you?"

"No, of course not, I've been up since nine."

"How come? I slept like a log and I've had my fill of croissants, toasted bread and jam and they even brought me some cheese. Do they eat cheese here even in the morning? Do you eat it for breakfast?"

"No, certainly not."

"What's the matter? You seem to be a bit down. What's happened?"

"Nothing, absolutely nothing's happened to me," Tonio replied without being able to conceal a hint of irritation in his voice.

There was a moment's silence and then Irene said, "I'm sorry Tonio, perhaps I shouldn't have phoned you. At times I can be a bit too intrusive. Everyone says so. I'm sorry that..."

"No no," he replied. "It's nothing to do with you...the fact is, if you want to know the truth...I've done nothing but think of you since I left you. And I've realised that knowing that you have to leave...knowing that you're about to get married...and that you've come into my life at this very time, pisses me off, excuse my language.

"Please try and understand me and above all, don't think that any of this has anything to do with you. Well to be precise, it certainly has something to do with you, but none of it's your fault. Do you understand? I'm confused damn it, and pissed off with myself. I'm older than you by how much? Ten? Twelve? Perhaps fifteen years. In fact I never asked you how old you are. And here I am carrying on like a young lad who gets angry because things don't go his way. We left each other a few hours ago and I can't wait to see you. I want to make love to you again. I can't believe that I've missed you so much and that...well...don't take any notice...I'm the one who should be saying sorry to you."

There was a pause and then Irene said, "Have you finished?"

"Yes."

"Then we'll see each other later. That's if you'd like to, of course. Do you want to?"

"Of course. You know that I want to."

"Then come by and collect us in about an hour. Then we can do that tour of Paris which you promised us last night. Are you up for it?"

"But of course, I'll see you later."

What was happening to him? His bad mood had vanished all of a sudden. The mere thought of seeing Irene once more made him happy and elated.

Tonio arrived at the hotel within the hour and got the *concierge* to telephone Irene. As soon as she came down to the lobby she said that Nunzia was not feeling very well and could not go out for the time being.

Seeing the disappointment on Tonio's face, she suggested to him that they go up and see Nunzia. At least they could be together for a while.

Nunzia was in bed, looking very pale. She said that she had a very bad headache and was not up to going out. Moreover she was sorry not to be able to go to Sunday Mass.

"Nunzia, perhaps you'll be better later, in time to go to an evening Mass. I'm sure that there will be one somewhere in Paris," Tonio said.

"Good Lord! I'm just not up to it. I'm feeling a bit dazed."

After a while Irene said, "Nunzia, I don't want to miss Mass. Tonio, could you ask the hall porter to see if we can attend Mass somewhere around here, and could you possibly accompany me?"

"Of course, only too glad to."

The porter informed them that there was a Mass at five at Saint-Germain-des-Pres in the Latin Quarter; a Mass which was very well attended, because of its excellent choir, famous for their Gregorian Chants. He advised that they should go soon if they wanted to find a seat.

After having reassured Nunzia that they would return as soon as possible after the service, they set off as happy as two young school children. Having arrived in Place de la Concorde, Tonio pointed out the stately Champs Elysees.

"Marvellous isn't it?"

"It's fantastic. And where do you live?"

"Over there," he said, to her indicating vaguely towards the Tour Eiffel, which was looming up imposingly and distinctively amongst its surroundings.

"It's a small apartment but it suits me fine. In Rue Blériot on the bank of the Seine."

"Will you show it to me?"

"What, now?"

"Yes, now."

"But what about Mass?"

"It means that I'll have to go to confession and not only for not going to Mass, I'll have to do a double penance!" she said with a mischievous smile. "I'm really quite shameless aren't I?"

"No, not really. If you must know the truth, I was racking my brain to find an excuse to be alone with you. I'm dying to kiss you."

They went to Tonio's place and made love with renewed passion.

This time, however, knowing that they were totally alone, and consequently could abandon themselves completely to each other without inhibition, Tonio taught her many new things, which made sex even more pleasurable between them. He showed her new positions, and how to caress a man in certain areas of his body. He found Irene an attentive pupil with great eagerness to learn.

At a certain point she said to him, "I enjoy these…these prohibited frenzies of sex…but I think that I wouldn't be able to do this with another man, I'm sure of it. Well, at least not like…this. I'm completely at ease with you; I've never felt like this with anyone before. Let alone with a man. And if I think that we've known each other for only a few hours, that makes it all the more incredible…Tonio, I also thought of you for a long time before falling asleep last night, and my first thought on waking this morning was for you. And there is another thing I must tell you: please don't think of me as a slut or whatever, but

I really don't regret what I've done. I don't know what the consequences of all this will be for me or for my future life, but I'm happy now. And nobody can take this away from me." She said this in a deep voice but almost in a whisper looking him straight in the eye.

When they returned to the hotel it was almost nine o'clock. They found an extremely worried Nunzia up in Irene's room. From the way that she looked at them, Tonio had the distinct impression that she had understood everything. He saw Irene blush profusely, and noticed she avoided Nunzia's stare as she went back into her bedroom without saying a word to Irene.

Irene said, "Tonio, I think it's best if you were to leave now, things are not too good here. It's best if I try and calm the poor woman down, tomorrow morning we're leaving early. I'll phone you when we arrive at Saint Malo."

Tonio went straight home, arriving just in time to hear the telephone ring. Irene said to him, "Will you think of me again tonight?"

"Well to tell you the truth, I don't think so," he joked. "I'm waiting to hear from three or four girls who I've had to put on hold while seeing you this weekend."

"Do you really want to finish up facing a *lupara*?[*] Don't forget I'm a Sicilian lass. Watch it or I'll send a couple of *picciotti*[**] round to you, and they'll give you a good going over – get my drift?"

"Donna Irene, I've got the message, loud and clear…now listen here *picciotta*, when are you getting married?"

There was a moment's silence.

"Must we really talk about this now? I've hardly given it a moment's thought over these last two days…it's as if I've erased it from my mind, at least for the time being…Well, it's obvious

---

[*] A sawn-off shotgun often used by the mafia
[**] The lowest rank in the mafia hierarchy

that it's always there, but it's as if I've shelved it for the moment. I suppose in a few days' time I'll have feelings of remorse..." There was a long silence. Then she continued, "Do you know it's odd, but at this very moment I feel as if I've wronged my father, rather than Peppino."

"But do you love Peppino?"

"Look, I'm marrying him in a month's time!"

"Yes, but you haven't answered my question."

"Why do you want to know?"

"Nothing, just...out of curiosity."

"Tonio...Tonio...are you jealous?"

"No, I don't have any right to be jealous...it's only to...to know you better, that's it." And after a while he added, "Well then? Do you love him?"

"I'm very fond of him...I don't know...I believe it's love."

"I understand."

"What do you understand?"

"Nothing, I understand...are you sure that you're not doing this just to please *babbone*?"

"Look I should really take offence at what you've said...no, it isn't like that...of course I know that *babbone*'s pleased. But I'm not doing it just to please him."

"But you and Peppino..."

"I beg you Tonio, stop it now. I don't feel like talking about Peppino, *babbone*, the wedding...no, not tonight, please...it's best if we turn in. Moreover I've heard some sounds coming from the other room. I hope Nunzia hasn't heard anything."

"Yes you're right...goodnight...*amore mio*."

"Goodnight...Tonio?"

"Yes?"

"I'm twenty-two."

4

It had taken him more than half an hour to drive only two kilometres.

At the junction for Le Mans, the gendarmes were forcing all cars to turn off the road; the motorway had been closed to traffic because of an accident. After consulting his road atlas, he decided to carry on along Route Nationale 138 in the direction of Alençon. He would then take the N.176 as far as Saint Malo. If the weather worsened, which seemed likely, it could take him more than four or five hours.

After about an hour he stopped at a service station to fill up, and he made the most of the stop by telephoning Irene. In the *pension* where she was staying, they told him that she had gone out, but they assured him that they would pass on his message to say that he would be delayed.

As forecast, the weather worsened. By now it was sleeting more than it was raining.

Tonio slowed down because he felt the car, which was not particularly suited to the bad weather conditions, had skidded a couple of times.

On the N.12, after Alençon, the road began to climb and with the snow, which was falling increasingly heavily, he found it difficult to read the road signs. He almost missed the turn off for the N.176.

He was forced to reduce his speed further. If things continued like this, he would have to abandon his journey.

By now it was after midday, he decided to stop and have something to eat. The traffic was very light. After about twenty minutes he noticed a sign for the town of Domfront, only three kilometres away.

At that very moment he was overtaken by a large, dark, Mercedes whose wheels splashed snow and mud onto the lower Triumph. Tonio lost sight of the road ahead for a few seconds. Swearing, he had to brake hard, causing the car to skid violently. He followed in the wake of the Mercedes, which gradually left him behind.

Having arrived in Domfront, the town seemed to him to be larger than it appeared on the map. It was lunchtime and the weather was bad. The few shops that there were all seemed to be closed. He caught sight of a sign indicating the castle on the hill, but there was not a soul to be seen on the road.

He drove through Domfront following a narrow winding route, which was all bends until finally he noticed a board: *Le Coq Normand, Bar Restaurant à 1 km.*

It was just what he needed.

Near the restaurant he noticed that the Mercedes was stopping. The small car park in front was full of cars and there was even a coach there.

He managed to find a parking space between the coach and the restaurant's van. He reached the entrance to the restaurant at the same time as the owner of the Mercedes, who was carrying a brown leather document case with him. The two men entered the crowded restaurant at precisely the same moment; a waitress came up to them and thinking that they were together, showed them the only remaining free table.

Tonio pointed out to the girl that in fact they were not together. She said to them, stretching out her arms and looking around her, that that was the last free table. Then she explained that all those people in the restaurant were Belgian tourists who were travelling by coach on their way to Mont St. Michel, but they had decided to stop off there for lunch. Therefore...if *Messieurs* didn't mind, they could eat at the same table. Tonio and the owner of the Mercedes looked at each other, and with a shrug of the shoulders, said to the girl, almost in unison, "*et pourquoi pas*?"

As soon as they had sat down, while the waitress went to look for the menus, the man introduced himself to Tonio in French, which had a slight hint of a foreign accent, which Tonio thought to be German.

"*Enchanté, Pierre Haber.*" Tonio shook hands with him, introducing himself in his turn.

"*Enchanté, Antonio Brignani.*" Tonio felt that it was a firm, but at the same time, warm handshake.

"Are you Italian?" Haber asked him in Italian, almost with no trace of an accent.

"Yes, it's easy to guess, isn't it? And are you German?"

"Oh no, Good Lord no, I'm Swiss…I hope that we can eat well here, all this driving in the rain has whetted my appetite."

"Me too," said Tonio. "Anyway, in order to play it safe, I think I'll order a lovely steak with chipped potatoes. I think the French are in a class of their own when it comes to cooking them."

"Not a bad idea," the other agreed. Then he added, "I see that you drive a British sports car. How come? Being Italian I would've expected you to drive – let me see now – an Alfa Duetto or a Fulvia Coupé."

Tonio observed his companion at the table more closely. He was a handsome man, very tall, well-built, but slim at the same time, perhaps around sixty years of age. He was wearing a blue cashmere jacket with a white crew-neck jersey and dark-grey trousers. He had grey hair which was combed back, blue eyes, and a wide smile which inspired an immediate sympathy towards him.

Tonio at once thought of Curt Jurgens, a German actor who often played the part of a Nazi officer or a university professor in those black and white films, which he liked so much.

Precisely at that moment a man, who seemed to be the owner of the restaurant, approached their table bringing two menus with him.

Haber said to him, "There's no need for a menu. We're ready to order. We'd like two steaks, cooked rare, with a mountain of fried potatoes, which only you French know how to cook."

"Fine," said the man smiling, "and to drink?"

"I'd say a red wine, what do you think Signor Brignani?" he said turning to Tonio.

"Messieurs," interposed the man, "we have a good selection of bottled wines, Bordeaux, Burgundy, Beaujolais, Côtes du Rhone…but if I may suggest, I'd advise a house wine, which we serve by the carafe. It's a *petit vin* produced locally and is really quite good. If you don't like it you can always order a bottle of wine…"

"Let's go for the *petit vin,*" said Haber. "We must celebrate this meeting. Don't you agree Antonio?" Then when the owner of the restaurant had moved away from their table, he continued, "Let's use the more informal 'tu' form. We're about to have something to eat together…call me Pierre. I know that I could be your father, but I'm not one for standing on ceremony. Well then…about this British car?"

It was because of this question that Tonio told him how, when he had left Naples three years before, a friend of his had suggested to him, that since he and his wife were expecting their third child, Tonio should buy his 1964 Triumph sports car from him. Since Tonio was a bachelor and was about to leave for Paris, where he was due to work for an Italian bank with quite a good salary, a sports car just fitted the bill.

"So not only did I buy the Triumph off him, but also his collection of three hundred bottles of rare wines."

"And how did you manage to bring the wines to France? You didn't take them in the car did you?"

"No," replied Tonio smiling," the bank arranged to send them together with a few sticks of furniture, which I had in Naples."

The restaurant owner returned with the carafe of wine and waited for the two men to taste it.

"What's your name?" Pierre asked the man.

"Pascal, *Monsieur*."

"Well Pascal, you're right. This wine is really rather good. Let's hope that the steak matches it."

After Pascal had moved off, Tonio asked, "And what about you Pierre, what do you do?"

"I'm a consultant in the industrial sector…especially in the metallurgical field. The company I work for is located in Switzerland, but we have dealings in various parts of the world…in fact, I'm on my way to Rennes in order to meet a few partners; and you, where are you heading for in this foul weather?"

"I'm trying to get to Saint Malo this evening for dinner time, weather permitting."

"Saint Malo's a nice place. I was there as a student many years ago. Can I ask you why you're going to Saint Malo?"

"Well, if you really want to know the truth, I'm going to see a girl I met in Paris last week; she's Italian and she's there for a few days to learn a bit of French."

"She must be really worth it for you to undertake this dreadful journey…ah, how nice to be young…"

"Yes, I think so…she's really worth it."

"I'm curious to know more," said Pierre. "How did you meet her? Do you feel like talking about it?"

Tonio consequently found himself talking to a complete stranger about his meeting with Irene and Nunzia, which provoked a deep, spontaneous and contagious peal of laughter in Pierre when he told him how the older woman got drunk.

He also told him – without going into too much detail naturally – how he found it marvellous to be making love to the girl.

Without realising it, almost as if he were speaking to himself, he revealed his true feelings for Irene – the confusion which had taken hold of him, and the fear of harming himself, but above all the girl, whom he considered to be young and vulnerable.

Pierre remained silent, sipping his wine, but it was clear that he was listening attentively, giving the impression that he was participating in and sharing Tonio's sentiments.

When the steaks arrived, together with the huge plate of chips, Tonio interrupted his story and said, "Pierre I'm boring you…the steak seems to be as good as the wine, let's get stuck in."

"Yes, the steak seems really good…but no, I'm not at all bored. Rather, I should thank you for confiding things to me which are so personal. You see Tonio, I admire people who aren't afraid of unburdening themselves and their true feelings, even to a total stranger, as is the case with us.

"In my opinion, this is a sign of interior strength, of someone who has nothing to hide, and who has an optimistic view of the world. I also admire your concern for this girl. You like her, but you'd be sorry to hurt her. Admirable, but let me tell you something, sometimes we have to bring ourselves to do or say extreme things in order to provoke a reaction. This can be the one that we had hoped for, or even the one which we feared would happen, or on other occasions, something completely new and unexpected, which leads us to consider an event or happening from a completely different point of view.

"I've the impression that you're an honest man, above all to yourself. Therefore you'll see the solution will come of its own accord.

"It's true that the girl is about to get married, but it seems to me that she didn't hesitate too much in going to bed with you. It's possible that she's searching for something too, if not a relationship, she may be looking for something beyond what she's yet found within the narrow confines of her house in Sicily. Having said this, sermon over and…ah, here's our friend Pascal."

"Messieurs," said the man, "I don't know whether you've realised it, but by now there's at least ten centimetres of snow out there. Fortunately a snowplough is on its way in a few minutes. I'm not chasing you out of my restaurant, quite the contrary, you're welcome to stay here until dinner, if you want. But if you have to travel far, I'd advise you to get behind the snowplough."

"Pascal, *mon ami"* said Pierre. "Thanks for the advice…a coffee to keep us awake and we'll be off straight away."

Tonio took advantage of the brief wait to go to the telephone kiosk and call Irene. When the operator passed her over to him, Irene said, "*Tunuzzu*, how happy I am…here it's an awful bore, where are you, when are you coming?"

Tonio told her about the difficulties caused by the bad weather, but that he hoped to be with her by dinner time.

The coffee arrived after a few minutes. Pierre and Tonio exchanged business cards with the promise that they would look each other up if they happened to be in their respective cities, Zurich and Paris. Pierre insisted on paying the bill. When they were taking their leave he said, "It's been a great pleasure to have met you, Tonio. I mean this most sincerely. I'm sorry that our paths have to go in different directions so soon."

Pierre could not have even remotely imagined just how mistaken he was in making this statement.

5

Tonio left the restaurant car park and followed Pierre's Mercedes. The snowplough had just passed but a thin layer of snow had already settled on the road.

He also got the impression that there was ice on the road, because he immediately noticed that the Triumph was less stable.

He began to ask himself seriously whether he should abandon his journey, although he would be very disappointed not to see Irene.

He thought once more about what Pierre had said. Perhaps he had been right: the girl, without realising it, was probably in search of something. After all, he thought, she was so young, full of life and happy. Perhaps the prospect of an impending marriage did not really appeal to her. Perhaps she was going through with it only to please her father. He was not convinced that the love she had for this Peppino was really the love of her life. But what was he to do about it? And what if he asked her to stay in France and to blazes with everything? What madness! Not frenzies of sex, dear Tonio, but rather frenzies of someone with a screw loose…

At that moment the road began to descend. It was a gentle slope, but Tonio had the feeling that the car no longer responded adequately to the steering wheel. He slowed down even further, by now he was using the gears more than the brakes to slow the car down.

All of a sudden the Mercedes, which was in front of him by a hundred or so metres, began to skid dangerously out of control.

Tonio saw the brake lights come on and the skid became even more serious.

Everything happened in a flash.

It was clear that Pierre had lost control of the car. It was quite a tight downhill bend. The Mercedes continued straight on towards some metal poles which served as markers, indicating the edge of the road.

To his horror, Tonio saw the car knock down the poles, mount a small bank of snow and mud thrown up by the snowplough, and disappear from sight.

He changed into second gear and gently stopped as soon as he could after negotiating the bend. Tonio hurled himself out of his car and rushed towards the scattered poles.

What he saw took his breath away: beyond the mound of snow there was a fairly steep embankment. The Mercedes had come to rest in a clump of low bushes, dangling perilously over the edge of a near vertical drop, a good ten metres further down.

Tonio did not think twice about it. He began to climb down, ignoring the undergrowth which was lashing his face, and the deep mud into which his shoes were gradually sinking. He went down almost stumbling, clinging on to the branches of low-growing shrubs in order not to lose his balance, at the same time shouting out Pierre's name.

It took him a little over a minute to get to the car. Reaching the side window, at first he could not see anything, then he was able to make out that Pierre was slumped to one side.

As soon as he tried to open the driver's door, the car tipped dangerously forward. Dragged down by its weight, the Mercedes was gradually slipping on the mud down towards the bottom of the steep embankment!

Tonio looked more closely towards the front of the car, and he noticed with a shudder of fear, that the wheels of the car were practically suspended in mid air. Tonio heard the sound of running water further down. Almost certainly a stream or river. A drop of at least ten metres!

Tonio realised that the situation was even worse than he had imagined. He had to hurry in order to release Pierre from the car before it fell and plunged headlong into the river.

He thought of climbing back up the embankment to seek help from a passing vehicle. However, first of all, he wanted to reassure himself of Pierre's condition, as he was not responding to his shouts.

After a few attempts and after tugging forcefully, the car door opened half way. Pierre was lying outstretched on his right side on the passenger seat, his legs trapped under the steering wheel.

Tonio called him, touching him on the knee.

"Pierre can you hear me? Are you able to move?"

There was no reply. Being extremely concerned, he stretched his arm out towards Pierre's wrist and he tried to feel his pulse. It was beating at a regular rate. Somewhat encouraged by this, he began to call out to his friend once more.

"Pierre, Pierre, can you hear me?" Nothing. The car moved slightly again.

Tonio was in the grip of terror once more. It was absolutely essential to drag Pierre out of the car as soon as possible. He heard a weak cry of pain.

"Pierre, can you hear me? You've skidded off the road, and now we have to get you out of here."

"What?" said Pierre, "what did you say?"

"Pierre, listen to me! You have to try and get out of the car. I really don't like the way the car is positioned. It's slowly slipping downhill. Do you think you can make it?"

"I don't know," moaned Pierre." I can't move."

"You have to force yourself, Pierre. Grab my arm and I'll try and pull you out."

Tonio offered him his arm and Pierre seized it with all his strength and he began to heave.

At that precise moment the car jolted and slipped down a good half metre and tilted forwards even more. Pierre screamed.

"Christ!" Tonio shouted, "it's not possible, dammit!"

He felt that he was being gripped further by panic. He was short of breath.

"Pierre listen to me, I don't know what to do…I'm afraid that this shit of a car is going to fall." At that very moment he heard a car passing by on the road. He could not see it. He began to shout.

"Help! Help! Hey stop, help! Down here." But the car appeared to carry straight on.

"You bastards…*arretez!*" he shouted at the top of his voice, but the sound of the engine grew increasingly fainter, until it disappeared.

Downhearted, he turned to Pierre.

"Listen," he said. "The only thing I can try and do is to climb back up to the road and stop the first passing car. Somebody's bound to help us surely…they could go to the nearest phone and call the police, an ambulance…"

"No Tonio, no police!" exclaimed Pierre with a new and unexpected vigour.

"What do you mean no police?" Tonio replied. "Well, who do you want to call then? Why no police?"

"No…nothing…it's just that…"

"What Pierre, it's only what? I think it's a good idea don't you?"

"Yes…of course," Pierre gasped, grimacing with pain, "but…I think they'll take hours to get here…do you realise just how busy they'll be in this bad weather?"

"But who gives a damn! You've had an accident. You need help…"At that moment the car moved a little further.

Tonio reflected for an instant. Perhaps Pierre was right, there wasn't enough time. He decided to try once more to drag Pierre from the car. He grabbed him by the arm once more and pulled him.

Pierre screamed from the pain.

"Aaaah, my leg!" he said, "my leg…my foot is trapped under the pedals…I can't move it…I can't feel it!"

Tonio poked his head between the door and Pierre's body, and saw that his left foot was trapped in an awkward position between the brake pedal and the accelerator, and with his right foot crossed over it and resting on the floor of the car.

He attempted to get to Pierre's left foot to try and free it, but he could not reach it – Pierre's body and the half open door blocked his way.

Looking more closely, Tonio realised that perhaps by lowering the brake pedal, Pierre would be able to free his foot. But how could he reach it? He looked around about him to see whether he could find something which might help. He saw a branch, broken off a shrub by the Mercedes during its precipitous downward path. He picked it up, stripped it of its foliage and inserted it into the car. Now with the aid of the branch he was able to reach the pedal.

"Pierre," he said to his friend, "listen to me, you have to make an effort now. I'll push the brake pedal down with this branch and as I do so, you have to try and free your foot. Do you understand?"

Pierre nodded in assent, "OK, I can try…"

"Yes that's it, come on push, now!" Tonio pushed the pedal with the branch. Pierre tried to move, but he cried out from the pain, "I just can't do it, it hurts too much…"

"Listen Pierre, listen to me carefully. Don't push with your left foot, it's trapped and I wouldn't be surprised if it were broken. Listen, when I move the pedal, you push with your right leg. I think it should work then. Right then, let's try again…now!"

Tonio pressed the brake with the branch and Pierre, screaming, pushed his right leg with all his strength.

His left foot came free. Pierre was able finally to sit upright on the car seat. Tonio looked at him; he was as white as a sheet. His hair was dishevelled and was falling down over his eyes and a drop of blood was flowing from his nose.

Tonio slipped his arm around his shoulder and he began to pull.

"Pierre, help me. Push with your right leg. That's it!"

With one last effort, groaning, and almost on the verge of tears, Pierre pushed while Tonio helped to drag him out of the car.

After a few more minutes, which seemed interminable, at least half of Pierre's body was extricated from the car. With his little remaining strength, Tonio pulled even harder until Pierre was totally free, at which point he fell with all his weight on his friend, who had to prop himself up and support his arms and legs so as to avoid sliding downwards.

He lay down panting for a few seconds, and then he raised himself on his knees, and dragged himself towards Pierre, who was lying on the ground motionless. He appeared to have fainted.

"Pierre," he called. Not receiving a reply, he moved closer to the man's face calling out to him once more.

"Pierre?"

The latter opened his eyes and said in a whisper, "We made it…I don't believe it…we made it!"

"Yes Pierre, we made it…but now what are we going to do? You can stay here while I call someone or…"

"The bag!" exclaimed Pierre "Where's my bag? It was on the back seat. We have to get that bag, Tonio. I can't leave it…"

At that very instant, the Mercedes started to move once more, this time it did not stop. It gathered speed falling through the bushes and shrubs, which had hitherto restrained it, and after a rocking motion, dragged down by the weight of the engine, it fell forward and plummeted down. For a few seconds they could hear nothing. Then the sound of a deafening crash reached the two panting men.

After a moment's silence they looked at each other incredulously. Then Pierre said, "Tonio you...you've saved my life…the car…did you see? It's fallen down…Tonio…but do you understand? You've…"

"Forget it," said Tonio, who only then fully realised what had happened. "Now we have to think how we're going to climb up. And to cap it all it'll be dark soon…" He looked up towards the road and continued, "I can't hear any cars going by. I've a feeling that we're going to have to do this all on our own. Do you think that by pushing bit by bit with your right leg, you'll be able to climb up this embankment? I can help you, pulling you by the arm."

"We can try," Pierre replied. "But I'm afraid it's going to be tough going."

6

It took them over half an hour to climb back up the embankment.

Gradually, with Pierre pushing with his right leg, and Tonio pulling him by the armpits, they succeeded in getting to the top at the level of the road.

Still panting, Tonio said to Pierre, "Now you wait here, I'll go and get the car. Do you see? It's down there past the bend."

Pierre made a sign that he had understood. He seemed to have no strength left.

Tonio went towards the Triumph, put it into reverse and stopped just a few centimetres from where Pierre lay, on the passenger side.

"Now we have to make one last effort, Pierre. You have to try and get into the car. I've moved the passenger seat back as far as it'll go. You'll have to prop yourself up on your right leg. I'll raise the other one…let's try, push!"

After numerous attempts and screams of pain from Pierre, the latter finally succeeded in sitting in the car. Tonio helped him to lift up his left leg. When he saw his friend finally sitting in the passenger seat, he breathed a sigh of relief. He was exhausted.

As soon as they had set out on their journey, Pierre exclaimed, "Tonio, the bag! We must retrieve the bag…we can't…I can't leave it behind down there!"

"Don't even think about it, Pierre. The car has fallen into a deep ravine. I wouldn't even know where to begin to look for it. And what's more, it'll soon be dark. Above all, you need medical attention, I'm sure. Forget about the bag for this evening."

Realising that Pierre was shivering with cold, he put the car heater on full. It was only then that he appreciated the state they were both in: mud everywhere, in their hair, on their faces, on their clothes. Scratched hands. Fortunately the blood which had been flowing from Pierre's nose had stopped.

The snow had stopped falling, but the temperature had dropped even further, forming ice on the road.

After driving for a quarter of an hour, Tonio saw a sign which indicated they were entering Mortain.

It appeared to be a village perched upon a hill. Tonio carried on for a few hundred metres more and found himself in what seemed to be a mediaeval village, with ancient houses on both sides of the road.

There was not a soul to be seen. Having gone past the centre of the village, he saw a sign: *Au Bon Vent, Hôtel Restaurant, Rue du Rocher* with an arrow pointing to a narrow side road. Tonio took the turning and found the hotel a short distance away.

He stopped the car right in front of the hotel and went inside. There was nobody behind the small reception desk in the lobby. He rang the bell which was clearly displayed on the desk, and after a few seconds a woman appeared who had clearly been eating in the back room.

"*Bonsoir, Madame,*" Tonio said. "Excuse me for disturbing you, I'd like to know…"

The woman's eyes opened wide on seeing the state he was in. He continued, saying that his friend outside had skidded off the road a few kilometres from Mortain, and that he had helped him, but he feared that his friend had twisted, or even worse, broken his foot, so they needed two rooms for the night, preferably on the ground floor, and sooner or later a doctor who could examine him.

The woman replied that yes, there were two rooms free on the ground floor, and that she could call a doctor.

They went to the car, but when the woman saw Pierre's condition she went to call her husband to help.

The rooms were large, clean and with all that was required to make their stay a pleasant one. Clearly it wasn't the Ritz, thought Tonio, but it was more than acceptable.

They sat Pierre in an armchair, after having spread some newspapers on it so as not to dirty it. The lady went out to call the doctor, whilst her husband asked about the accident.

After a little while the wife returned, and said that unfortunately the doctor was out on some calls, and that she feared that they would not be able to see him until the next day. The woman suggested that she should call her daughter, who was a nurse at the hospital at Caen. She would know what to do.

They decided to take Pierre's shoes off; his ankle was swollen, with a massive bruise on it. One did not need to be a doctor to understand that there was probably something broken.

Tonio suggested that Pierre be put to bed after a shower, or at least after a wash.

Pierre was at the end of his tether, and everyone could see it. After the woman had left the room, Tonio took Pierre's shirt and trousers off, and he was left in his vest and underpants, and with the help of the other man, they took him into the bathroom. They sat him on the edge of the bath and washed him as best they could. Then they put him to bed. Pierre was panting as if he had run an obstacle race. Tonio placed his hand on his forehead; he was running a temperature. He asked the man who had remained with them in the room what his name was.

"*Hubert Le Cardonnel, Monsieur, et ma femme c'est Annick.*"

A few minutes later when Madame Le Cardonnel returned with her daughter, a woman in her thirties, who was quite pretty and had rather a no-nonsense attitude. When the latter realised the condition Pierre was in, she decided to give him a good dose of painkillers, and then immobilised his leg with two lateral splints bound together with very tight bandages. After that she advised that they call for an ambulance to take Pierre to the hospital.

At this point Pierre opened his eyes, and weakly said to the girl with gentle gestures so as not to offend her, that he would prefer it if a friend of his, who lived in Rennes, who he'd been travelling to see before the accident, could take care of the whole situation. He only had to telephone him. The girl said that this was no problem, but she strongly advised him to go to the hospital.

She also told him that the only available telephone was in the hotel reception.

Tonio warmly thanked the Le Cardonnel family for their invaluable assistance, giving the impression that this would not be forgotten at the time of their departure. He also ordered a light supper for Pierre, to be served in his room.

When the others had left the room, Pierre asked Tonio to call a number in Rennes, and to track down a certain Bruno, and tell him about the accident, and urge him to come with an ambulance the following day. Tonio promised to do this immediately after he had changed. He fetched his travel bag from the car and took a warm shower.

He changed and went back to Pierre. The latter was sleeping deeply. Evidently the pills had had their effect on him.

Tonio tiptoed out and went to the telephone. At the reception he asked Madame Le Cardonnel to serve him dinner in the restaurant, and to let him make a couple of phone calls.

He first telephoned Irene. It was almost ten o'clock and very probably she was asking herself what could possibly have happened to him.

Tonio told her about Pierre's accident, how he had helped him and how they were now in a small hotel in Mortain. He told her that he would have to cancel his trip.

Irene's disappointment was clear. She asked him to phone her again the following day. Before hanging up she said to him, "You know Tonio, I knew that you were a good and generous person. You are giving all this help to someone you hardly know..."

"Irene, I don't think it's a question of being kind or generous. Anyone in my place would have done the same...and then, although it might seem strange to you, this man, this Pierre...seems a very nice person and is really quite interesting too. When we have the opportunity I'll tell you what we said to each other over lunch today."

"All right then, call me tomorrow...it's strange, but I've really missed you. Ciao, goodnight."

Then Tonio dialled the number which Pierre had given him. A man's voice answered.

"I'd like to speak to Mr Bruno, please," Tonio said.

There was a hesitant moment of silence. Then the man said, "Who is asking for him?"

"Good evening, I'm Tonio Brignani. I'm calling on behalf of Mr Haber. Pierre Haber. I'd like to speak to Mr Bruno."

"That's me, go ahead." Tonio noticed the same hesitation in the voice as before.

"Well, you see, Mr Haber has had a car accident. He skidded off the road and he's injured himself. He's not able to walk. I've helped him to book into a small hotel here at Mortain."

"How is he now? Is it possible to speak to him directly?"

"No, it's not possible. There isn't a phone in the room. In fact he's asleep now, and I think he has a high temperature. He urged me to call you and ask you to come here early tomorrow, and to arrange an ambulance to take him to the hospital in Rennes."

Tonio gave him all the directions to get to the hotel, and went to eat.

During dinner he reflected on the day's events. He had liked Pierre right from the start, and he wanted to get to know him better. At the same time, he had a strange feeling that he could not explain to himself, or where it came from.

It was like a small worm hidden in the labyrinth of his mind which was gnawing away at him. He tried to concentrate on everything that had happened, and on everything which had been said, but without finding an answer to his questions.

Before going to bed he looked in to see how Pierre was, the door had been left half open. He found him awake. The pain in his foot seemed to have calmed down. He sat next to him on the bed.

"Have you phoned Saint Malo?" asked Pierre.

"Yes, and your friend Bruno, too. He'll be here tomorrow morning."

"Tonio," said Pierre. "I have to ask you another big favour, even if it means delaying your arrival at Saint Malo a bit longer."

"Don't worry about that, I've given up any idea of going there. With the roads in this state, I could only stay there for a few hours. I absolutely have to be back in Paris by tomorrow evening. I have to be in the office early on Monday morning."

"I'm sorry Tonio. Really I am. I regret that on my account your plans have fallen through…"

"Don't think about it …accidents happen when you least expect them. Come on then, tell me, what's on your mind then?"

"I'd like to ask you to accompany Bruno to the scene of the accident tomorrow. I absolutely have to recover that bag. You see, in it there are documents which are essential for my business…original contracts, work plans and other things, not to mention my passport and some money. If you were to leave early and were able to find and climb down that ravine, you might be able to make it in a couple of hours, or maybe even less."

After a minute's silence, Pierre asked, "Where's your family? In Naples? What are you doing in Paris?"

And so once again, Tonio found himself telling Pierre many things about his life, including some things which were of a very personal nature.

He told him about his childhood in Brazil; about his father who had remained there, and about whom he had no further news. About the sacrifices made by his mother in bringing him and his sister up, and her death a few years earlier. About the girl who had dumped him at the same time; and how he first entered the bank; and how he was transferred by them to Paris, thanks to his aptitude for foreign languages; and finally about his career ambitions and some of his frustrations at work.

He had no difficulty whatsoever telling Pierre all these things. In fact he seemed to be completely at ease with him. Pierre was an attentive listener, who only rarely interrupted him.

Tonio felt that a distinct bond had been established between them, which went far beyond the boundaries of mere acquaintance. Moreover, this was not only the result of the accident, in which they had both narrowly cheated death, but also because they both felt, for different reasons, a subconscious wish, at that precise moment, for something or someone who would mark a turning point in their lives.

They talked for a long time.

However, when Tonio asked Pierre about his family, he was rather dismissive. He was a widower and had an only son, Rainer, who was thirty-five years old, the same age as Tonio, and who worked in one of the companies in the same group, but whom he did not see very often.

Tonio detected a certain degree of bitterness in his voice, but he did not insist on asking further questions.

Later in his room before going to sleep, that same feeling of unease, as if there were something which did not quite add up, returned to him. However, try as best as he could, he was not able to find an answer.

7

When Tonio awoke the following morning, he heard some noise coming from Pierre's room. He looked at his watch, it was six o'clock. It was still dark outside.

Thinking that his friend needed some help, he dressed quickly, knocked on Pierre's door and went in.

"Come in Tonio," Pierre said smiling, "let me introduce you to my good friend Bruno Gravier. He arrived a few minutes ago with reinforcements."

In fact there were two other men in the room standing near the window.

Gravier got up from the chair next to the bed and shook Tonio by the hand.

"Bruno, this is Tonio, my saviour," said Pierre, and then turning to Tonio, "I was just telling Bruno how you literally saved my life."

Tonio shook hands with the other two men but they did not introduce themselves.

"Well," said Tonio, "let's say that we've both been lucky. Had that car fallen into the ravine only a single minute sooner, it would have dragged both of us to kingdom come. Thank God we're here to tell the tale. More to the point, how are you feeling this morning?"

"My foot's hurting a lot, but I think I'll survive. Yes, what you say is true Tonio. But without your help and your determination…"

"All right, let's forget it for now. The important thing is that someone takes care of your fracture. The ambulance?"

"It'll be here in a couple of hours' time," Gravier replied.

"OK," said Tonio, "then all that remains to be done is to go and retrieve this famous bag."

Twenty minutes later they left for the scene of the accident in a Land Rover, which did not have the slightest problem in negotiating the icy roads. Tonio sat next to Gravier in the rear seats while one of the two men who had come with him drove. Tonio noticed that from the first moment he had met them, they had not uttered a single word.

During the journey Gravier informed Tonio that Pierre had told him in great detail about the previous day's adventure.

"Even though I have seen the extent to which Pierre is grateful to you for all that you have done for him up till now, I too would like to thank you personally."

"Think nothing of it. Have you known him a long time?"

"An eternity. Pierre and I know each other from when I was sixteen. At that age I had – how should I put it – gone off the rails a bit. I had a lot of problems both at home and outside it. I don't wish to bore you with the story of my life, but Pierre took me off the streets. He gave me a job. He helped me to grow up, not only as a man, but professionally too. He has taught me a lot. I'm very close to him."

"How did you get to know each other?"

"It's a funny story," Gravier replied. "We met for the first time when I was trying to steal his car radio." Seeing Tonio's expression, he continued, "Yes, just like that. He caught me red-handed. However, instead of having me arrested, he began talking to me, asking me a load of questions. I told him where I came from, my situation at home, about the abject poverty in which I was living, with my father who had left my mother and five children. He made me an offer: he asked me how much I would have got for the radio, how many had I stolen that month etc., and then he offered me the job of being his errand-boy for a sum of money which was much more than anything I could have earned in a month, provided of course that I kept my nose clean.

"As soon as I put a foot wrong, not only did he threaten me with the police but he made it perfectly clear that I'd pay dearly for it. It was a really attractive offer. I accepted although with a few reservations, asking myself what he really wanted from me. But there weren't any problems and everything went smoothly. After some time he found a job for my mother as a home help and he even helped out with my younger brothers' schooling."

In the meantime they had arrived at the scene of the accident. Tonio showed him where the Mercedes had gone off the road.

Bruno and the other two went down the embankment. They looked around for a while, and finally began to walk along the edge of the ravine towards the valley, until they disappeared from sight. Half an hour later, he saw them reappear at the same spot they had started from. Tonio noted for the first time that the bag, which Bruno had in his hand, was fitted with two large combination locks and a chain designed to be locked to the wrist.

Having returned to Mortain, they saw that the ambulance had arrived. Pierre was ready to leave.

Tonio realised that his friend was wearing the same clothes he had worn on the previous day, but that they had been freshly washed and ironed. Madame Le Cardonnel had worked miracles, certainly a point in the *Au Bon Vent*'s favour.

From that moment onwards everything seemed to happen very quickly. The bill, including Tonio's, was settled in a hurry by Bruno. Judging by the expression on their faces and the profuse thanks of the Le Cardonnels, Tonio realised that the tip that they had been given was a generous one.

Pierre was placed on a stretcher in the ambulance. A nurse sat next to him.

Just before leaving, Pierre wanted to speak to Tonio alone.

"I'd like us to remain in touch, Tonio. I'll never forget what you've done for me…now they're taking me to hospital. In the next few days, or perhaps tomorrow, I'll call you. Promise me you'll come and visit me at Rennes, where I'll certainly be stuck for a few days."

"Of course, I'll come and visit you. Ciao."

By now it was ten o'clock. Tonio went back into the hotel to collect his things and also to telephone Irene.

"I'm going back home," he told her. "I'm really disappointed. I wanted to see you so much, *piccola*. But that's life! I hope to see you when you return to Paris before going home at the end of the week. If we aren't able to see each other in town, I'll come and see you off at the airport."

He was a few kilometres from Paris, listening to Edith Piaf singing *Non, je ne regrette rien,* when Tonio was struck by a mind-blowing thought. Now he realised what it was which hadn't quite added up: the firm refusal on Pierre's part when he had suggested calling the police to ask for help down there on the embankment. He had been too adamant, almost violent. Tonio clearly saw once more the expression in Pierre's eyes at that instant: it was as if they were illuminated by a cold, clear determination. He remembered that a few moments later everything had become less important because the car had moved once more, slipping down towards the bottom of the ravine, and they had been forced to hurl themselves out in order not to be dragged down with the car.

Tonio knew that he was not wrong. His new friend had something to hide, he was sure of it.

While he was joining the Sunday traffic on the *Peripherique*, he could almost physically taste the bitterness that this thought left in his mouth.

8

The following week Tonio was very busy at work. He was handling a delicate international finance operation involving large sums of money.

His work was made more difficult because the international financial community had regarded Italian banks in an unfavourable light for a considerable period of time, because of some previous unfortunate episodes which had compromised their credibility.

A couple of years earlier, in 1982, the Roberto Calvi episode hit the headlines: as President of the Banco Ambrosiano, he was referred to as God's banker because of his links with the Vatican. He was found dead, hanging under Blackfriars Bridge in London.

It was quite an ugly story. Despite the fact that everything clearly pointed to murder, not least because Calvi was found with large stones placed in his pockets, curiously the police in London filed his case as suicide.

Later on, it came to light that he had been the subject of anti-mafia enquiries a few years earlier, and was only one of numerous people mixed up in a much more complicated affair, which involved the interests of organised crime, political groups, secret societies, drugs, and important financial institutions.

The most surprising thing was the role played by an institution little known to the general public, called the Istituto per le Opere di Religione (The Institute for Religious Works): the Vatican's official bank.

The collapse of Calvi's Banco Ambrosiano revealed that some highly-placed officials, both in the Vatican itself and the bank, had collaborated in setting up a network of fictitious companies in some tax havens, financed by credit facilities from the Banco Ambrosiano, into which hundreds of millions of dollars vanished into thin air.

In the wake of all this, other smaller banks were also subject to investigation, which revealed that some of them had been involved in fraud, illegal appropriation, funding of political parties and other nefarious activities which had nothing whatever to do with banking.

The consequence was that the reputation, which Italian banks had hitherto enjoyed abroad, took a severe downturn, and it became increasingly difficult for them to obtain loans from foreign banks to finance those international activities, which were so fashionable at the time.

Tonio, however, had been able to build-up friendly relations with some French, Swiss, English and American banks based in Paris. These had extended generous credit facilities to the Banca Nazionale dell'Industria, his bank, at least up to certain limits. It was not easy for Tonio to exceed these limits, but they were considerably higher than the credit levels extended to other Italian banks, even those bigger than the BNI.

The banking operation in which he was principally occupied in those days, the financing of an industrial project in North Korea to the tune of eight hundred million dollars, was led by a French state bank which, in turn, had formed a consortium of European banks in order to spread the risk in proportion to their investments.

The suggestion that Tonio take part in the consortium had come from the headquarters of his bank in Rome a few months earlier. The President of the Bank had personally called him to Rome in order to tell him that he had heard, in confidence, that the deal was at a preliminary discussion stage in Paris; and that he would like BNI to take part, principally because he had been informed that the financial returns to the bank would be excellent – without mentioning the prestige the bank would gain in the eyes of the worldwide financial community.

Tonio had been briefed to find out about these developments with a view to trying to get BNI to be invited to be one of the partners in the operation. It would then be up to the specialists in Rome to weigh up the risks and, if it were necessary, to grant permission for the bank to participate in the project.

On his return to Paris, Tonio had sounded out his banking friends for any further information on the project, and ascertained where the initial negotiations were taking place in order to get the project up and running. Not only had he succeeded in ensuring that his bank was one of those which received an initial invitation, but he was also successful and quick off the mark in ensuring that his bank was offered a large percentage of the financing itself, beating many other banks, including French ones, who would have been more than happy to participate, bearing in mind the rate of return and the prestige of being one of the initial backers.

However, the financing of the project turned out to be more difficult than had been anticipated, both because of the problems encountered in acquiring reliable information from North Korea, and because of the thousand quibbles thrown up by an army of lawyers on a daily basis, while drawing up the final document.

Tonio had been forced to take part in all the most boring preliminary meetings. Now it finally seemed that things were proceeding more smoothly. The only remaining obstacle was to take the final decision regarding the 'period of grace' given to Korea once the financing of the project had been committed, before that country had to start repaying the debt. The banks financing the loan proposed a period of one year, whereas the

Koreans were insisting on two years. It was probable that they would reach a compromise of eighteen months.

Tonio would return home every evening extremely tired, but before going to bed he had got into the habit of telephoning Irene in order to wish her goodnight.

He had thought that their separation would have diminished the intensity of his feelings for the girl. In fact, quite the opposite was true. The long phone calls each evening had contributed to deepening their knowledge of each other. The more he got to know her, the more he liked her, but also the more he considered himself to be an idiot after every call. He was convinced that he had entered into a blind alley with his head down, but that in the near future when she returned home to get married, he would run into a brick wall which would finally wake him up.

They had made an appointment to see each other at Orly Airport on the following Friday.

The Alitalia flight to Palermo was scheduled to leave at five in the afternoon, four hours after Irene's arrival in Paris from St Malo.

Tonio had also received a call from Pierre, who told him that there had been complications with his foot, and that he had to undergo an operation at the end of the week.

He promised once more to call him and to go and visit him in Rennes the following week.

On Friday, Tonio got his secretary to cancel all his appointments for the afternoon, and at two o'clock he was already at Orly as he had promised.

They met in the departure lounge of the airport.

When Tonio saw Irene arrive, accompanied by Nunzia, he felt his heart beating faster. He could not help but admire her bearing which he thought had a distinctly regal quality. From a distance, she gave the impression of being older than her twenty-two years. She was strikingly beautiful and at the same time, slightly reserved. She was wearing an ivory-coloured silk blouse with a pair of jeans which were slightly worn at the knees. She was carrying her fox fur nonchalantly over her arm.

Her black hair, flowing over her shoulders, contrasted with her light-coloured skin. Her eyes seemed to him to be larger and greener than he remembered. The golden streaks, which he had noticed at their first meeting, seemed all the more luminous.

While the girl was approaching, Tonio was conscious of admiring glances, especially from men, which her progress aroused.

They gave each other a kiss on the cheek in Nunzia's presence. The latter looked at him strangely as if it were the first time that she had ever laid eyes on him.

Since it was too early to check-in their luggage, they went to sit in a bar. After ordering coffee, Irene told him just how negative her experience at St Malo had been.

"It might be that once you have known Paris…" she said to him, looking him straight in the eye, "everything else seems dead or boring. And then there were too many Italian and Spanish students. All in all, I don't think I learnt much French there."

After finishing her coffee, Irene said, "Listen Tonio, I'd like to find a little present for *babbone* here at the airport. Take me to see if there's anything suitable around here. Nunzia, please, look after the bags, we won't be long."

Once they were out of Nunzia's sight, almost in unison they stopped and regardless of the people around them, they embraced each other and exchanged a long kiss.

"Ah, so you haven't forgotten me *Tunuzzu.*"

"How could I…I'm afraid you've cast a spell on me. You have completely bewitched me; I'll be your slave forever," he said laughing.

They became serious. They walked a little way in silence, holding each other by the hand.

Then she stopped again and said, "Tonio, I have to say something to you. You know, I've spoken to Nunzia…I couldn't keep everything bottled up inside…I've always told her everything, since I was a little girl."

"What did you tell her?" Tonio asked her. "Have you told her…everything?"

"Well not absolutely everything…almost everything."

"Hmm. What was her reaction?"

"She already knew…you see Tonio…when somebody is near you all your life…when she loves you like a daughter…you don't have to speak. She only needed to catch a glimpse of us that evening in the hotel to understand what had happened. She only urged me to think carefully about what I was doing, and above all, not to displease *babbone*."

There was another long moment of silence.

"I understand," Tonio then said. "I don't wish to upset your life any more than I already have. However, I have to say that my life isn't the same any longer since I met you. Well then…to speak of love can seem a bit excessive, and perhaps it is, but I don't know how else to define what I feel."

"Me too, I've never been so confused in all my life," she replied "but you know as well as I do, that I have to go back home to get married…once you asked me if I loved Peppino. Well, my answer is that I don't know. I thought I did, before I met you. I'm fond of him, that's certain. You'll tell me that's not enough in order to get married.

"I know that Peppino will do all he can to make me happy…even if he's only called me once in all the time I've been here in France…whereas you on the other hand…but the main thing is I want to remain near my father.

"I'm the only reason for his living. In the eyes of the big wide world he seems a strong man. But I know that he's very fragile inside. Nunzia has told me that deep down, he's never been the same since my mother's premature departure. He feels guilty over her death, and he tries to shower me with all the love he is capable of."

They arrived in front of the window of a jeweller's shop.

They went in. Irene bought some gold cufflinks for her father. Before leaving the shop she stopped in front of a case, which contained silver bracelets.

"These bracelets," she asked the assistant who understood Italian, "are they for ladies or men?"

"They're for ladies as well as for men: unisex," the lady replied, laughing.

"I'd like to buy one, please."

"Another gift-wrapped parcel?" the assistant asked.

"No, no parcel, thank you," and then handing it to Tonio, said, "this is for you."

"But… Irene…I can't…"

"Please…" she said.

Tonio put it on his wrist. "Thanks, I love it. I'll wear it always."

Then, after a brief silence, he turned to the assistant, "Listen, since they're unisex, I'd like to buy one too."

The woman looked at them with an expression which was comically dreamy, and sighed. "*Ah, l'amour…*"

Tonio gave it to Irene who remained silent.

They left the shop; she embraced him, and gave him a long kiss.

"Tonio," then she said, "we must be really mad. It's as if we've exchanged love tokens…all this is madness…but I too will wear mine forever."

By now they could see Nunzia, who was still seated at the bar. Tonio stopped once more and said to her, "There's one last thing I want to say to you…and it's important. Irene, whatever should happen to you in life, at any time, I want you to know that you can count on me. It sounds like one of those standard platitudes which people say to each other when they're feeling good but with the passing of time they forget…but believe me, that isn't the case with me. You only have to write or phone me, or better still, come… I want you to know that you have a friend you can rely on. Will you promise me?"

"There you go, you've gone all serious on me again…but yes, I'll promise you."

"And then, one last thing, I want to find a way of remaining in touch with you…even after your marriage. I want to know everything about you…share in your life, even from afar. Please find a way and let me know."

They approached Nunzia.

"I think it's time to go," said Irene, looking at the queue of people waiting at the check-in. "We don't like long goodbyes, do we Nunzia?"

Nunzia did not reply. Tonio went up to her and said, "Nunzia, it's been a pleasure knowing you." He held both her hands and continued, "I've said it to Irene and I'll repeat it to you, consider me your sincere friend. You can count on me at any time. I hope that you won't need it, but in life…you never know."

There was a moment's silence and then the woman said, "Don Antonio, I know that you are sincere," and after having given a quick glance to Irene said, "you deserve a good *mogliere.*[*] Find a nice French lass who's down to earth, and you'll see that your life will be even more lovely and interesting. You seem to me to be an honest man."

Perhaps he was wrong, but Tonio seemed to detect a note of sadness in her voice.

---

[*] Wife

9

While he was travelling back to the city centre, Tonio could not get Irene out of his mind.

A strange sadness came over him, accompanied by a feeling of jealousy towards a man he did not know, but who could embrace Irene in his arms whenever he wanted to.

Thinking back to what they had said to each other during those days, he felt a growing sense of protection towards the girl.

He returned to his office and decided to make two telephone calls.

The first was to his friend Achille Salemi, Deputy General Manager of the Banco di Sicilia in Palermo.

Before returning to Sicily, Salemi had been the head of his bank's branch in Paris and the two had become close friends, often exchanging useful information about their business activities.

"Don Antonio, *eminentissimo,*[*]"drawled his friend in his Sicilian cadence, "to what do I owe the honour of a phone call from Paris, no less?"

"My dear Achille, the women of Paris – but what am I saying, of all France – are still mourning your departure."

"Forget it! With a wife and three children, Paris is the last thing on my mind…but rather I should compliment you on what you're doing. I've heard about the Korean operation. Well done. And how can I be of help to *vossia*?[**]"

---

[*] Most eminent

[**] Your Lordship

"Well now, I'd like you in strictest confidence as always, to give me some information about a certain Sicilian person. I must point out first of all, that this hasn't anything to do with the bank. It's…how should I put it…a personal curiosity, which I'd like to satisfy. What can you tell me about a certain Giuseppe Cantera…I think he might own a few sulphur mines in the region of…"

"Who? Do you mean Don Peppino Cantera? Who doesn't know him here in Sicily! Mining sulphur is the original activity his family is known for, but this has now become overshadowed somewhat by other commercial activities. As the only son, he inherited everything from his father Tommaso, God rest his soul.

"Peppino Cantera owns quite a few construction companies; he has several contracts for the building of council estates in the Province of Siracusa, but he is mainly involved with the reconstruction of the Port of Gela. A business worth millions. It's said that he's very closely tied in with local politicians. You know, and I wouldn't be telling you anything that hasn't already been reported in the newspapers. He's been investigated a couple of times for having dubious links with the mafia, but he has always come out unscathed. He is considered by many to be the golden bachelor and the best catch in the whole of Sicily. He has very extensive lines of credit from many regional and national banks. That's more or less all I know about him."

"Very efficient and always well informed, as usual, our Achille. Many thanks. Listen, as you're there on the spot, what can you tell me about Calogero Consalvo, the owner, I think, of food processing companies and producer of the drink *amaro* Consalvo digestif."

"Ah! Our good old Brignani, always one step ahead of everyone else…Consalvo's a pillar of the community! A true gentleman of the old school. I seem to remember a few years ago, he lost his wife in a car accident, which at the time many thought had been arranged by the mafia, maybe because notoriously he's always held out against them. Rumour has it, at least in Sicily, that the two families Consalvo and Cantera are about to unite their fortunes through the wedding of their two children. I've heard it said that Don Calogero's daughter is an absolute knockout...and our friend Brignani in Paris, already knows everything. I won't even ask you why you need this information."

This news left him rather puzzled. He could not imagine Irene with such a man. The trouble was, he reflected, he was not able to imagine her with anyone else.

The other telephone call was to Franco Müller, one of the directors of the Crédit Suisse Bank in Zurich.

Tonio and Franco had met on the same course on specialist banking techniques in Lugano a couple of years earlier. They had immediately become friends, sharing a common interest in British sports cars, and they had remained in touch ever since. They had even spent a couple of holidays together on the pistes at St Moritz, where Franco had a small chalet.

"I knew I'd find you in the office at this time. Don't you go home early even on a Friday?" Tonio said to him as soon as he had been put through.

"And what about you then?" the other replied. "Where are you going tonight? To the Moulin Rouge, or are you going to be a peeping Tom at the Crazy Horse?"

"To tell the truth, I'm going to both! Joking apart, I need a personal favour. Last week I met a fellow countryman of yours, and I'd like to know a bit more about him. His name is Pierre Haber. Have you ever heard his name before?"

"Well," the other replied, "if we're speaking about the same person, I can tell you that the Pierre Haber I know, is a Swiss industrialist who is beyond reproach. He's the head of Technical Engineering Consultancy, which has many business interests under its wing, ranging from steel production to cereals brokerage.

"One of the branches of his group operates in the military sector. His contacts are, therefore, at the highest government levels. And, if I'm not mistaken, he seems to be a small percentage shareholder in my own bank too. Listen, if this is the person you're interested in, I could supply you with more detailed information by consulting our archives..."

"No, no forget it, what you've told me is more than enough, it was just to satisfy my personal curiosity."

So then, his new friend Pierre is a Swiss industrialist above reproach, Müller had said. That feeling of unease, which he had experienced a few days previously, returned to him once more.

He thought that perhaps he had given too much importance to something, which had been said in a moment of stress.

He decided to go and visit Pierre the very next day.

The following morning he caught an express train to Rennes. Having arrived at the hospital, he asked to be directed to Pierre's room. When he knocked on the door, he heard his friend's voice inviting him to come in.

"Tonio, what a lovely surprise, you said you'd be coming next week..." and then, turning to the man sitting next to his bed he said, "Rainer, this is Tonio that I've talked to you about. Tonio, let me introduce you to my son Rainer, he's arrived from Geneva today."

The two shook hands. Tonio's immediate impression was that of having touched a slug: Rainer's handshake was weak and moist. He was about twenty centimetres taller than Tonio; he had washed-out, blond hair which barely hid the fact that he was prematurely bald. He was meticulously dressed and gave the impression that he was looking down his nose at everything, and this was not just on account of his height.

Pierre was pale, but all things considered, he seemed to be in good form.

"I decided to come today, because I think I'll be in Rome for the annual budget next week. But, more to the point, tell me how did your operation go?"

"Well, to be honest, better than expected. You know, that damned brake pedal has caused a lot of damage. But with a good plaster cast, some physiotherapy and a couple of crutches, they tell me that I'll be back doing the hundred metres in a couple of months. But this is nothing compared to what could have happened. Once again Tonio, I don't know how to…"

"Come off it, Pierre, forget it. Its water under the bridge, more to the point think about…"

"I too would like to thank you, as well as everyone else for what you've done for my father," interposed Rainer.

He said this in a formal manner, with the air of someone who has received a present, which is of absolutely no interest to them whatsoever. Then he turned to his father, and said something in German.

Pierre replied to him in Italian, throwing him a glance of disapproval for his boorishness. "No, there's no problem. We can carry on that conversation some other time."

Tonio, realising that he had interrupted an important conversation between them, said, "Please do carry on talking. I'll go down to the bar for a coffee, which I really need. I'll come back in ten minutes."

"No Tonio, don't bother. We can…"

Rainer, however, interrupted him. "Would you mind terribly? Ten minutes should be more than enough."

Tonio went out of the room, noting Pierre's angry expression.

When he returned twenty minutes later, he found Rainer putting on his coat. The atmosphere between father and son was glacial. Tonio felt ill at ease.

As Rainer was leaving, he turned and said to Tonio, "I'm sorry, but I have to go. I have an appointment, which I just can't miss. However, I see that my father is in good hands."

If, at first, Tonio had considered Rainer to be unpleasant, he now considered him to be utterly odious.

When Rainer had left the room, there was a moment of silence between Tonio and Pierre.

Then the latter said, "You must excuse my son. He's rather stressed out at the moment. However, when you think that it's been a full two months since we've seen each other…but, let's forget it…tell me, what's new in the *Ville Lumière*?"

They spent the whole afternoon together. Tonio told him about his meeting with Irene and about his work. Pierre seemed to be particularly interested in the initial setting up of the Korean operation, asking him several questions, which clearly indicated his deep knowledge of the procedures involved in international finance.

During those hours together, they were interrupted several times by telephone calls, which Tonio noticed were coming from several countries. He heard Pierre speak in German, English and French.

Towards evening, when Tonio was already thinking of leaving his friend, he asked him to talk about his work, naturally not telling him that he had already been generally briefed about his business activities.

Pierre told him that he had first started off as a young man, working for an import and export company, dealing in raw materials, particularly cereals. This had been while living in the Middle East with his father, who was a diplomat there. Then at only twenty, he had founded his first company, which imported used military equipment from Europe, to be sold on in small, local markets. He traded in used uniforms, camp beds, blankets etc. He had first found his suppliers among acquaintances of his father in Switzerland. Then, once the company was established, he had found other suppliers by himself, in other countries.

"These were golden times. The merchandise fairly flew off the market stalls like hot cakes. It was like manna from heaven. My father, however, insisted that I carry on with my studies.

"Subsequently I took my degree in mechanical engineering, which I must admit was very useful to me later on. In the space of a few years I created a network of five companies, which specialised in buying and selling various different products. My clients began to change. I moved from market stalls, to shops and then to wholesalers. In effect, even to this day the organisation of my business group is still modelled on that initial structure created many years ago. The only difference now is that it is under the umbrella of a holding company, the size of the turnover is rather different, and the customers often tend to be governments.

"Today, I have twelve companies in different countries, and I have about five hundred employees. The latest company is one which charters aircrafts. And the next one, which I'm still setting up, will be a company dealing with electronic engineering, a branch of engineering which I greatly admire, and for which I predict a brilliant future. That's a bit of a rough and ready sketch of what I do."

"Wow, Pierre, without knowing it, I've saved the life of an industrial magnate. I'm almost tempted to get you to open up an account with us...after all we're called BNI: Banca Nazionale dell'Industria," said Tonio laughing. "In fact, I'm surprised that nobody has thought of that before."

"Don't be surprised. As you well know, for us Swiss, discretion is extremely important; essential, I'd say. And I'm no different. For instance, I'm aware of certain transactions, some which were quite major, which have taken place between your branch in Milan and some of our companies in Lugano. Involving steel if I'm not mistaken."

They were interrupted by Bruno, who arrived accompanied by one of the two taciturn men he had met the previous week. He had a bundle of newspapers under one arm, and the famous bag in the other hand. He seemed genuinely pleased to see Tonio.

"Don't tell me, you've been able to keep him away from that phone all afternoon?"

"Well, not entirely, he has taken a few calls."

Bruno shook his head and said, "to think he promised the doctors that he would take things easy, and instead, just look at the pile of papers he wants to look at and sign."

Tonio understood that it was time to leave. Pierre clasped his hand in his, and looked him in the eye without saying anything. There was no need for words between the two men to understand the respect and friendship which each felt for the other.

On leaving the hospital, Tonio noticed a dark Mercedes, identical to the one involved in the accident, which was parked on the other side of the road. He thought it was the other taciturn man at the wheel, who appeared to be keeping a careful watch on who was entering and leaving the hospital.

10

A couple of weeks after his trip to Rennes, Pierre told Tonio that he was leaving the hospital and that he was moving to Paris for a while, where his TEC Group owned an apartment in Avenue Foch. It was the most practical solution for him, so he could have rehabilitation therapy on his ankle, and at the same time work freely. The TEC apartment was equipped with numerous telephone lines and a telex machine, so Pierre could meet business people in its ample office.

The two friends began to meet on a regular basis, and Pierre often invited him to dinner. On occasions there were dinners, which were also attended by members from the international industrial world or by directors of the TEC Group, but more often than not, they dined alone in the apartment, or at a Chinese restaurant not far from Avenue Foch.

It was a period during which their friendship went from strength to strength.

Thinking back to those times many years later, Tonio realised how two events which were completely separate from each other – his meeting with Irene first, and then the one with Pierre a week later – had resulted in a completely unexpected turn in his life.

Up till then, Tonio's life could have been described as 'normal' – not 'ordinary' in the narrowest sense of the word, but above all, 'normal'.

He had been born into a well-to-do family, which had deep roots in Calabria and in Brazil.

His grandfather, nicknamed *Il Grande Antonio*, had been sent by his father to Brazil to procure wood for the family sawmills, which supplied sleepers for the newly expanding Italian railway companies at the beginning of the century.

Tonio's great-grandfather had taken this decision when he realised that trees for felling were becoming increasingly scarce on his lands in Calabria.

In that distant country *Il Grande Antonio* cut down an enormous number of trees. He built roads, schools and hospitals in the Mato Grosso, a region which was still semi-wild at the time.

He created a myriad of other commercial activities and set himself up as the sole importer of Ford motor cars into the region.

He even found the time to get to know a pretty Brazilian girl of noble Portuguese origins, whom he married and by whom he had no fewer than ten children. Half of them were born in Brazil, among whom was Fernando, the first son, Tonio's father, and half in Italy, most of whom were born in Naples to where the family had moved in the early 1930s. At that time, *Il Grande Antonio* expanded and consolidated the family's business empire, setting up leather factories in Italy, which supplied shoes and boots to the Italian Army, as well as several companies importing and exporting raw materials.

During one of his lengthy study periods in Italy, Fernando met Luciana, the daughter of a stockbroker, who was much younger than him. He fell in love with her, married her, and after the birth of Tonio he took her to Brazil, where he thought he could offer her a well-off, comfortable life in the bosom of a family, which was well-known and extremely wealthy.

Unfortunately, after the death of *Il Grande Antonio* only two years later, things began to take a turn for the worse. In fact the two eldest brothers, Fernando and Domenico, who had taken over the reins of the business empire, realised that they were not up to the task of profitably managing their father's businesses. They delegated the administration of the companies to some dubious characters, who claimed to be friends of the family, but squandered their immense fortune in the space of a few years.

Fernando was forced to find himself a job, but never having worked before, and not having the business shrewdness of his father, he embarked upon several initiatives, which regularly failed. His dream of restoring the family to its former glories was miserably dashed.

Not seeing any other alternative Luciana (who, unlike her husband, possessed a strong and practical character, and who in the meantime had given birth to a daughter), returned to Italy to her father's house, and put into practice what she had learnt from the nuns at her girls' college many years previously by opening a dress-making business, which soon became the best in the city, and claimed a great part of the Neapolitan nobility among its clientele.

It was through his mother that Tonio had received a thorough Catholic education, having attended various religious institutions in the city. After getting a degree in economics he went into banking where, partly because of his marked flair for international finance, and partly because of his good command of English, he was to build a brilliant career.

After the death of his mother, to whom he was very close indeed, Tonio decided to increase his international banking experience by accepting foreign postings. By now he had been in Paris a good four years.

One day Pierre asked Tonio how the North Korean project was proceeding. Tonio informed him that it was in the final stages of negotiation. The Koreans had been really insistent in their demand not to begin paying back their loan for a full two years, contrary to the eighteen-month period which the funding banks were ready to concede. This had left a slightly bitter taste in Tonio's mouth, but it did not seem to worry the other banks.

The copious loan documentation had been sent to Rome two weeks earlier, and was now being closely scrutinised by the International Credit Office, which was weighing up the risk factors. The reply to the lending banks had to be given within ten days; otherwise the BNI would be excluded from the operation.

Two days later, Pierre invited him to dinner the following night. However, instead of the usual hour of eight, he asked him to come at around midnight. Tonio found this rather strange, but accepted the invitation nonetheless.

When he arrived at Pierre's house the following evening, Pierre was in the company of an elderly man with oriental features, whom Tonio took to be Chinese.

"Tonio, allow me to present Mister Li to you. Mister Li has agreed to have dinner with us," Pierre said in English. His tone although matter of fact was very serious.

As soon as they sat down to dinner, Pierre said, "Tonio, I'd like you to know that Mister Li is Korean, and that he is one of President Kim Il Sung's closest collaborators.

"Mister Li was a General in the Korean Army, and in his capacity as personal adviser to the President, he is aware of everything which concerns his country. Mister Li, naturally, knows of the financial operation which your bank wishes to participate in.

"I've known Mister Li for over twenty years, and I can guarantee that he is a wise and honest man.

"I've asked him to come here this evening, because I'd like him to tell you something of great interest to you. In accepting my invitation, he is literally risking his life. And believe me, I'm not exaggerating! Nobody must know that he's come out of his hotel tonight.

"I've asked Mister Li to return a big favour, which I did for him in the past, and an even bigger one I'm about to do him in the not too distant future."

Tonio was bewildered; he did not understand what was going on. Those words resounded upon him like a premonition of bad news, which, in fact, was not slow in coming.

In a subdued voice and in not very good English, Mister Li told him a story, which at first Tonio could hardly believe, but which gradually, as Mister Li progressed, began to fill his mind with all its enormous implications.

First of all, he said that his real name was not Mister Li. He preferred not to reveal his true identity in order to protect himself and Tonio too.

He told him that the eight hundred million dollar fund, which was about to be deposited in the vaults of the Central Korean Bank, was the greatest robbery in history. It was a swindle of worldwide proportions.

Once the money had been deposited, it would not be used for industrial reconstruction, which the country sorely needed, but rather would have been earmarked almost exclusively for nuclear research, which Korea kept very secret.

Not to say that a large tranche of the money would have finished up in Switzerland in the personal accounts of the President and a few officials.

Two years later, perhaps less, Korea would officially declare that it was not in a position to service her debt, and would have asked for a moratorium.

The experience of other countries with outstanding debts, which had declared bankruptcy, in their turn appeared to indicate that the re-negotiation period for the loan could well last several years. To conclude the whole matter could well take up to ten years or even longer, in order to reach some sort of compromise, with the end result clearly being that only a small fraction of the initial debt would be repaid, and only then over a very long time scale.

When Mister Li finished, there was a moment's silence. Tonio, still incredulous, could barely comprehend and imagine the consequences of what he had just heard.

His bank would have sustained enormous financial damage and Tonio's reputation would have been torn to shreds.

He was speechless. He felt as if he had received a massive punch in the stomach. A thousand questions crowded his mind. He was on the point of asking one when Mister Li got up and, without waiting for the dessert or the fruit course, took his leave with his eyes downcast.

At the last moment he turned to Tonio and only said, "Sorry…" Pierre accompanied his guest to the door, while Tonio remained seated in his place, his eyes wide open in amazement, and his mind in a turmoil.

"Tonio," Pierre said, when Mister Li had left. "What you have witnessed tonight is a small token of my gratitude to you. You still have time to drag your bank out of this unholy mess.

"However, I will say this to you: be very careful, no one, I repeat, absolutely no one must ever know the source of your information. If it ever came out that your source was Mister Li, who officially doesn't exist, or was me, I'd be the first to deny it. Find a way out of it for yourself. I trust you, so I can tell you the background to this story.

"Mister Li and I have done a lot of business together during the time when he was the head of the Korean armed forces. Mister Li now wants to break off all ties. He no longer has any trust whatsoever in Kim Il Sung. He considers him to be merely an ignorant warmonger, who, during many years of his tyranny, has been able only to reinforce the army and the cult of his personality.

"North Korea is extremely poor. The people clearly go hungry. That's just about it, they don't have enough food. I've seen them with my very own eyes quite recently.

"Only the army is well fed. Infant mortality is at an alarmingly high level. On the President's strictest orders, news about this state of affairs must on no account go beyond the border. Even South Korea isn't aware of what's going on beyond the Demilitarised Zone, which runs along the thirty-eighth parallel. China, the historical ally of North Korea, is beginning to distance herself from her former friend, as she continues to follow her policy of opening up much more to the West.

"North Korea is a country destined to become even more isolated than it already is. When you told me about the operation which you are setting up, I tried to find out where that godforsaken country would have found the funds to repay such a large debt.

"When I found out that Mister Li was in Paris for a couple of days to be examined by a French surgeon, I forced him, yes, just as I say, I forced him to come here this evening in order to speak to you.

"In exchange, I'll keep my word and the promise I made to him a few months ago, that after his heart operation which he'll undergo probably in a few weeks time here in Paris, Mister Li, who will be accompanied by his wife, won't be going back home. He'll ask for political asylum and will resettle in all probability in the States with a new identity. And I'm the one who's organising all this for him. That's it, I've told you everything. It's up to you now to make the necessary moves. In my view you've still got time to get out of it."

"Thanks Pierre," Tonio said. "I'm speechless. I've got so many questions to ask you, but I understand that you can't tell me any more. I'll leave you now.

"I have the feeling that I'm in for a few days which are going to be very…how shall I put it…intense."

Driving home – it was almost dawn – Tonio realised that he was experiencing the very same sensation he had felt towards Pierre a few weeks earlier.

The man he had come to respect, and for whom he felt a deep affection, had revealed himself to be more and more unpredictable, and he felt that he was still hiding something from him. It was clear that Pierre was moving in a universe which was very different from his. It was also clear that there were some mysterious aspects in Pierre's life which Tonio promised himself to uncover.

11

The following afternoon Tonio found himself sitting in front of the President of the BNI.

"Brignani, you're telling me that we have to get out of the Korean operation. And you don't want to tell me why? I hope you're joking! Please tell me it's a joke."

"Unfortunately not sir," Tonio replied, "I'm not joking in the slightest. The information which has been brought to my attention has come from a reliable and impeccable source. I've promised not to reveal his identity. I've given my word. It's an extremely delicate matter. If you take my advice, I guarantee you won't regret it."

"I don't understand, Brignani. Up to yesterday you've bombarded the International Credit Office with requests to give absolute priority to this investment. But today…what's happened in these few hours? You have to give me something more in order to get me to change my mind. You understand that don't you?"

"Look sir, I can only tell you that if what I've discovered becomes common knowledge, all hell will be let loose. I'll take all responsibility regarding you, the bank and its shareholders. I don't think I've ever let you down. I beg you to believe me. I ask you to put your trust in me once more."

"Christ, Brignani! Do you realise what you're asking me to do? Apart from the loss of profit, what kind of impression will we make on the other participating banks and on the international financial community?"

"I've thought of that as well sir, and I've thought out a plan which will allow us to leave the project without too much loss of face. I've worked on this most of the night and during my flight here."

"Brignani, I don't like this whole affair. Either you tell me what you've heard, or we go ahead with the project. If you wish you can stay out of the negotiations."

"President Aletti, I expected this reaction from you. It's more than justified and I understand your position.

"Unfortunately it's not just a matter of loss of profits or of face. We're dealing here with very serious matters, which will have far reaching consequences for the politics of that country and well beyond its borders.

"Believe me, one day you'll be glad that you weren't involved. I'm sorry but I can't tell you any more. If you don't believe me, I'll have no other alternative but to tender my resignation. I'm not bluffing. I don't wish to be involved with this operation. My name has been associated to the project right from the beginning, and I too have a reputation to uphold.

"If I'm forced to resign, I'd like you to know that I'll do it this very day, and in my letter of resignation I'll add a note in which I'll explain my reasons, together with my reticence in exposing the BNI to the risks in this operation.

"Quite frankly I don't know how the bank's shareholders will react when they see a large sum of money go up in smoke after a large financial operation like this has collapsed."

There was a long silence between the two men. Then Tonio noticed a perceptible change in the President's expression and he understood that he had won the battle.

"Well then, Brignani, do you even resort to blackmail now? I've known you long enough to understand that you're deadly serious. Well then, what's this plan you have in mind?"

"It's very simple, you'll have to play the part of the ultra-cautious banker. Not that you aren't, of course, but the 'get out' will be provided by the Koreans themselves.

"You'll have to insist on the repayments beginning to be made in eighteen months time. You'll ask for further information which I already know, nobody will be able to provide you with. I personally will draw up a list for you.

"You'll have to put the poor chaps in the Credits Office through their paces, who in turn will pass the hot potato to me in Paris. I'll react very annoyed and embarrassed in having to ask for the re-opening of the dossier, which the original funding banks consider to be already closed.

"In other words we have to stall for time. A lot of time. We will get back to them just after the official entry deadline has expired, without having reached a decision. We'll be shut out.

"Certainly, in the immediate future, we won't have covered ourselves in glory. They'll say that we weren't prepared for an operation on this scale and that President Aletti's a pain in the arse, excuse my language.

"As for the funding of the project, don't worry about it because unfortunately, it'll still go ahead. There are at least three or four other banks ready to take the BNI's place. Please believe me that when the shit hits the fan in a few years or perhaps even in a few months' time, you'll be covered in glory."

On the return flight to Paris, that same evening, Tonio went over in his mind what had happened recently. He could still scarcely believe that recent events could have so dramatically affected his job. In fact, he realised that a few hours earlier, he had gone out on a limb putting all of his future professional life on the line.

At the end of the day, all this was based on what had been suggested to him by a person he had only met a few weeks before. He felt confused and excited at the same time. He had placed his bet. Now he awaited the outcome of the game.

12

It didn't take a long time for the 'bomb' to explode. A mere eight months after the loan had been sanctioned, the world came to know of North Korea's nuclear programme.

This happened barely three months after Mister Li's defection.

The CIA had published a document which confirmed that North Korea was developing nuclear facilities based on the processing of plutonium at a base in Yongbyon, one hundred kilometres from the capital Pyongyang.

It became common knowledge that with the help of the Soviet Union, which had supplied the machinery, and with the assistance of hundreds of Chinese and Pakistani scientists, a nuclear power station was being built on the base with an output of five megawatts. This would annually process sufficient uranium to generate seven kilos of plutonium, enough for the production of one single nuclear weapon per year.

The reaction of the West was furious. After many entreaties to the Korean President, urging him to desist from his projects, things passed to a second stage: economic sanctions were imposed against North Korea. Urged by their respective governments, the banks which had arranged the loans for industrial rebuilding, demanded their money back.

Not only did Korea ignore their requests, but she made it known through the Central Bank of Korea, that the country was unwilling to pay back one single dollar until the economic sanctions had been lifted.

Everything which Pierre had predicted actually happened.

A few weeks later, Tonio was summoned to Rome by President Aletti, who thanked him for the advice about avoiding the danger and for the considerable kudos which he had gained. Aletti informed him that it had been decided to promote Tonio to the grade of Central Director. He would be in charge of the Foreign Service, taking responsibility for all the bank's international affairs. This would make him the youngest Director in the bank's entire history and would entail his return to Italy to work at the bank's headquarters in Rome. The move was scheduled to take place in a month, allowing sufficient time for a handover to the new head of the Paris branch.

A fortnight after that trip, while Tonio was busy showing some paperwork to his new replacement, Madame Marchand, his secretary, asked him whether he wished to take a call from a certain Signora Consalvo. At first he did not understand who it was, then with his heart in his mouth, he answered the telephone.

"Is that you Irene?"

"Yes Tonio, it's me, how are you?"

"Fine, fine, but where are you calling from, are you in Paris?"

"If only…no, I'm in Butera."

"Butera? Where's that?"

"What, do you mean to say you don't know where Butera is? Butera is…is…the Paris of Sicily, surely you know that?"

"OK, I get it. But tell me how are you? How are you getting on…as a married woman?"

There was a moment's pause, then Irene said, "Well…it's OK. It's…different from what I'd expected. But I've called you not to talk about me, but to congratulate you on your promotion and on your success."

"And how do you know about that? It's only just happened…who told you?"

"Nobody. I read it in the paper. You see, Peppino buys lots of papers, which he hardly ever reads, and leaves them all around the house. And I, who have little to do, I even read the financial ones. In yesterday's *Sole 24 Ore* there was an article about your bank and also about your promotion. They say that you're going to be transferred to Rome. Is it true?"

"Yes, in a couple of weeks' time…tell me about you. I'm really delighted you called. How long…it's been over a year…"

"Twenty-one months," she interrupted him.

"Yes, you're right…twenty-one months…it seems only yesterday…well then, tell about yourself."

"Well, the most important thing is that I've had a son. His name's Giovanni."

"Congratulations! I'm sure that you're a marvellous mother and that little Giovanni is very beautiful if he's taken after you."

"Yes, he's beautiful…and how about you? Have you found your French lass as Nunzia advised you to do?"

"No, come off it, no French lass. I've been too busy. More to the point how's Nunzia?"

"She's here, next to me. She sends her greetings. Unfortunately she's not feeling too well. I'm going to have to take her to Rome for a check up in a few days' time."

"To Rome? But then we might be able to meet up if I've moved by then. Here, write down my office phone number in Rome. Otherwise I can phone you…may I?"

"No, it's better if you don't…I'm phoning you from a public phone…it's better if I call you, but I wouldn't want to disturb you…"

"Come off it, don't be silly. Call me whenever you want to…you must promise me. And tell me if there's anything which I can do for you or Nunzia in Rome."

"I promise you. I'll call you again. Ciao, Director."

"Ciao, *piccola*. See you soon…I hope."

Tonio remained silent for a moment, thinking about the call. Then he went into the adjacent office and said to his colleague who was to take his place, “Roberto, this evening I want to take you out to dinner. We must celebrate!”

“Great. Celebrate what?”

“Life. Life’s lovely surprises!”

Before going out that evening, Tonio took a road map of Italy and looked for Butera in Sicily. He found it difficult to locate. When at last he found that small dot on the southern coast of Sicily, not far from Caltanisetta, he could not help but ask himself what Irene was doing in that godforsaken hole.

13

Tonio and Roberto went to dinner at the *Sans Culottes* in Rue Guisarde in the Latin Quarter, one of Tonio's favourite restaurants.

It was run by two Italian brothers; the food was good and the prices reasonable. Above all, Tonio liked the atmosphere there. The restaurant stayed open until daybreak and was a magnet for artists, singers and nightclub dancers, who would go there to dine after their shows. It was there that Tonio had always met women who, like him, were not looking for relationships which would be too serious. Generally these affairs only lasted a few months.

The two men stayed in the *Sans Culottes* until late, and it was almost three in the morning when they decided to go home. When Tonio parked the Triumph outside his apartment, he noticed two people talking near the entrance to the block where he lived. They looked like two night hawks, who were bidding each other farewell.

When he inserted his key to open the main door, the two, with a sudden movement, threw themselves onto him hurling him into the building.

Before Tonio was able to recover from this surprise move and open his mouth, he found an arm gripping his neck and a knife a few centimetres away from his eyes.

He let out a throttled groan and tried to free himself. The man in front of him growled, "Don't breathe you piece of shit. You see this knife? If you move I'll poke it in your eye. Got it?"

He spoke French with a strange accent. He was tall with curly hair and was wearing a dark jumper. He was perhaps North African. His breath smelled of beer. Tonio had difficulty breathing.

He dug his heels in, trying to free himself. This time it was the one behind him who spoke, "You turd, haven't you understood that you mustn't move? If you try again I'll break this shitty neck of yours."

With an enormous effort Tonio was able to emit some sounds which resembled words: "wallet…pocket…jacket…"

"What ya' talking about, you bastard. I've told you to keep quiet."

Tonio tried again, "Money…in pocket…jacket."

"Money?" said the one in front of him. "Who, you prick, wants your shitty money? We don't want your money!"

The man was just a few centimetres away from his face. In the shadows of the lobby Tonio caught his eye and was afraid.

The man had an expressionless face, as if what he was doing was something he did every day. A cold expression, indifferent to everything around him. Tonio knew with absolute certainty that this man would not hesitate to stab him in the eye with the knife.

"Listen to me, missy," the man continued. "I'm not interested in your money. And I want to be sure that you understand what I've got to tell you."

The man must have guessed that Tonio was at the end of his tether because of lack of oxygen.

A glance to his companion was sufficient for him to loosen his hold slightly. Tonio was able to breathe in a mouthful of air into his burning lungs.

'But is it possible that nobody passes by here?' he thought. Then he remembered that it was actually three in the morning.

"Well then, my friend, open your ears carefully. And pay attention to what I'm going to say to you now, 'cos I don't want to have to repeat it again. Understood?"

Tonio agreed with a slight nod of his head.

"You have to deliver a message. You have to deliver a message to your Swiss friend. To that fine dickhead Haber. Are ya' listening to me?"

Tonio did not move. He did not understand. 'What's this got to do with Pierre?' he thought to himself.

"*Mademoiselle* Brignani, are you listening to me? Have you heard what I've told you?"

Tonio's surprise increased considerably. 'How come they know my name?' he thought. This put things under a completely different light: it was clear that he was not dealing with a couple of muggers. The situation had taken a totally unexpected turn. Tonio began to be seriously worried.

"Hey you, you ugly turd, have ya heard what I've said to you?"

Tonio nodded once more.

"Good boy. Listen then," the man continued, resting his knife on Tonio's cheekbone directly below his eye. "The message you have to deliver to your son of a whore friend is this: he has to stop playing the shit with Multari. You have to tell him that Multari's money is as good as anybody else's; he's made a commitment and now he has to honour it. You must tell him that Multari's fed up and he'll give him a week to deliver the goods. Understood? And if he doesn't do it, he'll find himself in a load of trouble. This thing tonight is only a warning. Understood you bastard? Make a sign to show you've understood."

Tonio looked at him with hatred before nodding slightly.

"OK. That's how I like you. Now I want to tell you something else which you can pass on to your big-arsed Switzer. Do you know why we've chosen you as our messenger? It's because we know that you and he are as thick as thieves. We know that he'll listen to you. And watch it, you'd better be good at convincing him because, dear *Mademoiselle* Brignani, if you don't manage to convince him, we'll come and call on you again. And then we'll really have some fun with you, especially him," he said, looking at the other man. "My friend here goes mad over arses like yours..."

Having said this, he made a sign to the man who was standing behind Tonio. The latter released his grip on his throat and pressed his hand over his mouth, pulling Tonio's head towards his chest. The other man in front of him, with a very quick gesture, moved the knife downwards, cutting the skin for a couple of centimetres.

The whole thing happened in the batting of an eyelid.

Tonio did not realise straight away what had been done to him. Only after a few moments did he feel a burning sensation on his face, followed by a shiver which after a split second transformed itself into a searing pain.

He could not believe it. That man had cut his face! A few seconds later, he felt blood flowing down his cheek which trickled down between his shirt and his neck.

"That's a little souvenir which I'll leave you with. Just so you won't forget us," the one with the knife said, who seemed to be the leader. Then he added, "We're leaving now. Don't get any strange ideas into your head shouting out like a young woman who's had her bag pinched.

"Anyway nobody'd hear you at this time. If you want to call the police, be our guest. By the time they arrive we'll be well away anyhow. But before you do it, I'd advise you to consult your friend Haber, I'm sure he wouldn't be too pleased.

"He likes to keep well clear of the cops. Too many explanations to give...too many questions...*Au revoir ma cherie*."

Having said this, they opened the entrance gate, and instantly disappeared into the night.

Tonio remained standing for a few minutes, pressing his hand against his cheek, still shocked by what had happened. He went slowly towards the lift, with his blood dripping on the floor. He entered his apartment, went into the bathroom, washed and disinfected his wound and put a plaster on it. Then he walked out onto the landing and cleaned, as best he could, the floor in front of his door and in the lift which was still at his floor. He went back into his apartment and poured out a good shot of whisky in the hope of gathering his thoughts. He sat on the side of the bed, trying to make sense of all that had happened.

Thinking back to the 'message', which had been given him by the two thugs, a blind rage began to take hold of him.

Little by little, as he relived the scene, he realised that he had been used for something which did not really concern him, and over which he began to ask himself many questions.

After a few minutes, the rage reached an unbearable level in him, it transferred itself to his muscles. Tonio began to tremble and to grind his teeth. He barely restrained himself from shouting out at the top of his voice. There was only one thing for him to do: he went to the telephone and dialled the number.

At the fifth ring Pierre answered. The voice sounded sleepy, and at the same time, betrayed a certain degree of annoyance. "Hello, who…"

Tonio did not give him the time to finish his sentence, "I need to see you. Now!"

"But do you know what time…"

"I don't give a damn. I'm coming to see you." He did not give the other time to reply. He slammed down the receiver, put on a sweater and went out. It was almost dawn.

14

It did not take him much more than ten minutes to reach Avenue Foch. Number 23, halfway up the road between Place de l'Etoile and the Bois de Boulogne, was a small building in the Haussman style, with a small garden around it protected by a high gate.

Technical Engineering Consultants, who had leased it for years in order to accommodate Pierre or others travelling to Paris, had bought it outright a few months previously. Tonio knew that they had paid an astronomic price for it because of its prime location.

Pierre had transformed the ground floor and the basement into offices, where some ten people worked. On the first floor there were some reception rooms, while on the second floor there were two very comfortable apartments, which were completely separate. Pierre's apartment was on the top floor. He now spent more time in Paris than in Zurich.

After parking his car nearby, Tonio approached the gate. He found Francis, the Corsican caretaker who was almost two metres tall and had a pockmarked face, waiting for him. Francis said to him in his usual polite voice, "*Monsieur* Haber is waiting for you on the third floor."

"Thank you, Francis. I see you've strengthened security. Is that CCTV?" Tonio asked, noting the equipment at the corners of the building.

"*Oui Monsieur*. Installed a week ago!"

Tonio ran up the stairs. He found Pierre waiting for him on the third floor landing. He was wearing a blue silk dressing gown, and his hair looked as if it had been combed in a hurry.

He had stubble on his face. He appeared to Tonio to be older than his usual self.

"How are you Tonio? How come…heh, what's happened to your face? Have you cut…?"

"Forget about my face," Tonio interrupted him, striding into the apartment in front of Pierre. "Now you're going to sit down on that chair, and listen carefully, because I've got a message to give you." He said this in a low voice, throwing a threatening glance at his friend.

"Hey, hey, calm down…a message?" the other replied "What message?"

"A message from your friend Multari. And it's a signed message to boot. Do you see the signature?" Tonio said pointing to his wounded cheek. "Here's the signature! A fucking cut made with a knife an hour ago, right outside my door."

Pierre became visibly pale. He was looking at Tonio, but it was as if he did not see him. He was wringing his hands. He seemed to be lost in thought, speechless.

"Well then?" Tonio shouted. "Do you want to hear the message?" His voice was trembling. He was no longer able to control himself. His accumulated rage exploded in a torrent of brusque and cutting words. "He says that you have to deliver the goods. But what goods are we talking about? And what the fuck has it got to do with me? Could you bloody well tell me what the fuck it has to do with me? Multari sent the message via those two bastards, that his money is as good as anybody else's. And he's giving you a week to deliver the goods. What the fuck is he talking about, can you tell me?"

Pierre slowly lowered his head and covered his face with his hands.

Tonio began shouting again. "What are you doing, why are you hiding your face? That's not going to cut any ice with me. Look at me!" He moved closer to Pierre and began to shake him by the shoulders. "It's best if you begin to talk, my friend, because I'm not leaving here until you've told me everything. And do you want to know another thing? Those bastards told me that if I wanted to phone the police, it would be better if I checked with you first, as you'd certainly prefer that I didn't phone them, so as not to have to give too many explanations. Can you tell me what the fuck's going on? Tell me what you have to hide!"

Pierre did not move.

Tonio, exasperated, gave him another sharp shake. "Speak up dammit!"

Pierre remained seated in silence for a few moments longer. Then he slowly lifted his head and looked at Tonio.

"I'm sorry," he said. His face was as white as a sheet. His eyes were lifeless. He had a slight tremor at the corner of his mouth.

Tonio had never seen him in this state before. He seemed a different person. He gave the impression of an old and defenceless man.

"You're sorry?" said Tonio. He had regained control of his voice. After a moment he continued, "I bet you're sorry. But it's best if you start talking. I'm serious. I'm not leaving here until you tell me everything...and do you know the funny thing about all this? It's that according to this Multari, I'm the one who's supposed to convince you to deliver the goods. But do you realise? That son of a bitch...what the fuck has it to do with me?"

Tonio did not like using foul language, but under the circumstances it came to him spontaneously. It helped to get the rage out of his system.

He went to sit down in an armchair in front of Pierre. They were in his study, which was finely decorated. On antique items of furniture, there were objects of value with a provenance from several countries, mostly Oriental and African. In the centre of a low table, there was a silver frame displaying in black and white, the only photograph in the room, of a very beautiful woman. Tonio knew that it was Pierre's wife, who had died very young of a brain tumour.

Tonio waited. Quite a few minutes elapsed. Then Pierre got up and took a few steps towards the window, turning his back on him as he did so. Then he turned round slowly.

Tonio noticed a transformation in his friend's expression, which had taken place in those few moments. His eyes had regained their sparkle. He had squared his shoulders. There was a new man in front of him. He realised that Pierre had taken a decision. His friend began speaking in a firm and resolute voice.

"Yes, I'm sorry Tonio. I'm very sorry for what's occurred. It shouldn't have happened. But you're right. You've a right to know. I want to talk to you and tell you everything. Not only about Multari. Multari's not worth a bean. You see Multari…"

"He's not worth a bean? What do you mean…?"

"Please let me speak. I promise to tell you everything. I want to tell you everything right from the beginning. However, I want you to understand that you'll not like all you'll hear…on the contrary…I know that you'll find it hard to accept some things. I know you. You're an upright person, solid, respectable with sound principles. I admire you a lot, Tonio. Furthermore I can say that I'm as fond of you as a son. I'm not exaggerating. From the day of the accident, up there in Normandy, some things have changed in my life. For the better I think. And you, without knowing it, have had a role in this change. But I'd like to explain that to you on another occasion, if you'll let me. Now it's only fair that you know more. Talking about it will be a liberation for me too…and by the end you'll know who the real Pierre Haber is. I don't expect you to understand everything straight away, but I beg you not to come to any hasty conclusions about what I'm about to tell you."

Tonio was not expecting a speech of this kind. He had listened to him with a frown on his forehead. He did not understand what Pierre was driving at, but at the same time he was pleased to hear these words which demonstrated an affection which Tonio shared.

When Pierre had pronounced the word 'son', Tonio did not consider it to be out of place. He automatically looked at Pierre, unconsciously asking himself whether he could ever have regarded him as a father. And he realised with a certain amount of relief that the thought did not trouble him. But he was different; he was a friend above all. Perhaps he was the friend which he had always longed for in his father, but had never had.

For an instant he remembered Pierre's son, the real one, with a hint of jealousy. He could not help noticing that in the room, there was no photograph of Rainer.

Pierre was looking at him. The shadow of a smile appeared on his face, as if he had guessed Tonio's thoughts. He then said, "Today I need your time, Tonio. I need to spend a few hours with you. In order to tell you lots of things. I'll need more of your time, much more of your time, over the following days. I'm asking you as a big favour. The biggest favour I'll ever ask you."

Tonio opened his arms as if to say 'Here I am at your disposal. You have all the time you need.'

Then Pierre added, "You won't believe it, but I'd already decided to speak to you, to tell you about some aspects of my life which you don't know about. I was only waiting for the right moment. Well, today's events have put an end to the wait, despite what I would have liked to have done. But it's better like this. From now on there won't be any secrets between us, I promise you."

He approached Tonio and he held out his hand, "Still friends?"

After a moment's hesitation, Tonio shook his hand. But all the questions which had taken him there that morning were still etched on his face.

Then Pierre added, "Come on let's go to the kitchen…we both need a cup of good, strong coffee."

15

They crossed the length of the apartment and entered the kitchen. An ample, well-appointed room, which looked onto a small, but perfectly maintained garden. Tonio knew that Francis looked after it lovingly and had begun to introduce some changes to it, bringing some plants from Corsica, which he hoped would survive in the much colder Parisian climate.

The kitchen was the undisputed kingdom of Janine, Francis' wife. She was a petite woman with very dark eyes and hair, which indicated strength and determination. Tonio had no doubt who wore the trousers in that household.

Janine's greatest concern was that Pierre, and especially Tonio, who had been adopted by her from the first day they met, did not eat enough, with the result that the portions of food she served were always enormous.

When the two friends entered the kitchen, they saw that the coffee had been freshly made and that Janine was taking some ring-shaped cakes out of the oven.

When she turned round to greet them, she was speechless at the sight of Tonio's face. A glance from Pierre, however, sufficed for her not to ask questions. The two men sat down and had breakfast in silence, each one immersed in his own thoughts.

Tonio's rage had abated, replaced by a restlessness caused by having to wait to hear what Pierre had to say to him.

After breakfast, Pierre went to have a shower while Tonio waited for him in the office.

When Pierre returned, a quarter of an hour later, he was wearing a tracksuit. He had shaved and had obviously put on a fragrant after-shave.

He began speaking even before sitting at his desk. Tonio sat on a sofa next to the window.

"While I was having my shower," Pierre said, "I asked myself where should I begin this story.

"Naturally the obvious reply is always the same: from the beginning. Therefore my dear Tonio, I'll begin by telling you some facts about my life, which go back a long time, to the period when I was fifteen and living in Beirut, in Lebanon.

"It's important that I begin there, in order for you to understand what's happened, and how I've arrived at where I am today.

"My father was posted to that beautiful city – well, it was then anyway – by the Swiss Authorities, as commercial attaché at the Consulate.

"They were the golden years for the Lebanon and especially for the capital, Beirut, which was called the Paris of the Middle East, with its boulevards built by the French after the First World War. And just imagine, Lebanon was also known as *Sweezra al Shark*: the Switzerland of the Middle East!

"There was a continual flowering of banks, luxury hotels, casinos…and lots of beautiful women. I'd finished my schooling in Zurich and my father was proud to enrol me into The American University of Beirut, a first-class institution, which was on a par with the best universities in Europe. I enrolled in the Faculty of Engineering and I graduated four years later in 1964."

Pierre was interrupted when the telephone rang. It was somebody from the office downstairs. "No" he said, "no phone calls. I don't want to be disturbed. Speak to Bernard about it." Bernard was the manager of the ground floor office.

Then half closing his eyes, almost as if he were concentrating on the story he had begun to narrate, he went on.

"They were golden years for me too, believe me. Above all, I had all the freedom I wanted. My father, who was always busy and always travelling, let me do whatever I wanted, so long as I carried on with my studies.

"That's how I became friends with quite a few undergraduate students. We formed a close-knit group of about ten students from different ethnic origins: American, Lebanese, Armenian and even Palestinian, the sons of political refugees. All these lads were on the ball. I learnt a lot from them: their customs, traditions…their different aspirations. One thing that united us was the common goal of doing something substantial to make the world a better place. It goes without saying that we discussed politics a lot. Ah…the sleepless nights!

"Do you know, I'm still in touch with some of them. We had an easy life, but we also saw a lot of people making a pot of money in the most disparate ways.

"One day, one of the Palestinian lads took me to a small market in the suburbs of the city where, he said, you could buy the strangest things at absolutely rock bottom prices. It was in fact an open-air *Souk*, where you could buy almost anything, although it was mostly second-hand junk. It was there that I noticed that several stalls were selling old military uniforms, some in a lamentable state so they were almost rags. And the interesting thing was that they seemed to be selling like hot cakes!

"My friend explained to me that these uniforms were often used as work clothes, but they were also much appreciated because at times, if you wanted to be enlisted in one of the militias which flourished in the Middle East, you had to have a uniform. Any old one would do as long as it was green or grey.

"It was then that I had a brainwave. A few days earlier I had heard my father speaking on the phone to someone in

Switzerland, who wanted to find an importer in Lebanon, willing to sell military materiel, especially second-hand uniforms. I heard my father reply that he didn't know of anyone who imported that sort of thing, but that he would find out about it for him.

"I asked my friend to ask the sellers where they got their supplies from. They complained that, unfortunately, they were in the hands of people who weren't professional; who didn't keep their word, and who weren't reliable because they themselves had problems sourcing their merchandise. To cut a long story short, I got in touch with the man in Switzerland, who was an agent for the Swiss army. I founded an import business; rented a warehouse and began bringing in used military equipment such as uniforms, blankets, sweaters, socks, boots…on a regular basis.

"In the space of a few months, I had the monopoly in distributing this kind of material, to such an extent that I had to rent another warehouse. Then requests started coming in for more specific items: spares for military vehicles, tyres, tents and so on. The fact is that by the time I graduated, in 1964, I had two companies to my name. I owned five warehouses and I had twenty people working for me. The number of my suppliers had also increased.

"I'd also been successful in cutting out the middlemen. At this stage I was importing from the American, French, and British armies…in brief, on the one side they wanted to get rid of their surplus and on the other, there were people who were willing to pay good money for these goods. I had a distribution network also in bordering countries. Things went from strength to strength for months, indeed for years.

"Then one day in 1968, a university friend of mine, Sarkis, an Armenian, asked me whether I'd be willing to import a limited number of arms from Bulgaria, destined for South America. He told me that it was a perfectly legal operation with government documentation approved at the highest levels, and it was a transaction which had the complete blessing of the United States.

"As proof of this, he arranged a meeting for me with the American Consul who confirmed everything. The Consul told me, in reply to my many questions, at that particular moment, the United States could not expose itself directly for political reasons, but that they would approve the involvement of another intermediary with a good reputation such as me. Finally, and this was the icing on the cake, he outlined for me the profit margin: astronomical. And that, my dear Tonio, is how I became a military consultant, or if you prefer it, an arms merchant."

"An arms merchant?" Tonio did not believe his ears, "are you joking?"

"Oh no, my friend, I'm deadly serious."

"Wait a minute, wait a minute, Pierre. You're telling me that you became an arms dealer. Do you mean to say that you're *still* one?" Tonio asked.

"Yes," the other replied.

Tonio looked at him incredulously. He got up, stood in front of Pierre and said, "Look, you're not taking the piss out of me are you? I really don't think this is the right time for that."

"No Tonio, I'm not taking the piss. It's the truth, and I can prove it to you."

Tonio went back to sit on the sofa. He did not know what to think. He looked at the clock. It was almost nine. He got up again and moved towards the desk saying, "May I make a phone call?"

Pierre pushed the telephone towards him. Tonio phoned his secretary to tell her that he'd be in the office later. Then he went back and sat down on the sofa once more.

"So," he said, "Technical Engineering Consultants are in this too?"

"Oh, no, no," replied Pierre. "TEC hasn't anything to do with this whatsoever."

"Well then, how do you manage to…to…buy or sell…arms?"

"Well, for this kind of activity, unless you are a producer or a government, you can't just set up a company whose business activity is 'Arms Wholesaler'. I have to do it personally."

"You mean to say that you *personally* buy arms…I don't follow…how do you buy them? Who do you buy them from? Who do you sell them to?"

"Well, you must understand that these transactions aren't…what shall I say…ordinary. They take time to bring to fruition. You have to be very patient. The participants must know each other very well but above all, they must trust each other completely. In the beginning you have to work a lot on the phone. Then there's the documentation stage which is not always easy to finalise. Then at the end there are 'companies of convenience', which are able to help when undertaking transactions involving international finance. I use a small company registered in the Cayman Islands called Universal Trade and Shipping. It has practically no personnel apart from a legal section which takes care of the contracts and all my financial transactions, and they are very significant."

There was a brief silence, then Tonio exclaimed, "I don't know what to say. Everything seems so…so…surreal…Pierre, these are things we see in films!"

"Well, unfortunately they are real, you'd better believe it! This is a very flourishing trade unknown, for good reasons, to the majority of people."

"Excuse me Pierre, but are you talking about arms, real ones which shoot and kill people?"

Pierre nodded. There was a serious look on his face which made Tonio remain silent for a few minutes.

After a while Tonio spoke again. "Listen, you understand, don't you, that it's difficult for me to believe all of this. That's to say…I mean…it isn't that I don't believe you…but I know you…or at least I think…I thought I knew you…"

Pierre was quiet, and there was another long silence. Then Tonio got up and turned to the window. He looked down at the few pedestrians on the Avenue Foch; some seemed to be going to work, others were students, or young women pushing prams in the direction of the Bois de Boulogne. He heard Pierre's voice behind him. "Shall I continue with my story?"

Tonio did not reply straight away. Then he said, "I'm not sure I want to hear the rest, but tell me one thing…this Multari, does he have anything to do with…with this activity?"

"Yes."

"I understand…well, I still don't understand where I fit into all of this. Perhaps it will be worth my while listening to the rest of your story."

"Well, there's not a lot to say, except that my 'specialist' activity has grown out of all proportion over the years. It's a trade undertaken in a parallel world to that of ordinary legitimate business. The protagonists operate at a variety of different levels. I'm not trying to justify myself in your eyes, but I can say that I've always tried to play the game fairly. In the beginning I was blinded by the enormous profits to be made, and I was unscrupulous. It was always a case of small orders which went directly from the manufacturers to institutional 'users' always at the suggestion or proposal of the American authorities."

"Do you mean to say," Tonio interrupted him, "that you stayed in contact with the Americans who gave you your first business opportunity?"

"Oh yes, Tonio, I'm still in contact with the Americans…except that they're not the same Americans from way back then…you see my greatest…how can I put it…employer in this field is the government of the United States."

"The government of the United States?" Tonio's amazement increased markedly.

"Absolutely," Pierre said, happy to have caught Tonio's interest. "You see, this activity is based entirely on trust and on reputation. I've always kept my word. I've never taken on responsibilities I wasn't able to carry out. All my transactions have always gone well, with genuine documentation. The Americans, and others, have appreciated my qualities. I've also turned down some business, which would have been extremely lucrative, because the final destination of the goods was not clear. Unfortunately these transactions were carried out later by others. People who have fewer scruples…"

"Like Multari?" Tonio interrupted him.

"Yes, like Multari. Look, Multari's a small fish, a new arrival who is making a big noise. He belongs to a new generation of operators who think that they can get everything at once, and with little work…don't worry about Multari…he won't give us any more trouble…"

"How do you know he won't trouble us any more?"

"Because I phoned Bruno before I took my shower. He'll arrange delivering *our* message to Multari…"

"What do you mean?" Tonio interrupted him. "Have you too got thugs armed with knives?"

"No, Tonio, nothing like that at all. Multari will today receive a phone call from someone who'll tell him to stop his shit, otherwise he'll never work with anyone. He's risking becoming a complete pariah. If he wants to work he'll have to play by the rules…otherwise sooner or later Multari will tread on someone's toes who doesn't think the same way as me, and he'll finish up badly."

Tonio reflected for a moment about what he had heard and said, "Pierre, I can hardly believe my ears. Do you realise what you've said? And how you've said it? I seem to be listening to the words of a Mafia Godfather."

"Well, I'm sorry if I've given you that impression, but things are just as I've said they are. This parallel world is a world with strange but very precise rules. You have to operate within certain limits and within the law wherever possible. You can't go round threatening people. Look, I'm fed up with being indoors. Let's go for a stroll in the Bois. We can talk as we walk."

16

They went out of the gate and walked towards the Bois de Boulogne, under the line of chestnut trees, which decorated both sides of the Avenue Foch. It was pleasant to walk in the sun, which was not too warm in that early part of June.

Tonio could not help but admire this road each time he walked along it. With its width of one hundred and twenty metres, it was the widest in Paris. An air of opulence reigned there, of imperial *grandeur*. Sadly it was also notorious, because during the German occupation, number 84 was the headquarters of the Gestapo, and housed their torture chambers and command centre.

After a few minutes, when they had almost arrived at Porte Dauphine, Pierre began to speak once more.

"I've a feeling that I ought to be grateful to Multari. Were it not for him this conversation wouldn't be taking place. Well, at least not today. It's been my intention to tell you about all this for quite some time now. But I delayed…I put it off. And do you know why? Because recently some things have happened, which at first sight didn't seem important, but which have given me cause to reflect. Barely perceptible signs…I feel like an animal in the forest, which has smelt a slight whiff of burning, and has begun to wonder whether there's a fire or not."

"What things?" Tonio asked.

"Difficult to explain. A few chance words picked up during a conversation, glances which were more insistent than usual, slight pauses in replies…now with what's happened to you, although it *might* not have anything to do with this…you see, I don't believe in coincidences and I want to know what's going on…and something *is* going on."

"Is that why you've had the CCTV cameras installed outside?"

"That's part of it. The main reason is that both on the ground and the third floors, there are too many sensitive documents, which would be very attractive and useful to many competitors."

"Documents on the business of buying and selling arms?"

"No, no. Those are safe with my lawyers in the Cayman Islands…those are my insurance policies…no, I mean the TEC documents. We are in the process of making new acquisitions…but I don't want to talk about those now."

They crossed Place du Maréchal de Lattre de Tessigny and went into the Bois.

"Listen," Tonio said. "A little while ago, at your place, you began to speak about your dealings with the Americans, in fact you said that they are your largest employers. I don't understand this. Why do they want to use you in this business?"

"For many reasons," Pierre replied. "At the beginning they entrusted me with a few minor operations, alongside others which were much more important. They had me take part in transactions which were already under way, almost as if they were testing out my professionalism and my efficiency. This carried on for a couple of years to our mutual satisfaction.

"Then, towards the end of 1974 during a trip to Washington, I was informed that in a few months, things in Lebanon would change drastically. That political stability would end. Since I'd shown myself to be a trusted friend, they advised me to close up shop and to return to Europe, or to the States, if I wanted to. I knew that the information was reliable because it came from a member of the American Congress."

"No less! And what did you do, did you believe him?"

"Of course, I didn't have any reason not to. Also in a smaller way, I had my own informers. These had told me that since Palestinian refugees in Lebanon numbered more than three hundred thousand, the country was becoming a pressure-cooker, which was ready to explode. There had already been skirmishes between the Lebanese regular army and the Palestinian militia headed by Yasser Arafat.

"I followed their advice and within a few weeks I sold up and went back to Switzerland.

"Just in time – because right on cue, a few months later, there was a serious government crisis which escalated into the civil war which lasted until '78. In effect, all I did was transfer my businesses from one place to another. And all of them took off in an exponential fashion; on the one hand my commercial businesses diversified into the present group structure comprising steel, cereals and shipping; and on the other my specialised but very sensitive activity, the supply of arms."

"But how have you, or rather how are you, able to combine both?" Tonio asked. "This activity of supplying arms, as you call it, doesn't seem to be well-known to many people, isn't that the case? Perhaps it wouldn't be well received by everyone to know that you're an arms trafficker."

"Please Tonio, I hate the word trafficker. It's a derogatory term...applied to someone involved in illegal trading...similar to the terms wheeler-dealer, trickster, cheat, swindler. I prefer the word merchant, which is a term used to describe someone who carries out a commercial business, which is what I've done all my life. I like to be associated with those merchants of fabrics, silk merchants who came from the Far East...and to the grain merchants in mediaeval markets. It's the only thing I really know how to do well. I like dealing, negotiating. In the Middle East they consider it to be an art! After prolonged negotiations which turn out well for both parties, you get to know each other better, new friendships are formed, you learn about new traditions. Just think, there's a chap in Saudi Arabia with whom I've done a lot of business, who now considers me his brother! Do you know how I'm known in all the Middle East and beyond? The Merchant. *Al-Tajer*. Haber Al-Tajer."

They walked along the *Lac Inférieur* and then sat down on a bench in the *Alée des Dames*, not far from Auteuil race course.

Tonio asked, "Who knows about all this? You can't be working alone, surely."

"Bruno naturally, and a few others. You don't need a large organisation for a business of this kind. The important thing is to have people around you that you can trust with your life."

"And Rainer, your son? Is he also part of this restricted group?"

Pierre's face darkened for an instant. "Rainer? No, Rainer knows only a bit about this work." He remained silent for a while, and then he said shaking his head slightly. "I've always tried to keep him out of the business because, I don't think that he's cut out for this profession. He's…too impulsive…impatient…he doesn't have the qualities of a negotiator. He likes to play and he likes to win all the time. He takes unnecessary risks.

"A few years ago, I helped him set up an investment company, but I've had to bail him out on more than one occasion. Last year I put him in charge of a small company which was formed to develop new technology for mobile phones, in which I'm a firm believer, but I don't think he was particularly committed. The only thing he's interested in is this business, this, what shall we call it, my secondary business. He's fascinated by this world, by the arms and the political intrigue, but I believe above all, he's attracted by the large sums of money floating around. He's constantly asking me to let him join the business."

The two men got up from the bench and walked back to Pierre's place. Tonio began to feel the fatigue of a sleepless night.

Pierre continued, "Do you know that Rainer isn't my son?"

Tonio was amazed. "What do you mean by that?"

"It's true. When I married Erika, as soon as I graduated in 1965, she was twenty-five and was already a widow with a son of seven. Rainer is the same age as you. You were even born in the same month – May.

"Even back then he was a difficult character. He was ill-tempered, he quarrelled with everyone at school and he didn't want to study. When Erika died three years later, Rainer became impossible. It's clear that the loss of both his parents created major defects in the boy's personality.

"I did my best to alleviate his suffering. Travel, presents, parties, but above all I tried to keep close to him as much as possible, while recognising the fact that I could never take the place of his father. Nothing helped.

"In the end, two years later, I was forced to send him to a boarding school. First in Switzerland, then in England, trying to give him the best possible education. I don't think he's ever forgiven me for this. Just imagine, one day he even accused me of the death of his mother. He said that I hadn't done enough to save her from the illness..."

After a few minutes' silence, Pierre stopped and turning to Tonio said, "Since I've stated that I'm going to tell you everything, I'd like to let you know of a drastic decision I took some time ago: I've decided to finish with this business, with the supply of arms."

"Really. Why?"

"It's been a mental process that's been slowly maturing. It began a few years ago. I was no longer at ease, nor am I at present, carrying on with this activity. Things have changed over the years. People change, administrations change.

"I'm under the impression, although I can't be certain, that many players aren't above board any more. They've used me, and continue to use me, for their own hidden agendas. I've begun to dig deep and get more information, and what I've found out I haven't liked.

"The day of the accident in Normandy, the day you got to know me…having brushed with death…something happened to me, and made me open my eyes. I found it difficult to look at myself in the mirror. And that's a bad sign...so I've decided to call it a day."

"Well," Tonio said, beginning to walk once more. "If you want to know, I'm really pleased. Just the thought that my best friend, The Merchant, was also an arms dealer…I prefer to think that you are linked with the buying and selling of cereals, steel, transportation, and so on. But how are you going to get out of it?"

"There's the rub. And that's why I've been wanting to speak to you about this for some time now. I need your help."

"My help? How come?"

They had arrived at the gate to the villa.

"Well it's complicated, but I've got an idea and I'd like to talk to you about it. Not now. It would take too long to explain. Come to dinner this evening. Or tomorrow, as you wish."

"OK, Pierre, but I really don't see how I could…"

"Please," Pierre interrupted him. "It's very important to me. I wouldn't be asking you if I didn't know that you're the only person who can help me."

They decided to dine together that same evening.

Tonio went back home, had a shower and a sandwich, and went to his office.

Throughout the afternoon, he could not get what Pierre had told him out of his mind. He continued to ask himself how he could help get his friend out of business activities, which he did not know the first thing about. He thought about Pierre's nickname – The Merchant, *Al-Tajer*. All things considered, he liked it.

17

Janine had prepared lasagne with Corsican goat's cheese. A little on the heavy side, but delicious. The main course was an enormous mixed salad. After serving dinner she disappeared, leaving the two men alone.

They were in the smaller of the two dining rooms, the one that Pierre used when he was on his own, sitting at a circular mahogany table which was in the Louis Philippe style. Tonio preferred eating there rather than in the large room, which was too austere for his taste.

Pierre was pensive, taciturn, almost peevish. Tonio noted that he barely raised his head at Janine's parting greeting.

"Well then, Merchant, tell me about this plan of yours," Tonio said in a lively tone, in an attempt to brighten up the atmosphere.

Pierre filled Tonio's glass and invited him to taste the red wine, also produced in Corsica by one of Francis' cousins.

Tonio tasted the wine with appreciation, and waited.

After a few minutes' silence, Pierre began speaking. His voice was little more than a whisper.

"You see, I don't think I've made many mistakes in my life. Believe me, I'm not conceited. I've always tried to behave in a consistent way, above all being true to myself. Sometimes I've overdone things a bit, it's true, but I've always believed that nothing was really too important or irretrievable."

He paused for an instant and then continued, shaking his head and turning his eyes towards Tonio. "But that time when I accepted the first deal which Sarkis proposed to me, and then later in the business transactions immediately following that deal, I now think I made the biggest mistake of my life. I was very young, dazzled by the money which arrived by the sackful, but above all, I forgave myself because everything seemed to be done openly in the light of day and for good reasons."

"For good reasons?" Tonio interposed. "How could you think that selling arms could be justified?"

"Well, you see in 1973, at the time of my first business ventures, we were all pro-Western, pro-American. We admired everything that came out of the United States, despite the Vietnam War, which we didn't have a very clear picture of at the time. Initially I didn't ask too many questions. The reassurance of the Americans was enough for me.

"When I received an invitation from their Consul in Beirut, I even went to Washington, where I met people with key positions in Congress, and even an agent from the CIA.

"I repeat, I was literally dazzled. This continued for several years. They convinced me that what I was doing was nothing more than helping the United States to pursue their noble aims in the struggle against communism. Later on, I discovered that my first delivery was sent to Chile. And even then I didn't worry too much about it. It was only a long time later, thinking about it, that I discovered who had really received those arms. I was shocked to learn that they'd been used, together with much larger shipments supplied by others, in order to destabilise the government of Salvador Allende. The same happened with other shipments. I've sent arms to Nicaragua, Mobutu in Zaire, Roberto d'Abuison in El Salvador, Noriega in Panama and even to Saddam Hussein in Iraq."

"But Pierre! Those are all dictators, scum who've persecuted their own people and are still doing so."

"I know, Tonio, I know. But at the time I didn't know this. Nobody did. Let me finish, let me explain. I'll try to get you to understand how things developed, how I found myself in a spiral without a way out.

"You see, during those years, when you were only fifteen or so, there were two blocs: the Americans and their allies on the one side, and on the other, the one formed by the communist countries headed by the Soviet Union. We, under the American umbrella, were convinced that we were in the right, and that we'd been invested with the mission to spread democracy to the world; they on the other hand were the demons inspired by Marx, the godless, the stiflers of individuals' rights.

"And those who weren't with us, or rather with America, were against us. But there were, and still are, many countries in Asia, Africa and South America who have started to find a certain degree of political stability, through more or less democratic elections, after years of civil wars, uprisings and so on.

"Many of these new governments experienced the disapproval or even the anger of the United States, when they proclaimed their politics of 'self-determination', as the English call it: an approach born of the desire to follow a different political agenda to the USA's model. They showed their ambition to free themselves from political, economic and cultural dependence on the United States. Sometimes they refused to reduce their relations with the Soviet bloc to a bare minimum, or to suppress the number of their left-wing political parties at home, and were unwilling to open up their doors to military installations on their soil.

"During those years this was the principal mission of American foreign policy. In other words, the USA, which never had an enemy in their own 'back yard', found that they had a world-wide enemy: communism. The Cold War expanded from Europe to Asia, to Cuba, to Nicaragua. But the official line was that they weren't fighting the communists in Cuba or Nicaragua, they were fighting those countries because they were considered to be agents of the Soviet Union.

"And who provided this information to those who had to take the decisions? The CIA naturally, which wielded enormous power and funding after the end of the Second World War – the only organisation authorised to conduct clandestine operations abroad, while keeping the American people in the dark.

"But they never declared war against any of these nations, oh no. America couldn't be seen to appear a warlike nation, a provoker, a destabiliser. No, it sent in mercenaries against them. Mercenaries armed by people like me."

Pierre paused and pushed away the plate of lasagne, which he had only half eaten, and held his head in his hands.

"I can't find any excuse for this Tonio. It was convenient for me. I liked the world I was moving in. I loved the element of risk, the frisson, being involved in these games which were bigger than me. I liked the adrenalin which flowed through my veins before a deal came to a successful conclusion.

"And naturally, the money. The money brought power. And I liked that too.

"I had my doubts whether what I was doing was always above board, but I trusted the Americans. A bit like you, when you trusted the large banks who proposed the Korean deal to you.

"Then the stories about Allende's successor, General Pinochet, started to circulate; his terrible dictatorship, the *desaparicidos,* – then the stories about Noriega and his drug trafficking, and Saddam Hussein and the Kurds…

"When I began to try and find out what was really going on, I found myself in a labyrinth of lies amongst people who were only pulling the wool over my eyes. I began to realise that I'd become one of the many pawns used by a band of presumptuous and ignorant warmongers.

"I therefore began to slow my activities down, only agreeing to supply ever smaller 'lots'. This was noticed and someone's nose was put out of joint. The pressure applied by my 'employers' increased, forcing me to enter into an even bigger ball game. I was no longer supplying small arms or semi-automatic weapons like pistols, rifles, AK-47s or anti-tank mortars. The stakes had been raised dramatically, and how! We were now talking about missiles, F16 jet fighters and the rest..."

"Excuse me Pierre," Tonio interrupted him, "was it so easy to get hold of these bloody arms? Where did they come from?"

"Dead easy! Once you've made the right contacts and built up a good reputation, the doors open up easily.

"A bloc of countries in the East: Bulgaria, Poland and Hungary were my best suppliers for decades. You have to know how to use the right political channels.

"At that time you had to go through the Soviet Union, but Russia didn't want to be directly involved. She didn't want to be caught red handed. So they suggested I should go to Bulgaria and other countries in that area.

"There I could choose whatever I wanted. Any arms whatsoever. Following the Second World War there was an immense arsenal available. And they – all of them – with Russia first in the queue, needed money. Not roubles mind you: dollars. Dollars from Lebanese or Swiss banks from clients in Iran, Iraq, Argentina, Chile and many African countries. Sarkis and a few others were the middlemen. That's where the dollars came from. And everybody knew, as they know today, that they were working under the protection of the USA.

"The money also arrived from other clients, such as Libya, which notoriously helped other countries, terrorists and the like, who I've never wanted to deal with."

"And you received your commission on every deal?"

"Of course. Ten per cent!"

"Wow! A fair chunk considering the amounts..."

"Well, some traders ask for fifteen, twenty per cent; others, the small guys, are happy with seven per cent just so that they can take part in the game."

"And things have always gone well for you? I mean, has there ever been anyone who made a mistake, or who didn't keep his side of the bargain?"

"Yes, once, an order for twenty thousand AK-47s destined for Peru, finished up in the hands of Columbian guerrillas. I was accused of not having kept my side of the bargain. But I was able to prove that the order had been delivered into the hands of the highest military authorities in Peru. After which my responsibility ceased. You see, in this business it's important to have a document that's been signed and countersigned by buyers and sellers which is called *End User*. I had this document signed by all the right people and with all the correct official stamps and seals; but the consignment still finished up in Colombia. That's your problem, I said to everyone. I can't be there to supervise whether you've actually distributed the arms to your troops."

Tonio finished eating his salad. Pierre hadn't touched his.

"Well then?" Tonio asked. "What do you intend doing now?"

"I've decided to stop completely!" Pierre replied resolutely.

"Good, I'm pleased. Really I am!"

"But it isn't that easy."

"And why not?"

"Because there are a few things…how shall I put it…complex details…which have to be resolved…and that's where I need your help!"

"Go on then, get it off your chest."

"Well, in order to help you understand, I have to take a step backwards. A little while ago I told you that I took a ten per cent commission for every deal. Well, in recent years, instead of being paid in dollars, I asked to be paid in…arms."

"In arms? What do you mean?"

"Well, not to put too fine a point on it...I wanted to speculate. In order to make even more money. You see, in this profession information is the basis of everything. You have to keep yourself up to date on many things, and by doing this you try and create your own personal network of informers everywhere you can. You get to know people at certain levels in several countries who can give you information on delicate political situations in their own country, or in neighbouring countries...and therefore the requirement for a certain product which might be needed quickly.

"In other words, I wanted to be in a position to supply this 'product' quickly without having to rely on traditional suppliers. To a certain extent I didn't want to be an intermediary but rather a direct seller, imposing my own price for a much quicker delivery. So, instead of getting my commission paid in money, which I didn't need any more, I asked to be paid in arms.

"I considered it to be a kind of investment. So I've built up quite a sizeable personal stock, which I now want to get rid of."

"I don't understand Pierre. Do you want *me* to sell *your* arms?"

Pierre smiled. "No, certainly not. I want to destroy them!"

He stopped, seeing the astonished expression on Tonio's face. Then he went on.

"You heard me correctly, I want to destroy them. But I can't do it on my own. You see, there's only a small number of people who know that I've got this quantity of arms. But it isn't as if I can just go to the warehouse, strike a match under some gunpowder, and then BANG!"

"But what are you talking about? How much stock is involved?"

"A lot, a huge amount of stuff...small arms, semi-automatics, mortars, tons of ammunition, anti-tank mines, anti-personnel mines..."

"Anti-personnel mines…you must have really gone mad!"

"Yes…I suppose so."

They went into Pierre's office and after a while he began to speak again. "Well, this is my plan: I want to spread the rumour that I'm ill, very ill and that I want to…I have to retire. I want it to be known that I don't want anything further to do with this business, that I'm throwing in the towel. At the same time my activities at TEC will begin to diminish drastically. I've already found some buyers who are interested in acquiring a large portion of my group shares."

"It seems a bit of a drastic decision," Tonio interrupted him.

"Yes, it might appear drastic but it isn't really. If it's not generally seen that I'm reducing my holding in the TEC Group there wouldn't be any reason for anyone to believe that I'm ill. And that's where you come in. I'd like you to be a faithful collaborator, one of my representatives charged with convincing all those, who still want arms from me, that I'm no longer in a position to supply them."

"Me?" Tonio interrupted him once more. "But why me? Why not Bruno or even Rainer?"

"Please, I've already told you, forget about Rainer. He'd be only too happy to get his hands on the stuff, to do God knows what with it. And Bruno, no. Bruno wouldn't be able to. I trust him a lot, that's true, but he couldn't undertake such a delicate mission. You're the ideal person. You're a negotiator too, with the skills of being also – how shall I put it – a diplomat. You know English well, and French, and you get by in Spanish…"

"Pierre, are you telling me that you're asking me to go round and convince a lot of people that you're ill?"

"Yes, exactly that!"

"It all seems so absurd to me…and your arsenal, what'll happen to it?"

"That's just it – while all eyes are off me I'll load all the arms on some old hulk of a ship and sink her in the open sea. All planned – no noise or danger for the crew, our men of course, who'll be saved by another ship which'll be nearby."

"And how much will all this cost you? Have you worked it out?"

"Of course. About forty to fifty million dollars. Ship included."

"That's a pretty sum!"

"Yes, but a mere pittance if it clears my conscience."

They remained silent for a long period of time. Then Tonio spoke. "I don't know Pierre. It all seems so unbelievable…so…so…unreal…all of a sudden I discover a new world. So different from the one I'm used to. I don't know…you'll have to give me time to take all this in. I have to give it some careful thought. You realise, don't you, that this is a shock to me…"

"Of course I realise this, and how! But I also know that you're a person who understands when somebody is in need of help. You don't think twice about risking yourself to save a man from the brink; like that time in Normandy…I'm asking you to save my life a second time."

18

It was past midnight when Tonio got back home. He went to bed but he found it difficult to get to sleep.

At a certain point he decided to call his friend. Pierre replied almost immediately.

"Pierre, I've been thinking about all you've said and there's still something I don't understand. The change in your life will be total. If I've got it right, you're going to get rid of everything you've built up over the years. It's a decision which is awfully drastic! Not to put too fine a point on it, I'm under the impression that there's more; is there still something else which you're hiding from me?"

"Tonio, I've told you everything! I haven't kept anything back from you regarding my kind of business. And by asking me that question it goes to show once again that I'm right to ask for your help. You're the sort of person who wants to see things through to the end. And I like that.

"Yes, something happened which definitely made me open my eyes, something which struck me like being hit by a baseball bat.

"It was while I was convalescing after the accident in Normandy. I was confined to my bed, so I had more time on my hands to watch television. One evening I saw a programme, perhaps it was the news, which talked about the work of that organisation called Médicins Sans Frontières.

"One of the things they showed was how their doctors were committed to helping people who were the victims of local wars in Africa.

"At one point I saw a child, he was less than ten years old. I think he'd lost both legs. He'd stumbled on an anti-personnel mine. It was as if I'd been punched repeatedly in the stomach. It was as if I'd been struck by lightning.

"I'll never, I repeat never, be able to forget the expression in his eyes. They showed an unexploded mine they'd found. It was the same kind I supplied. I felt personally responsible. I remember I cried that night. I'm not ashamed to say so.

"The image will always remain etched in my memory. Often I wake up at night, I can tell you, and see the look on that child's face. That's it, now you know. My decision has been taken and won't be changed. Stopping is the least I can do."

They remained silent for a while. Then Tonio said, "You've made the right decision. We all make mistakes. I think that every one of us has done something in life which we aren't exactly proud of. The important thing is to realise it. To admit it, and take care not to make the same mistake again. To be genuinely sorry."

"If that's what you want to know, I can reassure you that I'm sorry, really sorry!"

There was a moment's silence then Pierre asked, "And you Tonio, have you ever done anything which you've regretted later?"

Tonio thought for a while and then said, "Well, yes. I also have a skeleton in the cupboard. Not on your scale, but I did do something of which I'm not very proud."

"Well, well," Pierre said. "You too, eh? What was it, can you tell me?"

"Well, since we're dealing with private matters, I can tell you. In fact, I've never told anyone else.

"It happened a few years ago, roughly six months before my transfer to Paris.

"At that time I was working in the international branch at the bank's headquarters in Rome. I was an ambitious officer like many others.

"The head of the bank's international service had a secretary who was a knock-out. She was married. I flitted around her like many others, but I decided to take her to bed. And that's what happened. After a relentless courtship, good old Maria finally gave way, and taking advantage of a time when her marriage was in crisis, heading for the rocks, I persuaded her to spend a brief holiday with me.

"We went to Tunisia where, in fact, we didn't even leave the bedroom, let alone the hotel.

"Without asking her, she told me many things about the office: gossip, matters concerning other departments, and so on. One of the things I learnt from her was that the post of head of the Paris branch was soon going to become vacant, since the existing manager was about to retire.

"At the time I didn't pay much attention to the fact. However, when I got back to Rome, the idea of moving to Paris began to grow on me. But I didn't know how I could put myself forward, because Maria had given me that information in the strictest confidence, and I didn't want to create problems for her.

"A few weeks passed. Our meetings became more frequent. Maria finished work later and later because, as the Director's secretary, she had to wait for the chief to finish his work, or for him to give her permission to leave. I used to hang around waiting for her so we could go home together, and often I'd look in at her office to see whether the coast was clear.

"A couple of times I caught her by surprise while taking off some headphones which, at first, I took to be one of those dictation playback gadgets, probably for letters which her boss had dictated previously for her on his machine.

"One evening I saw her using it in a rather furtive way. I asked her what she was doing. With considerable reticence and imploring me to keep the secret on pain of instant dismissal from both our jobs if it ever got out, she revealed to me that it was really a listening device monitoring her boss's office. He trusted her completely and allowed her to listen in on some of his meetings – those which he thought might be the most difficult or the most boring, or when he wanted to get rid of an unwelcome visitor. He would authorise her to listen in before a meeting and then during the conversation, after he'd used two or three code words previously agreed with Maria; she in turn would pretend to transfer an urgent call to him thus providing a good excuse to bring the meeting to a close.

"She even showed me where the device was located – in the bottom drawer of her desk.

"A few days later, my immediate boss – a good man who thought highly of me and didn't have any great ambitions in the bank – revealed to me that in a few days they were about to decide who to send to Paris; that very evening, after work, a meeting was to be held with the Director to decide on how to proceed with the selection of the candidate. He told me that he was putting my name forward, because of my knowledge of French and English, but he knew that there would be at least three or four other candidates supported by other section heads, and that some of these were strong contenders given their seniority and experience.

"I didn't think that the Director would keep Maria behind longer than necessary that evening, since the meeting was only an internal business one."

Pierre interrupted him. "I think I can guess what you did. Go on."

"Your guess is a good one, my friend. Maria went home and while the meeting was going on, I rummaged around in her office; I switched on the listening device and I heard everything. Since there was keen competition between the section heads, in that each was pushing his own protégé, the Director decided to organise a kind of competition – a test. He told the section heads to ask each of the candidates to prepare a report on how they would conduct business in Paris if they were appointed to the post. He even said that he wasn't expecting great things, and that everyone would probably concentrate on various commercial exchanges which were already current, and on the need for good relations with the other banks in France etc. But he then said he would like to see, for example, somebody mention the new strategies of the French *Banques d'affaires* who were trying to compete with the British banks.

"That was enough for me. Early the next day I was asked to prepare the report. I was given a week. In fact I worked day and night on that project. I bought all the Italian and French financial newspapers; I visited branches of French banks in Rome; I spoke with the commercial attaché at the French Embassy...in the end I had a report which covered a wide range of innovations, which I would have introduced in our branch in Paris. In the end I didn't have any rivals. And that's how I find myself here. Later on I felt pretty disgusted with myself for having taken advantage of that woman in order to further my career…"

"Well, Tonio, it seems to me that the bank didn't get that bad a deal in sending you here."

"Perhaps not, but this is something in my past which has always troubled me."

"Don't torment yourself so, my friend. It doesn't seem too serious to me. But I understand that it's important to you. We all have our own skeletons in cupboards. Some have big ones, some have small ones. Good night."

19

The next afternoon, Tonio received another call from Irene, telling him that she was going to Rome the following day. Nunzia's doctor had been able to fix an appointment with a specialist for a thorough examination of her digestive system. They would be in Rome for two or three days. She had called him to let him know, as promised.

"Tell me where you'll be staying. I'll try and come to Rome to see you."

"I'd like that Tonio…but I wouldn't want you to feel you're under any obligation…"

"Don't be silly. I'd planned to be in Rome anyway soon, and I'll find a reason to come a few days earlier. Where are you staying?"

"At the *Albergo Visconti*, the doctor suggested it. It's not far from the hospital where Nunzia will be admitted."

"Great. I'll call you at the hotel."

"Tonio?"

"Yes?"

"I don't want to give you the impression that I'm paranoid, but…I think I might be watched during my stay in Rome…"

"Watched? By who?"

"By my husband. It's a long story…I'll tell you what, when you call, tell staff at the hotel that you're Dr Benassi's assistant. That'll give the impression that it's something to do with Nunzia. Don't ask me questions for the time being. I'll explain it to you when we see each other…if we see each other."

"You can count on it, *piccola*."

Tonio justified his trip to Rome on the pretext that he had to go and see an apartment, which the estate agents had found not far from the bank, and which needed a quick decision otherwise he would lose it.

Instead of booking into the *Panama* where he usually stayed, he booked into the *Visconti* for the following day.

By taking the first Air France flight to Rome he was sure of arriving there before Irene.

It was incredible that he should feel so excited at the thought of seeing her again. He had not seen her for two years, yet he still had not stopped thinking about her. In the meantime he had gone out with other women, but none of them had given him the same sensations as Irene had. He had often thought of her, of the time they had spent together, and of how they had met. He could not forget her face, her eyes, her body, but above all he couldn't forget the warmth of her voice and personality.

He had spoken more about her to Pierre one day when he felt like unburdening himself a little. Pierre had advised him not to over-idealise a meeting which had only lasted a few hours. He would sooner or later meet another woman who would awaken in him the same emotions; but that had not happened. It was almost as if he had remained faithful to a simple image, to a dream. Hoping perhaps for a miracle. And lo and behold the miracle had happened – he was going to see her the following day.

During the flight his mind was galloping; if she had phoned him there must be a reason. This was proof that she hadn't forgotten him. She too wanted to see him, despite being married. He was a bit concerned she had told him she might be watched. Tonio thought of a jealous Sicilian husband, jealous as only Sicilians can be. But up to what point? He would find this out when he met her.

He arrived at the hotel at about eleven in the morning. Leaving his case in his room he went out, and from a nearby bar he telephoned the hotel, pretending to be Dr Benassi's assistant. He asked whether Signora Cantera had arrived. They told him they were expecting her in the afternoon.

Tonio seized the opportunity to go to the bank's headquarters to meet some of his future colleagues.

At about six that evening, he telephoned the hotel once more, asking for Signora Cantera. They put through the call immediately.

"Irene, I'm staying at the same hotel as you. I can be with you in less than an hour."

They met an hour later in her room.

After Irene had closed the door behind him, they hurled themselves into each other's arms, without saying a word. They exchanged a long kiss.

Then Tonio, drawing back his face from hers but still clasping her in his arms, said, "You haven't forgotten me!"

"No. But neither have you!" They kissed again.

"Nunzia?" Tonio asked.

"Over there," she replied, pointing to a door. "She knows that you're here."

Tonio drew back from her and looked her over. She had lost weight. She had a more mature look. She was wearing a black silk blouse with beige-coloured trousers. She had a single strand of pearls around her neck. He seemed to detect a look of sadness in her eyes. He thought she was really beautiful. He was immediately captivated again by her voice and by the intensity of her glance, which he found unchanged even after so much time.

He passed his hand through her hair. "You're even more beautiful!" he said.

"You haven't changed!" she said in reply.

They continued to kiss each other. After a while they separated and she said, "Come and see Nunzia. She's worried about tomorrow. She's worried that they might find something nasty in her stomach."

"*Signor* Tonio," Nunzia greeted him when she saw him, "It's a pleasure to see you again. This girl wants to look after this old woman. She's a saint!"

"Nunziatina, I'm sure that Irene does it willingly. After all, you deserve it. Don't worry. Everything will be all right, you'll see. By the way, which hospital are you being admitted to?"

Irene replied, "The Santo Spirito..."

"Well then, you're going to be in really safe hands there, my lass," Tonio said, in a light tone in an attempt to cheer Nunzia up. "Do you know that it's the oldest hospital in Rome and that it's had the best possible reputation for centuries?"

Tonio and Irene returned to her room. They sat down on a sofa at the foot of the bed.

"Tell me everything, Irene," he said. "Tell me about your life down in Sicily; tell me about your son Giovanni. By the way have you got a photo of him?"

"Yes," she said, taking a couple of photos from her bag. "I call him Nanni."

Tonio saw a smiling child, facing the camera, being held by Irene, who was looking up at him adoringly. The second photo showed Nanni on his own, sitting on a swing in a public park. He had an attentive expression, his lips tightly shut because of the effort of holding himself up while sitting on his own on the swing. Tonio noticed the dimple in his chin.

"You must be proud of him," he said to her.

"Yes," she said. "He's good, intelligent...he's got everything...all that a mother could wish for."

Tonio lowered his eyes once more to the photo. He looked at it for a while. He felt Irene's eyes looking at him. He slowly raised his head towards her. What he saw left him speechless.

"Irene," he said after a while. "Nanni...is..."

She nodded slightly. No words were necessary.

Tonio could not take his eyes off the photograph.
"He was born eight months after my marriage!"

20

After dining alone in the hotel restaurant, Tonio returned to the two women, who had eaten in their rooms.

They talked a bit about the days they had spent in Paris, then Nunzia went to bed in her room. She was tired from the journey and was nervous about what was waiting for her the following day.

When they were alone, Tonio asked Irene, “What’s this about someone watching you?”

Irene hesitated but then said, “Tonio…I don’t know where to begin. But I can tell you that my life is a living hell. My marriage was doomed from the start. Peppino isn’t the man I thought he was. He’s a completely different person. I definitely know that he married me because he was eager to get his hands on my family’s fortune, which will all come to me on my father’s death. I’m sure of this, because one day he told me so, to my face.”

“Jesus! What are you doing staying with a man like that?”

“For the time being, I’ve got to stay with him for Nanni’s sake, but also because I don’t want to disappoint my father, who’s ill.”

“I understand, but when did your marriage go wrong?”

“Right from the very first day, or rather, right from the very first night. You see…I remembered how…well with you…it was something beautiful, sweet, tender. I thought that I could have something similar with Peppino. I loved him even if I knew that there wasn’t any passion in my feelings for him. I wanted to be a good wife…I felt guilty about what happened in Paris with you.

I thought that I'd never see you again. Instead…right from the first night, it was very, very different…"

"In what way?" Tonio asked. "Do you feel like talking about it?"

"It isn't easy for me," she replied, "but I don't have any problem speaking to you. I should be ashamed of what I've done, or more correctly, for what I've been forced to do, but I feel that I can say everything to you. The only other person who knows the truth is Nunzia."

Tonio took her hands in his. In doing this he noticed the bracelet she was wearing round her wrist.

"You've still got it!"

"I've never taken it off…"

"Nor me, look." They kissed each other. "Go on," he told her.

"Well, that night after the wedding reception, we went to the suite in the hotel. I was expecting…well…you know…to make love like husband and wife. Just think, before and during our engagement nothing…how shall I put it…serious happened. Yes, passionate kisses…he touched me, he wanted me to touch him, but nothing…well, do you get the picture?"

"Yes I get the picture. And then? What happened?"

"There was a video cassette player in the room. He told me that he had a surprise for me. When he put the cassette on, I thought at first that it was just an ordinary film, even though, I must confess, it did seem a bit strange to me at the time.

"After a few minutes, I realised that it was a pornographic film. At first I began to laugh thinking it was all a joke, but it wasn't at all.

"Peppino was deadly serious and he told me to do exactly what those women were doing on the screen. At first I refused, telling him to switch off the TV, but he grabbed me by the hair and said to me, 'Now you're my wife, you do what I tell you, understand?'

"Imagine the shock! He could only get aroused by seeing those images. I was stunned, but I did what he wanted, hoping that he'd finish quickly.

"It carried on like this for weeks, and for months. There were always new cassettes, which he swapped with his friends, who are depraved like him. Once he took me to a friend's house where a real live orgy had been organised. I fled. When he got home that night he hit me with a belt, telling me that I'd made him lose face in front of his friends. It was horrible because afterwards he wanted to take me by force there and then on the kitchen floor."

"*Piccola mia,*" Tonio said, clasping her to his chest. "What a son of a bitch...but why didn't you escape to your father's?"

"I've done that twice. I told my father that we had had a row. I couldn't tell him the truth. Then Peppino would arrive with flowers and a *cassata*[*] to seek forgiveness in my father's presence. He believed our arguments to be mere tiffs between newly-weds.

"One day I realised that I'd missed my period. I waited another month and not having a period for the second month, I went to Caltanisetta on the pretext of doing some shopping, and I went to see a gynaecologist who told me I was three months pregnant. I did a quick calculation and realised it couldn't be Peppino's. I went back home and I told him that I was pregnant. He didn't seem to be particularly excited. The only thing he said was, 'It's OK. Make sure it's a boy'.

"At the right moment I would have told him that the child was born prematurely, but destiny wanted things to take a different path.

"One Sunday, on his return from a shooting trip, he entered the house and started slapping me without saying a word. I ran all round the house in order to get away from him, asking myself

[*] A type of Sicilian cake

what could have happened. Then he started shouting, calling me a whore, a tart, a slut, a sow…I don't remember what else. When I saw him take his heavy huntsman's cartridge belt, I ran into the kitchen and I grabbed a knife. I told him not to come near me. He must have seen my expression because he stopped in his tracks. And then he told me what had happened.

"On the hunting trip he'd met my gynaecologist, who had congratulated him on the child who was due to be born in July. Thinking that the doctor had made a mistake, he pretended that we'd had premarital sex, but the gynaecologist, while laughing, told him that we hadn't been careful enough. It wasn't too difficult for him to work out what had happened in Paris.

"He also remembered that when I was about to send out the wedding invitations, he'd seen your name on the list. At the time he'd asked for an explanation and I told him that you'd helped me buy the furniture. But I believe he must have seen me blush when mentioning your name. He told me that in his view, it wasn't worth sending an invitation to someone 'I'd only met in Paris for a few minutes'. I told him that he was right and let it pass. But that Sunday evening when he came back from his hunting trip, he understood everything.

"He didn't touch me until after Nanni's birth. He told me that I revolted him, I made him sick. He went with other women, he even started bringing them into the house. One night he seized me and literally raped me. It still happens every now and then.

"With the excuse that he's doing work on our house at Gela, we're now living in Butera, where he has a small family villa where his sister lives. I know he's moved us there so that he can keep an eye on me. His sister tells him every move I make, the telephone calls…everything. That's why I can only phone you from public telephone boxes. Fortunately, every now and then, I don't see him for days, but at times he comes home drunk and becomes very violent."

"Irene, you can't stay with a man like that. You have to go away. Take Nanni and come and stay with me. I'll arrange everything."

She caressed his face. Two tears gently rolled down her cheeks. "I've thought about it, my love. But I can't. Not for the moment, at least. My father's ill, I can't leave him alone. And then there's Nunzia..."

"Nunzia can come with you!"

"No, she'd never come...she too has a situation which is...difficult. You see she has a son who's a bit...how shall I say...simple. He's not mentally retarded he's...naive, that's it. He's forty, he's married and he's a bricklayer. A good person, but he's as poor as a church mouse. He lives with his wife's family. They're very poor too. Nunzia tries to help them out as best she can.

"Peppino wants to get rid of her, because he knows that she's my only ally. I want to protect her. I'm trying to help her buy a small house at Mazzarino where her son lives. But I've got to do it on the sly. I have a friend who's helping me do this. Now and then I ask *babbone* for a bit of money, he thinks I'm using it for something frivolous. I'm trying to put by as much as I can. When my friend Marta comes to see me at Butera, I give the money to her without anyone else knowing, and she in turn gives it to the owner of the house who is patiently accepting these partial payments."

"Irene, you can't go on putting up with this violence, you've got to go to the police, you can't be all alone in this situation. There has to be a way out."

"Yes, yes, I'm thinking of one. Moreover, this little house of Nunzia's could be a future refuge for me, if things get really bad."

"For God's sake, Irene, you've got to do something straight away...how much do you need to buy this house for Nunzia?"

"No, Tonio, don't even think about it. I don't want you involved in this situation."

"Irene, listen to me. I'm already involved. It's just as well that you get that into your head. I'm involved because I love you. Yes, I love you. I've never stopped loving you, even if we haven't seen each other for a long time. And then there's Nanni, another reason for loving you!"

Irene was sobbing by now. His words had touched her soul to the core.

"Don't cry, *piccola*," he said, clasping her to his chest once more. "You're not alone…any longer. Go on tell me, how much do you need?"

"Well…I've paid ten million lire, all my savings…but I owe another ten."

"Holy mother!" he exclaimed, "Is that all? Irene, you only have to tell me how to get the money to you. Believe me, it's not a problem. You'll make me a happy man if I can contribute, even in a small way, to help you get out of this mess."

"All right then, *Tunuzzu*, I'll give you Marta's phone number. She's guessed what's going on in my house and she wants to help me."

"Do you trust this Marta?"

"Oh, yes. She's a childhood friend. We went to school together. She married a policeman, would you believe it. He's also a good friend of mine…"

"But hang on, this policeman, if he's your friend, can't he help you to…to…can't he arrest your husband for violence?"

"I don't know…perhaps. But you know, it's not that easy. I'm sure that there has to be some proof, some witness statements. I'll try and speak to Marta."

"Yes, I really think you should. Go on then, give me the telephone number so I can give her a call tomorrow."

Irene gave him the number and Tonio said, "Well, I'm pleased to hear that there's at least someone you can speak to down there in Sicily, even if only now and then. Tell me a bit about these friends of yours. I don't know them, but they seem to be nice people."

"Ah, they're the salt of the earth. When we were at primary and secondary school together, we were an inseparable group of four: Marta, Carlo, now her husband, Oreste and me. Marta and I always stayed in Sicily, while Carlo after doing his military service, entered the police force and has quite recently been promoted to Police Inspector at Gela – not bad."

"And the other one, this Oreste, where did he finish up?"

"He's here in Rome. He's a priest."

"A priest? You've got a friend who's a priest?" Tonio asked, smiling.

"Of course. Oreste is an excellent priest. If I can, I want to go and see him after Nunzia's been admitted to hospital." Then Irene continued, "Now that's enough about me, please. Tell me a bit about you. Are you happy that you're coming to work here in Rome? You're becoming a big shot, Director."

"Yes, I'm happy, it's true, but there's something new that's happened over the last few days which has created a big problem in my life. And I have to resolve it quickly. I'd like to talk to you about it. I think that by discussing things with you it might clear my thoughts. Perhaps you can help me reach a decision."

That was how Tonio told her about Pierre; how they became friends after the accident in Normandy; and the respect and affection he had for him. He told her about the assault and how it had taken place, and how after that he'd found out about Pierre's activity as an arms dealer.

He spoke to her about his friend's crisis of conscience after seeing a child on TV mutilated by a mine, and how Pierre had asked him to help him to get out of this double life.

He spoke for over an hour. Irene was attentive. She did not interrupt him. When he finished he asked her an unspoken question with his eyes.

"Tonio," Irene said to him after a while, "this is a decision which you have to take alone. All I can say is that your friend Pierre is at his wits' end and desperately needs your help. I don't know what to say to you." She remained silent for a few seconds, then continued, "You know, now I come to think of it, if there's one person who might be able to give you some advice, it's my priest friend – Oreste. He's an exceptional man. If you want we can meet in the Church of the Sacro Cuore, near the Termini railway station. I'm sure you'll like him. What do you think?"

"Fine by me. Let me know at the office. The phone number..."

"I've learnt it by heart," she said. "I don't leave anything written down in the house. But now come here and kiss me. I want to make love to you. From the moment I knew that I'd be seeing you again, I haven't thought about anything else."

"Me too, *piccola*."

They made love passionately, knowing that they had to make the most of their few hours together. Irene reached her orgasm almost immediately. At the height of her pleasure, she opened her eyes and fixing them on his, said, "I'm...here...with you...with you..." And she abandoned herself completely. When it was his turn, Tonio made a sign that he was about to withdraw from her, but Irene kept him inside her, murmuring, "Stay...it's safe..." Tonio understood and abandoned himself to an intensity of pleasure that he had seldom experienced before in his life.

Afterwards they made love with tenderness, without tiring of looking at each other, caressing each other, finding each other again. At dawn, before falling asleep with Irene in his arms, a thought crossed his mind which made him open his eyes widely – 'Nanni, Giovanni...my son.' He fell asleep, smiling.

21

Approaching the Church of the Sacro Cuore the following afternoon, Tonio could not help but notice how striking the building was. The fact that it was situated in the busy and congested Via Marsala, in front of the Termini station, made it plainly visible even to the most distracted of visitors. Added to this, the large gilded-bronze statue of Christ on the very top of the high bell-tower made it a clear reference point from several vantage points in the city.

Tonio entered the church and was immediately struck by the calm which reigned there, in stark contrast to the chaotic traffic in the street.

He made his way along the central nave, lined by granite columns, admiring marble statues, stuccoes, gilding and paintings.

Since he was a little early for his appointment with Irene, he sat in a pew from which he could comfortably admire the transept and the cupola.

In the quiet of the church he tried to remember the last time he had gone to Mass; it had been Christmas Eve in Naples, when he had spent a few days with his sister.

Tonio had received a Catholic education, but he did not feel guilty if he did not go to church every Sunday. His relationship with God was based on a mutual agreement, which he tried to keep to. I live according to Your teaching, trying to help my neighbour, being honest in my work and with myself, without lapsing into the hypocrisy of many Christians; but You must not impose too many rules on me. He knew that he was not a good

Catholic and that he could not invent a religion *ad personam* for himself. If everyone else did the same, there would be chaos. At times he turned his thoughts towards God, not in formal prayers or invocations to obtain something, but almost like a conversation, in order to understand better the meaning and sense of things around him.

That morning, for example, going to the bank in a taxi, he had reflected on everything that had happened in Irene's life. Should he feel responsible for what had occurred in Paris years before? That episode had later set off the spark which had precipitated things between her and her husband. Certainly, he was at least partly responsible. He was also positive that the perversions of her husband, hidden so well before the marriage, would have become apparent as soon as he had got what he wanted.

Furthermore did he, Tonio, have any right to enter so overbearingly into Irene's life once more? At first, perhaps not, he said to himself. But now there was Nanni, his son, and she was the woman he loved. 'Do not covet your neighbour's wife…' came into his mind. 'But now it's too late for me to pull back', he thought, 'according to your Commandments I'm sinning, rather we're both sinning, because I know that Irene loves me too. What should I do? Ask for your forgiveness and promise not to do it again? But I wouldn't be sincere, because I'm not sorry for what I've done or for what I'm doing now…well, at the end of the day, You sort it out.'

He also thought about his conversation with Marta, Irene's friend, that morning.

"I was waiting for your call," the woman told him. "Irene called me a little while ago. Here are the details of my current account with the Banco di Sicilia where you can deposit the money. You're very generous, wanting to help Irene in this crisis…"

"Marta, it isn't a question of generosity, believe me," he said. "I'm doing it because...because...I feel I want to do it, that's it. I'd like Irene..."

"I know," she said, "you don't have to say anything else."

Tonio was grateful for her discretion and said that he would transfer fifteen million lire that day.

"But Irene only needs ten."

"I know. Please keep the other five for Irene's needs. You never know, it could come in handy one day...perhaps in an emergency. Thanks Marta."

"Don't thank me, Tonio; Irene and I are like sisters. Even though she doesn't tell me all that goes on at home, I sense that things are pretty bad. She tries to play things down, but she can't hide everything. I'm also worried because I've noticed some bruises on her arms and face...perhaps I shouldn't be telling you this, at the end of the day I don't know you. But she seems to trust you a lot."

"Thanks, Marta. Try and keep close to her as much as possible, and if you can, mention a few details to your husband...perhaps his intervention...the police..."

"It's a very delicate matter...I'll try."

Tonio was lost in thought when he saw a young priest coming out of a side door and approaching him with a smile on his face.

"Hi, you must be Tonio. Irene has just called me. She said that she'll be a little late. I'm Oreste."

He had a firm and dry handshake. Tonio was taken aback at his height; he estimated that Oreste was almost two metres tall. His cassock made him look even taller. His voice, though a whisper in the silence of the church, was warm and deep. His hair was black and curly. Tonio's surprise increased when he noted his eyes were light blue. He decided that Oreste's smile came more from his eyes than his lips.

"Hi there," Tonio said, looking at him. "I'm pleased to meet you...Father...Don Oreste."

"Come, let's go over there to my temporary office. We'll wait for Irene there. And forget the 'Don' – just call me Oreste."

They crossed the sacristy and went out into an enormous courtyard. On the right there were some doors. Oreste opened one of them and they went into a room, not too large, which had been turned into an office. Behind a table which was serving as a desk full of papers, there was an enormous crucifix, which took up a large part of the wall, out of proportion to the dimensions of the room. Tonio thought that it had probably come from one of the chapels in the church.

"Irene has told me about how you were at school together in Sicily," Tonio said, as soon as he was seated.

"Yes," said Oreste "we were very close. We were a really good group of friends. Just imagine, a couple of years ago, Irene, Marta and Carlo dragged almost our whole class from Caltanisetta to Turin for my ordination ceremony! It was fantastic!"

"And now you're here in Rome?" Tonio asked. "Is this your church? By the way, what order do you belong to?"

"The Salesians. Do you know that this church was built by Don Bosco, the founder Saint of our Order? I'd like to become a missionary. For the moment I'm here in Rome and my job consists of the co-ordination of the work undertaken by the Salesians in various parts of the world. Sooner or later I'm leaving too. I hope it'll be soon...I prefer to get my hands dirty in Africa or South America, rather than being here among these papers, chasing up banks who delay transferring funds to people who need them urgently..."

"I expect that also happens with my bank, the BNI."

"Ah, I didn't know that you worked for a bank. Well, yes, yours too..."

At that moment, after a couple of knocks on the door, Irene entered. "Sorry to be late," she said. "I'm pleased that you've already met."

Then, turning to Tonio, she said, "What do you think, isn't he the most handsome priest in the world?" She went up to Oreste and embraced him warmly and continued, "You can't imagine how many hearts he's broken! I advised him to go to Hollywood, but nothing doing, he decided that the cassock suited him better!"

"Well, while on the subject," Oreste replied, "look who's talking about broken hearts. Tonio, do you know what this wretch used to do when she wanted to dump some boy who was trying to court her? She used to say that I was her boyfriend. I can't even remember how many times we were supposed to be engaged and then broke it off in the eyes of those poor boys!"

Tonio did not need much convincing that there had been a large number of suitors. Irene was wearing the same trousers as the day before and a tight pullover under a beige linen jacket. Her hair was gathered up in a single plait which fell halfway down her back.

The two men asked after Nunzia's health. She was to be discharged from hospital the following day, after receiving the results of the tests carried out on her that morning.

Then Irene turned to Tonio, and asked him to speak to Oreste about his problem.

At first Tonio had some difficulty telling Oreste about his arms merchant friend, because he imagined that much of the priest's life would have been dedicated to soothing the suffering caused by such weapons.

Tonio spoke at length, leaving nothing out. He finished his story saying that he was more than certain that Pierre had repented his past life, and that he needed his help to get out of the arms trade. He had an important decision to take.

Furthermore, he didn't know how he was going to reconcile his work at the bank with what Pierre was asking him to do.

When Tonio finished speaking, they remained silent. Oreste got up and began walking up and down the room with his hands in his pockets.

After a while he stopped in front of Tonio and said, "I don't think I'm the best person to advise you. I wouldn't be impartial."

"And why?" Irene intervened.

"Because I'm partly involved."

"How come?" Irene asked.

Tonio began to understand what Oreste had in mind.

"I'll explain, by showing you something," Oreste said. He went to some metal cabinets along one of the walls of the room, opened up one of the drawers and pulled out a thick folder. Tonio noticed that the label said 'Ciao Africa'.

"This," he said, opening up the folder and taking out a file, "is one of the many organisations which we support. Its principal function is to look after, care for and support babies and children who have been the victims of the many local wars. Your friend probably saw on TV an image similar to the countless ones here." He pushed the file towards Tonio. The latter opened it and found himself looking at a smiling boy missing both an arm and a leg.

"This is Odiambo. He's seven now. He was five when a mortar exploded a few metres from him."

Tonio chose another photograph from the file. He saw a young woman in a hospital bed. Clearly, she must only just have been admitted since her body was covered in very severe burns which had not yet been attended to.

"This is Saada. Fifteen years old. She tried to save her brothers who were trapped in a hut being bombarded by heavy artillery in Kenya. We weren't able to save her. She died three days after we took this photo."

"This is Keyah," Oreste said, taking another photograph from the pile. "Eleven years old. We found her, purely by chance, on the outskirts of a village in Sudan, which had been ransacked and completely burnt to the ground, one month after the incursion of guerrillas. After burying twenty members of her village as best she could, among whom were her family, she survived by eating roots and drinking stagnant water. She's still in a bad way, but perhaps she'll get better. And just think, her name means 'in good health'."

Oreste continued for quite a while. Tonio was speechless. All the horror ran over him like an express train. At a certain point he turned towards Irene and saw that she had tears in her eyes. Oreste noticed it too.

"Forgive me," he said. "I didn't mean to distress you. But when I talk about these children, I wish the whole world knew what was going on. That's why I'd like to go there as soon as possible, and it's why I can't advise you, Tonio. I'm too involved. Even while I'm here, handling these papers, I'm totally committed. There are hundreds of these photos, and not only from Africa. In other drawers there are examples from Asia, Brazil, Nicaragua. The decision is yours alone. One thing I will say to you, if there is anything you can do which will keep even one rifle or one mine away from these children, you would only be doing your duty as a human being and as a Christian."

While Oreste was putting the folder back into the drawer, Tonio said, "I'd like to carry on talking to you, and to you Irene. Can I invite you to dinner this evening? I'd really like a good pizza if that's OK with you?"

"Unfortunately I can't," Irene said. "One of Peppino's cousins has phoned me. He's coming with his wife to the hotel, and we'll have dinner there. A bit of a bind, to tell the truth. I've only met them once, at my wedding. I'd also like to speak to Nanni before he goes to bed. Why don't you two go to dinner.

But before you go, I'd like to spend some time with Oreste. You don't mind, do you Tonio?"

"Not at all. I'll wait for you in the courtyard," Tonio replied, and he went out.

Tonio waited on a bench. It was almost dark. Some boys were playing football. Another group were sitting in a circle a little further away. There was another young priest with them, and Tonio wondered whether he too was dreaming of leaving in order to 'dirty his hands'.

A quarter of an hour later, Irene and Oreste joined him. Tonio had the vague impression that Irene had been crying again.

After she had left, Oreste invited Tonio to follow him. They went to a nearby pizzeria, which boasted that it served the finest pizza margherita in all Rome.

After ordering a pizza and a beer, Tonio asked Oreste to explain to him how the Salesian aid operations operated.

Oreste's eyes lit up. "Well, for one, I can tell you that there are numerous organisations like our own in Italy, and in other parts of the world, which do more or less the same thing.

"We're Salesians, so perhaps we're a bit different in that we tend to concentrate on looking after youngsters. And the continent of Africa is where we concentrate most. Just think, over half the population of Africa is under twenty. We only started at the end of the last century, but our experience over the years has taught us that Africa and the Salesians were made for each other. There's a mutual benefit for both. Africa enriches us with its abundant culture of values: the family, hospitality, its sense of religion, and also an immense capacity for suffering. We've learnt to renew our missionary dynamism and our approach, in order to get ever closer to the poor. We bring our Salesian charisma with its special interest in youth."

The pizzas arrived and the two men attacked them immediately.

"You see," Oreste continued, after a couple of mouthfuls, "I've only been there once, with a delegation organised by Unesco. That was enough for me to fall madly in love with the continent and with its inhabitants. If that's what they call 'Africa fever' then I'm incurably infected with it."

"I can see that, Oreste. I really admire you. But in practical terms what do these projects consist of?"

"Ah, there are hundreds of projects we're involved in.

"There are nutritional centres, for example, to take on the great famine emergencies. Children accompanied by one or two parents, by grandmothers or aunts, come to these centres, sometimes after walking for days. We distribute food to them. We weigh them, we keep them with us until they've regained weight and are healthier.

"Do you know that with ten dollars – just think with only ten dollars – we can provide food for a child for a whole month? Then we have centres where we gather up children who live on the streets. There are thousands of them in all the cities in Kenya, Tanzania and Zambia; they go around the streets looking for small jobs, or commit petty crimes.

"At night they sleep on the streets. We go looking for them, and we suggest to them that they come into our centres where they can eat, wash and sleep. Then we try and persuade them to attend school again, to find a decent job. With fifty dollars we can feed, house, clothe and provide medical assistance and schooling for a child for a whole month. Then there are canteens, kindergartens, which allow mothers to go to work leaving youngsters in safe hands, medical centres, field hospitals…in brief, dear Tonio, we have thousands of children and youngsters in our centres.

"But our funds are never enough. We receive very generous donations, but it's always too little. Often I have to say 'no' to some urgent request because there's another one which is even more urgent somewhere else. At times my work is really harrowing, believe me."

They finished eating and ordered coffee.

"Oreste," Tonio said. "I'm glad to have met you. I admire your passion, I also think that you've helped me reach a decision. Because here, this evening with you, I've decided to help my friend Pierre to 'redeem' himself. I'll ask my bank to give me six months' leave so that I can dedicate myself completely to his project. Thanks. Let's go back to your office now. I'd like to ask you for more information on 'Ciao Africa' and to see how I can help."

It was almost midnight when Tonio returned to the hotel. He was happy because he now knew what he had to do. He felt carefree and full of energy.

He knocked lightly on Irene's door, hoping that she was not asleep. She opened the door to him almost at once. "I was waiting for you," she said to him. And then looking him straight in the eye continued, "I see that you've made a decision. Oreste has infected you. I knew he would. Well done."

22

Tonio's request for six months' unpaid leave from the bank took the President of the institution and his colleagues by surprise. He cited personal reasons, without further explanation. The President grudgingly accepted his request, on condition that he remained at work for another month in order to make the handover to his replacement in Paris. The take-up of his new post in the international department in Rome was postponed.

Irene had left for Palermo with Nunzia in the late afternoon.

After putting his affairs in order at the bank, Tonio had called Pierre, informing him of his decision.

"But there are some conditions which you'll have to abide by, if you want me to help you," he told him. "And you won't like all of them. We'll talk about it tonight, when I arrive in Paris. In the meantime, I'd like you to send fifty thousand dollars to a charitable institution, the details of which I'm about to send you by fax. Send the money through my bank here in Rome, leave it to me to sort out speeding up the process to the beneficiary."

After having made sure with his colleagues in the international department that they would give the transfer top priority, he called his friend Achille Salemi at the Banco di Sicilia in Palermo, to tell him to expect the arrival of fifteen million lire for Marta's account. He asked him to credit her account as soon as possible, and he also took the opportunity to ask discreetly about Irene's husband.

"Achille, that Peppino Cantera I spoke to you about a while back, is he still a client of yours?"

"Unfortunately yes...but why do you want to know?"

"Well...you know, personal curiosity..."

"*Tonì*, as if I didn't know you well enough...if you're asking me about him there's something brewing. Look I'm not completely *amminchialuto*[*]."

"Don't worry about it, forget it."

"I understand, either you won't, or you can't, tell me about it. I don't know what your relationship is with him, but as a friend of yours I warn you, be on your guard...if he can put one over on you he won't think twice about it. He's swindled a lot of people. We have a proverb in Sicily which says *'a rubari picca si va 'n galera, a rubari assai si fa carrera'.*[**] I won't say any more and I don't think you need a translation. In my view, I think he's waiting for his father-in-law, old Consalvo, to die in order to sort himself out once and for all."

Tonio felt rage rise up in him. "No, I don't know him personally, but I too can confirm he's a first-class piece of shit."

He arrived in Paris at eight that evening and went straight to Avenue Foch. When Pierre asked him what had happened in Rome which had made him decide to help, Tonio told him about his meeting with Irene and Oreste. He mentioned his shock at the sight of the photographs which Oreste had shown him, and described what the Salesians were doing to alleviate the suffering caused by the arms sold in so many countries. The same shock he had experienced looking at the television programme about *Médecins Sans Frontières*.

"My conditions, which I mentioned earlier today, are designed not only to help you to get out of this terrible business, but also to help make amends, even in the smallest possible way,

---

[*] Brainless

[**] Robbing a little you go to prison, robbing a lot you advance in your career

for the suffering that, whether consciously or subconsciously, you have caused." Tonio spoke these words in an accusatory tone, even without meaning to.

Pierre listened, nodding every now and then. "I couldn't have asked for more," he murmured. "It's just what I wanted."

"Good. For the next four weeks I'm still going to the bank to hand over to my colleague. After office hours I'll come here every evening. I want you to show me all your paperwork. Everything, without exception. A list of all past business transactions, current ones, and those you've contracted for. I want to see all your notes, all your ledgers, if you have any. I want a copy of all those documents kept in the Cayman Islands, including those which you called your 'insurance policies'. I want to know in great detail everything about this business. I want to meet everyone who knows you're involved in this trade. I want to know how much money you've made and where it is. This money will be sent to Africa, Asia, South America…in fact we've already started doing this with those fifty thousand dollars …a mere drop in the ocean."

Pierre had been nodding all the time Tonio was speaking. At first he had a very serious expression on his face, then seeing his friend's determination, he began to smile.

He seemed a different man: like someone seriously ill who has just been informed that after all, he is going to live.

"No problem, Tonio. I'll have an office set up for you on the first floor. You don't know how happy I am having you at my side. Tomorrow I'll begin letting everyone know that you're on the team. And…thanks Tonio, I'm already feeling better."

"But now, Pierre, we must follow your plan to the letter. It's a good scheme. You have to pretend that you've got health problems, and give the impression that you're winding down."

"Spot on. In the next few days I'll go and see one of my surgeon friends who'll diagnose a problem with my heart, and he'll prescribe a cure and will advise me to avoid all stress. I'll leave home as little as possible. At every opportunity I'll publicise my gradual winding down of TEC for health reasons. You'll see it'll work. In this business news travels fast."

And this is how Tonio Brignani began to lead a double life. By day he was a bank manager, by night and at weekends he devoted himself to learning about the complex business of buying and selling arms.

23

It was not easy for Tonio to enter that completely new world. Having been used to operating within the rigid norms of the banking system where every document had to be accounted for precisely; where responsibilities were clearly defined; where in order to transfer significant sums of money one had to have various authorisations, in contrast the business of 'arms supplier' had several aspects which went against common sense.

The contracts for the various 'supplies' were documents which were quite specialised.

For a start, all the preliminary work to draw up an initial contract, leading to the final contract, was not documented.

Pierre explained to Tonio that during that phase of the operation, there couldn't be written contracts, and there were no official proposals and agreements on price, transport, delivery times and so on between the parties. Everything was done on the telephone or by face-to-face meetings. For this stage, all that was available were his notes or, at best, the recordings of telephone conversations made without the caller's knowledge.

The final contracts, when a 'clean' deal was going through – that is to say between countries producing arms and countries buying arms – these were signed by military authorities, or government departments or by private companies with strong governmental links.

In such cases, the job of the Merchant consisted of finding the right goods offered by various producers, which could meet the requirements of the buyer. As an intermediary, accredited by the government or group he was representing, Pierre would present his credentials to the company producing the arms, so that they could be scrupulously verified. Subsequently he would be permitted to enter reserved sections of a factory, where specialist technicians showed him the characteristics and workings of many products, and their effectiveness in different theatres of war. This was the case for small arms, mortars, portable surface-to-surface missiles, self-propelled guns, armoured vehicles, half-track trucks and so on.

"Often," Pierre explained to him, "it's actually the company which supplies the product which wants to use an intermediary. They try to offload the responsibility, if something goes wrong, on to the go-between. It goes without saying that intermediaries make sure that they get paid handsomely for this service, which at times can be dangerous. Some put a surcharge of twenty per cent on the final invoice. I personally thought that this was justified, even though I have never charged that much myself. These people who, to all intents and purposes appear to be businessmen, move in that area where neither government nor industry dares to tread – a true 'no-man's land'."

"And do you know these businessmen? I mean, do you have contacts with each other? How do they operate so secretly?" Tonio asked.

"Look, the majority of them operate quite openly when dealing with official operations. When they're operating undercover, clearly there isn't any publicity. You see their names in the newspapers. Perhaps the most well-known is Adnan Kashoggi, considered the arms dealer par excellence. He's become fabulously wealthy, thanks to his contacts at the highest level at the CIA, with people close to President Nixon, Arab sheiks and others.

"Take my friend Sarkis – Sarkis Soghanalian – he's an easygoing fellow with his family and friends, but when it comes to business he's really shrewd and implacable in negotiating commissions...then there's Manucher Ghorbanifar the Iranian;

Sam Cummings – the American – known for having recycled a lot of arms from the Vietnam war; and the Israelis Yaacov Nimrodi and Al Shwimmer, former members of Mossad, the Israeli secret service. More to the point, with the exception of Kashoggi who's often photographed in the company of beautiful women, they don't like publicity. Otto Skorezeny, for example, who was a courageous officer in the Nazi's SS, the man who was famous for freeing Mussolini from prison at Campo Imperatore in 1943, became an arms trader in the fifties and sixties but very few people knew this."

The signatures at the bottom of the final contract documents were those of generals, high-ranking officers, heads of security, government officials and sometimes local government ministers.

In the list of suppliers, Tonio noted the names of Italian factories producing light arms.

Then there were the 'dirty' deals, that's to say, where the Merchant was 'advised', usually by the United States, to supply arms to revolutionary groups opposing regimes in nations bordering countries who were hostile to the USA.

In these cases there would be light arms such as pistols, rifles, semi-automatic weapons, ammunition, anti-personnel and anti-tank mines, uniforms and tents; in other words everything that a small army needed. Sometimes he even facilitated the introduction of experts in guerrilla warfare into a country, to train local troops. For these cases the contracts were less official but always signed by some local authority.

However, all contracts had to have the vital document showing the *end user* attached to them. If the Merchant wasn't able to obtain it from those who were arranging the purchase and delivery, he expected it to come from the Americans. In his safe there were several documents from which it was easy to follow a trail leading to the CIA. Some of them even had the signatures of members of the American Congress on them.

Tonio was astonished at the quantity of arms Pierre had dealt in over the last ten years: pistols, Uzis, AK-47 and AK-74 machine guns, grenades, even 88 and 120 millimetre mortars, and tons of ammunition. And he was even more surprised to learn that the biggest buyers of these arms seemed to be the poorest countries on the African and South American continents.

Looking at the figures for buying and selling, and knowing that Pierre was only one of the intermediaries to whom these countries turned – and he was by no means the largest supplier – he reflected on the astronomical levels of finance, which were being denied to the development and social welfare of these countries, in order to build up their own arsenals.

Among the arms listed, the AK-47 automatic machine-gun, and the updated AK-74 version, were always present.

"Why is this weapon so popular? What's so special about it?" Tonio asked Pierre one day.

"Because it's a simple weapon to use, with a low production cost, light, reliable, and with few moving parts. The AK-47 has become legendary in the military and other sectors. In the cold war years the Soviet Union and China supplied these arms, often for free, to communist guerrillas like the Vietcong in Asia, or the Sandinistas in South America. Meanwhile, on the other side, the Americans were supplying the same type of weapon to the Afghans and the Mujahideen. It's a weapon that's had a production-run of over ten million. Just think, it's become so popular that it's diminutive name Kalash, short for Kalashnikov, is even used as a person's name in some African countries."

Tonio's knowledge in this field grew by leaps and bounds on a daily basis.

One evening when he was busy looking at some documents in Pierre's office, Rainer burst into the room, without greeting anyone. He began speaking to his father in German.

Pierre interrupted him, and said to him in French, “Rainer! Speak in French or English, you know that Tonio doesn’t speak German.”

Rainer carried on speaking in German as if he had not heard him.

“Rainer, French or English if you want a reply from me!” Pierre said in a cold tone, staring into his eyes.

Rainer turned for a moment towards Tonio with a look of hostility, and then turning back to his father said in French, “What’s this story about you being ill? You seem to be perfectly well to me; you’re here working.”

“They’ve found something wrong with my heart. The specialist says that I’ve got to be careful, try to avoid stress and…”

“And this story about selling up TEC? Is it true? Why haven’t you spoken to me about it?”

“Well, I see that you’re really concerned for my health,” Pierre said in an ironic tone. “And why should I discuss it with you? It’s my company and I don’t have to ask anyone’s permission if I want to sell it. Besides I’ve received some good offers and I need to take my state of health into account.”

“And…the rest?” and then turning to Tonio. “Can you leave us for a few minutes? I need to speak to my father in private.”

“Tonio can stay,” Pierre told him. “He’s become my collaborator and he knows about my business activity. All of it!”

Rainer turned his eyes once more towards Tonio, this time with an expression of surprise on his face. Then he turned back to look at his father.

“Well, how about that then…” he murmured.

At this point Tonio turned to Pierre and said, “I’ll go down to my office to make a call, which I’ll tell you about later.” He left without even looking at Rainer, who was still on his feet in front of his father’s desk. He was about to go down the stairs when he heard Rainer say, "Do you mean to say that he's got an office in this house?" He did not hear Pierre's reply.

A few minutes later, he could not help overhearing angry exchanges in a conversation, which was taking place on the floor above. It went on for a good half hour. Then Tonio heard a door slam violently, and Rainer's steps coming down the stairs. Rainer entered his office without knocking.

"Can you tell me what the hell's going on here?" he said in a threatening manner. "Was it you who put the idea of selling the group, and all the rest, into his head?"

"Look, I haven't put anything into anyone's head. Your father's only asked me to help him to..."

"Listen, my father's changed from the day of that damned accident; from the day you met each other. And I don't like these changes much," Rainer said pointing his finger at Tonio.

"Rainer, do you want to know something? Whether you like it or not, I don't give a damn!" Tonio said. He was beginning to lose his patience. "I'm doing the job which I've been asked to do: I'm only helping your father. So if you don't mind, let me get on with my work," he said, pointing towards the door.

Rainer went towards the door, but he turned back. He moved his face to within a few centimetres of Tonio's. "Yes, I'll let you work, I can see that you're carving out a nice career for yourself. From bank clerk to personal assistant to a big industrial magnate, my compliments! But you'd better know that from now on I'm keeping my eye on you. Try not to put a foot wrong. You can make a fool out of my father, but certainly not me."

Tonio was able to see the small red veins of his eyes behind his glasses, and a bit of saliva on the corner of his mouth. He decided to ignore the offensive remarks. "Listen Rainer, do what you want, but perhaps you haven't understood: what you think, what you do, what you are, I don't give a shit about. And now please go!"

Rainer left, slamming the door. 'What a piece of shit', Tonio thought. 'How can he be Pierre's son?' But then he recalled that in fact, he wasn't. He began to understand Pierre's reluctance to give him the task, which he was undertaking. He had not liked the expression in Rainer's eyes at all.

Later, in Pierre's office, the two men did not comment immediately on what had happened, but, before Tonio left, Pierre said, "Rainer'll never change…on the contrary, I think that our relationship has now reached a crossroads. I don't like having to say it Tonio, but from now on watch your back."

24

Over a month had gone by after the confrontation with Rainer.

By now, Tonio had an overview of the hidden side of Pierre's life, covering everything that had happened over a period of twenty years.

Pierre's willingness to give all the necessary information – even the most confidential documents – notes and bank statements – gave Tonio a complete picture of the Merchant's activities.

The exercise also allowed him to get to know his friend even better.

As he delved further into the documents, he had confirmation of his friend's ability to deal with the most disparate characters, from the American Congressman to the Sudanese guerrilla, from a major Head of State to the obscure military attaché of a Consulate in some godforsaken place. He also discovered another side to his character – a very personal sense of justice. He became aware of this by looking at some transactions which had taken place a few years previously. When Pierre had been approached by another intermediary, who was unable to supply one of the parties in a conflict, not only had he turned down the invitation but, without earning a penny, he had actually worked to help the opposite side, as he was not convinced by the pseudo-democratic theories of the rebel head. The result was that the government troops of the country regained control in that province, although they then put into force extremely repressive measures which resulted in many deaths.

Again, more recently, he had been asked to supply light arms and transport for troops in Morocco which, together with Mauritania, had invaded the Western Sahara after the withdrawal of Franco's Spain. The aim of the invasion was to repress the Polisario movement. Pierre had stalled because he wanted to find out more about this movement, whose aims were not well-known at the time. Through internal contacts in the Algerian army, which supported Polisario, he discovered that it was a group consisting of perhaps a thousand men who were fighting for their own land. These men felt that they had been betrayed by Spain and they had decided to pursue a guerrilla strategy against an enemy which had markedly superior forces.

Despite contrary advice from American emissaries, Pierre met one of the leaders of the movement – Mohamed Abdelaziz, who was to become the General Secretary, the highest position in the movement, and later the President of the Arab Republic of the Western Sahara.

Pierre told Tonio how he had become fascinated by this mild man, who condemned terrorism while maintaining that the guerrilla tactics of his Polisario movement should be considered a 'clean war', in that he tried to avoid involving the civilian population at all costs. From that moment on the Merchant, together with the Algerian forces, helped to transform his modest army which was initially equipped only with antiquated muskets and camels. By supplying them with modern jeeps and efficient weapons they were transformed, and caused major headaches to the Moroccan army.

It was already September and one evening Pierre entered Tonio's office and sat down astride a chair.

"I think the sale of TEC has reached its final stage. As soon as the lawyers have finished looking at the documentation, it'll be public knowledge. I think we'll have two to three weeks before that happens. Perhaps the time has come for us to bring our plan to its conclusion. You should soon meet two or three of those people I've had major dealings with. After that the news will spread itself – the Merchant is laying down his arms, and not only figuratively," he said smiling.

Tonio looked at his friend. He was wearing a Lacoste T-shirt and a pair of faded jeans. 'This man's changed', he thought, looking at him. 'He seems to have got younger. Only a few weeks ago, he seemed to be an old fogey who had lost his way. Now he seems to have found a new purpose in life'.

This change pleased him, and he forced himself to be optimistic about the final stages of the plan they had agreed on. On its completion Pierre had hinted that not only would he donate to charity all money raised through the sale of the arms, but would then use the huge amount due to be raised from the sale of TEC to go into a new business, throwing himself head first into a technological industry based on satellite telephones, which he was sure would be a big success. Some of the profits from this project were also earmarked for charity. He was already thinking of creating a foundation for the schooling of children and youth in the third world.

He seemed like a small boy whose eyes were gleaming, after opening one of those large boxes with a thousand pieces, to build a model aircraft or a sailing ship.

'The important thing at this time', Tonio thought, 'is that he mustn't go around looking so young and active. Nobody will believe he has a serious heart condition.'

"I'm ready," Tonio said, "but I think you should deal with the Americans. From what I've been able to see, and more to the point, from what you've already told me, they don't miss a trick. It's up to you to convince them that you can't stay in the game any more."

"That's right, I'd thought so too. I'll have to take a trip to Washington in the next few days to see the right people. Meanwhile we've got to start thinking how we can put the plan into action and make my arsenal disappear. The first thing I think we're going to have to do is to make a short trip together to Tunisia to meet one of my best friends. We'll go to his seventieth birthday party. I received an invitation a few days ago."

Two days later, Pierre left for Washington. He had a case full of medication with him.

The day of Pierre's departure, Tonio received a call from Irene. She was at her father's house at Caltanissetta.

"*Babbone* is not too well," she told him. "His leg is hurting him a lot and he has breathing problems too."

"I'm really sorry. He'll get better, you'll see…tell me about Nanni."

"He's a fantastic child, he's beginning to talk now and he can't stop for a minute. He's lively, happy…I think he takes after you. I'll try and send you a photo so that you can put it near the one you pinched from my bag before I left Rome. I'm going back there with Nunzia, next week. Do you think…?"

"I'll do my utmost," Tonio promised. "Yes, I don't need to think about it, I'm definitely coming."

On his return from Washington, Pierre told Tonio that the news of his retirement hadn't gone down too well in certain quarters. "As predicted, they already knew about the state of my health and that I'm selling off TEC, and it was no surprise to me to be asked what was to happen to my personal arsenal. They even knew about that.

Sarkis was right to tell me, many years ago, that whenever you drank a glass of water the CIA knew whether it was still or sparkling. When I told them I'd had exploratory talks about an eventual transfer, but that I didn't yet know who the buyer was, they revealed to me that it had been they who had given the information to the Sudan's People Liberation Army, the SPLA, and that the CIA wouldn't object to an eventual supply to them under the circumstances."

"Pierre, I think things are getting complicated..."

"It's just because of this that we've got to be on our guard. We'll probably have to adjust our plan in the light of this information. The man, who has contact with the SPLA in Sudan, is a trustworthy person, and we need to perfect the plan with his help. In my view, we have to pretend to be playing their game and to arrange the accident with the ship before delivery. It's even more necessary to go to Tunisia next week. My friend Nadhir will be able to advise me about it."

"That's fine. If you don't have any objection, I'll join you in Tunisia, but leaving from Rome. Irene will be there for a couple of days and I want to see her."

25

Tonio met Irene the following Monday in the same hotel, the Visconti. Almost two months had gone by since they had last seen each other. After dining alone, he knocked on her door, and was greeted with her usual affection. They kissed and embraced each other for a long time, even though Nunzia was present.

When finally they disentangled themselves, Nunzia approached Tonio and took his hand and kissed it. "May God bless you Signor Tonio. Thanks for everything. The keys to my house were handed over to me last week. My son's doing some of the painting. Remember that house is also your house."

"Nunzia, I did it with all my heart, but for the time being nobody must know about the house. It could serve as a refuge for Irene at some time in the future, you never know."

Nunzia went to her room. When, a little while later, Irene began undressing Tonio noticed the bruises on her arms and back.

"It's not possible!" he shouted. "I won't let you return to that stinking son of a whore. This time I'm coming with you and I'll knock that shit's teeth out!"

"Calm down, Tonio, don't shout," she said, embracing him "Yes, it's hell. But I'm hanging on in there. I'm learning self-defence. He came out of the last incident with a black eye."

"Jesus, but how can you go on living like this? Somebody has to stop him! You only have to show these bruises to Marta's husband…"

"Tonio, don't worry about it, really. I'm working on it. I've spoken about it to Marta, but I have to be very careful. He's even more cruel than he appears. He's threatened to do everything in his power to take Nanni away from me if I ask for a separation. And then there's my father who's not at all well..."

"What a scumbag, what's happened this time?"

"A strange thing, incredible in fact. Recently in view of his health, I've often been going to my father's house. One day, seeing that he had several meetings at home, I went to Caltanisetta to the house where Peppino had said he was having some decorating done. It's a two-storey villa on the outskirts of the city. When I arrived, there wasn't the slightest trace of any work being done on the place. I went in and saw evidence that not only women had been in his bed – although I'm not at all bothered by this now – but there was also evidence that men had been sleeping there too. I couldn't understand why the house was so filthy because we have a maid. It was clear that it hadn't been cleaned for some time. I even went down into the cellar because I wanted to see whether there was the odd stick of furniture, which I could give to Nunzia for her new house.

"You must realise that the cellar consists of four rooms, two large ones in front lit by small windows at street level, which are full of junk, and two smaller ones, towards the back of the house, one behind the other without any windows. You can only get to these via a small door, which you have to know is there, because it's hidden by an old office cupboard on wheels, which is easy to move. Peppino says it's a dry place and he therefore keeps some bottles of very old wine there which, he says, have to be kept in the dark.

"I had the impression that the cupboard had been moved recently. Curiosity got the better of me, so I went in and put on the bare light which hangs from the ceiling. The first thing I saw were two cases on the floor, without lids. I stared with my mouth open. My first thought, as quick as a flash, was of you and your friend Pierre by association, because they were full of arms!"

"Arms?" Tonio said alarmed, "what kind of arms?"

"Arms. Not that I know much about them. A few years ago *babbone* took me on a hunting trip and he taught me to shoot with a sporting gun. Once, he even taught me how to shoot with a pistol, which he had at home. I saw about a dozen pistols, some bigger ones which had magazines under them, and then shot-guns…I think some of them had sawn-off barrels…and a load of boxes of ammunition. While I was there, stupefied, looking at this stuff, I heard a noise behind me and I turned round straight away.

"In front of me there was a middle-aged man, who I'd never seen before in my life, even though his face seemed vaguely familiar. He had come out of the other small room and had a gun in his hand."

"Oh, Holy Jesus," Tonio murmured, sitting on the bed, "and what did you do?"

"Nothing. What could I do? He was there with a gun looking at me. Then he asked me, 'who are you?' It took me some time to gather my thoughts and I told him 'I'm the owner of this house. More to the point, who are you? What are you doing here?' Nothing from him, he didn't reply. I plucked up courage and said, 'I'm Peppino Cantera's wife. Put that gun away.' At this point, Peppino arrived. I can't describe his face. It was ashen. He took me by the arm and dragged me outside. We went up to the first floor. He started shouting. 'What are you meddling in? You always get in the way, showing me up completely! Sooner or later I'm really going to break your neck.' And then he began hitting me and I had to defend myself. I shouted out and he stopped. 'Quiet, you whore', he hissed, 'you haven't seen anybody or anything here today. If you tell anyone, you know that I'll get to hear about it straight away. And do you know what I'm going to do? It won't be you who'll be suffering the consequences, but that little bastard son of yours'."

"But what a shit, what a scumbag…"

"Yes, I know, Tonio. But now I've got something else which I can use against him, because I've discovered who that man is who's hiding in our cellar. He's wanted. He's a big wheel in the Sicilian mafia: Pasquale Colasanti, nicknamed Lillino Colasanti. I saw his photograph in the paper yesterday. He's wanted for masterminding several murders. When I get back home, I've got to find a way to trap him and Peppino. But I have to be careful. I don't want him to harm Nanni, you understand?"

"Of course, I understand. But I'm very worried. I don't like this one little bit. As soon as this job with Pierre is over, and I don't think that it will last very long, I'll have to go back to work at the bank in Rome. I want you and Nanni to come and live with me."

The following morning, Tonio went to see Oreste, who expressed his thanks for the initial fifty thousand dollars, and for the other funds which Tonio had promised.

"When I let Don Mario in Zambia and Don Savino in the Sudan know that they could have their health centres, they were almost on the verge of tears with joy. Tonio, what you and your friend are doing is fantastic…"

"Oreste, you know full well why all this is happening. Believe me, it's only a part of the compensation for so much damage caused."

The following afternoon, Tonio left for Tunisia, on the only direct Alitalia flight. After about an hour in the air, the captain announced that on this very clear day they could admire the Sicilian coast. Without meaning to, Tonio found himself trying to guess where his son and the woman he loved lived, especially now that he had decided to build a life together, stealing them away from another man, and uprooting them from their homeland, at whatever cost.

During the flight, Tonio was able to reflect on what events had recently taken place in his life.

The two projects he wanted to finish – helping Pierre to free himself from a past he was ashamed of, and building a new existence with his woman and his as yet unseen son – constantly occupied his thoughts. He had even forgotten his friends, and his contacts with his relatives were limited to brief weekly phone calls. As for women, which had up to then been indispensable in Tonio's life, they no longer generated any interest whatsoever after seeing Irene again.

He knew that in Pierre and Irene's eyes, he could give the impression of being a man of decision, resolute, always in touch with himself and with a clear vision of what his goal in life was.

However, they were not aware of his inner uncertainty, his weakness and, above all, his ever present fear of not living up to what those he loved, expected of him.

He did not show it, but he was constantly assailed by doubts, brought on by this sudden change in his life. A latent and undetectable anxiety accompanied him at all times throughout each day. One evening, a few weeks earlier, he was alone at home and he began to have violent palpitations in his chest. He called an ambulance, thinking that he was having a heart attack. They arrived a few minutes later, checked him over him, but they did not think that he was suffering an attack. They advised him, however, to consult a cardiologist. The following day, the cardiologist who examined him had not found any unusual symptoms in the functioning of his heart, but when he asked Tonio if there had been any sudden and significant changes in his life which could have produced stress…

'Changes?' Tonio said to himself, 'Within the space of a few weeks I've become a collaborator with an arms trafficker, the lover of the wife of a mafia boss and I've become a father. Not bad, by way of a few changes!'

He knew that he had to carry on, but he did not really have all the courage which others saw in him. He was getting involved with a world where violence was the norm. He had had proof of this a couple of months earlier, when he had been assaulted outside his apartment by Multari's men. He had thought about that incident on several occasions – he had been scared to death. A damned mother and father of a fucking fear. He'd read about it in thrillers. '...his stomach was gripped by fear…he was frozen by fear…fear took his breath away…' It was true! He recalled how his legs and the rest of him had trembled when those two had left him there, with the cut on his cheek.

He saw his face in a mirror when he got back home…and what he saw was certainly not the face of a hero!

26

The Sheraton Hotel in Tunis is modern, functional and is one of the privileged destinations of tourists and businessmen alike, since it is located in the diplomatic quarter, not far from the financial centre. Its elevated position gives it a magnificent view of the whole city.

During the taxi ride from the airport, Tonio had not expected to see a modern, clean and efficient capital, which was capable of presenting simultaneously, both an old and modern image of itself. It did not appear to him to be either very Arab or African, but neither was it very European.

On arriving at the hotel, Tonio found a message from Pierre's secretary, asking him to call his friend Franco Müller at the Credito Svizzero in Zurich.

After the usual jokey repartee, Franco said, "We here at the C.S. have noted that your bank has become the main bank for the whole of the TEC group. This happened after you asked me for some information about Pierre some time ago, do you remember? Despite what you think, that the Swiss haven't got any imagination, I've had an intuition. It's that you have your finger in this pie in some way or other. Up to now, no problem, and I congratulate you.

"Now, it transpires there's a Swiss prosecutor sniffing around, and he's beginning to ask questions about your friend, and my shareholder, Haber. I shouldn't be telling you all this, you realise that it's extremely confidential, but I know that you'll never betray me. Tell me, is there anything I should know? Is there something I can do to save my arse if there's a problem?"

"I wouldn't know," Tonio replied warily, "what sort of a question is that?"

"To tell the truth, I think this prosecutor is fumbling around in the dark. Somebody's caught wind of some accounts which Haber might have abroad, in some financial haven…and now it's public knowledge that he wants to sell the TEC Group, even if that's for health reasons, there are still a few who think they can smell a rat."

Tonio remained silent for a while. He did not wish to lie to his friend, but he certainly could not reveal the existence of the accounts in the Caymans. Over the last few weeks, he had gone over those accounts and money transfers with a fine tooth-comb, and he was certain that nobody could link those accounts to Pierre.

"As far as I'm aware there aren't any foreign accounts linked to TEC or Haber. I'm sure about this because, as I think everyone knows now, I'm helping in the sale of the Group. So I'm in a good position to be able to tell you this."

In the taxi which was taking him and Pierre to the house of Pierre's friend, Nadhir Haddad, he told Pierre about the call from Franco.

After reflecting for a while, Pierre said, "I can smell a rat too, Tonio. It worries me a great deal. I'll send out a few people to sniff things out too."

They arrived at Haddad's house, a small, plain white villa with blue windows in an oriental style. The party had already started. They were warmly welcomed by Haddad's wife Samira, a woman in her sixties, who was wearing a black oriental dress with violet highlights. She was not wearing much jewellery. Tonio thought that she must have been very beautiful when she was younger.

After introductions, Samira took the two men by the arm and led them to a courtyard in the centre of the house, where the guests were having a drink before dinner. Tonio immediately noticed the magnificent mosaics on the floor and the white and blue portico around the courtyard, the overall impression giving a sense of tranquillity and well-being.

"Come," Samira said, "I'd like to introduce you to some of my guests. You already know some of them, Pierre. The children are here too, and they'll be really pleased to see you."

"Tonio," Pierre explained, "by children, this beautiful woman means: Omar who's forty-three and Souade who's thirty-eight…Omar's at Morgan Stanley in New York, while she is an architect in London…ah, here's Nadhir."

Pierre had explained in advance that Nadhir was still, despite his age, The Secretary of State to the Ministry of Magrebin, Arab and African Affairs. It was a position he had held for many years. He was the principal architect of the good relations which existed between Tunisia and all African countries. A priceless ally of Pierre's. An inexhaustible source of information. They had got to know each other fifteen years earlier, during a 'clean' supply to the Tunisian army. They had become friends. Pierre had offered him hospitality several times in Zurich and had helped his son Omar to find his job with Morgan Stanley. Samira had taken him under her wing with the intention of finding a wife for him, sooner or later.

Tonio found himself in the presence of a thin, short man with thick hair, which was completely white. He was wearing a white kaftan with gold borders, which made him appear even more slender. He disappeared for a moment as Pierre towered over him in an imposing manner as they embraced.

Then he turned to Tonio, shaking his hand. "Pierre has spoken about you. I'm honoured to receive you in my house, which is your house." He had a mild and warm voice which, Tonio thought, reflected his personality.

Samira intervened. "Another bachelor! I wonder if this evening I'll have any better luck with you. For years I've been introducing this fop of a friend of yours to some of the most beautiful women in Tunis – but nothing, all he thinks of is working..."

Dinner, which was entirely oriental, was served in a long dining room which could amply accommodate the twenty guests.

Halfway through dinner, there was a toast on the announcement by Nadhir that he was to retire at the end of the year. He said that Samira and he would travel in order to visit all those countries they had dreamt of. And that he would be writing his memoirs, narrating his experiences during fifty years of political life.

Pierre's gift to him, a gold Mont Blanc fountain pen, seemed to be particularly appropriate.

Much later, when the last guest had left and Samira and the children had gone to bed, Nadhir, Pierre and Tonio went into their host's study.

It was a large room with dark wood inlaid furniture displaying innumerable photographs of Nadhir with famous people, or with members of his family. The desk was full of books and papers.

"I wanted you to stay behind a little longer because there's something I have to say to you. I'll say it in your presence, Tonio, because Pierre has assured me that you know everything, and I mean *everything*, about his business.

"Pierre has already briefed me about the plan you are working on to get him out of the military supply business. This is something which I approve of and which I fully support. Getting out now is a very wise move, and why? Because I don't like the winds which are blowing ever stronger from the Middle East. This wave of integralism and fundamentalism, as conceived by the new forces emerging from many Arab countries will, in my opinion, have disastrous consequences for the whole world. I'm happy to be leaving at the right time. And I'm happy that you too, Pierre, albeit for totally different reasons, also want to get out of the fray.

"However, there's something which does concern you closely, Pierre, which worries me. A few days ago I received a visit, completely unannounced, from your son Rainer. He came here late, out of the blue, two or three evenings ago. He told me that he happened to be in Tunisia and he wanted to call on me. I thought the whole thing was a bit strange, because it had never happened before…and with him…well, Samira and I have never had the same relationship with him as we have with you.

"I realised at once that there was something he wanted to tell me or ask me. For a start, he began talking about your shaky health, how he couldn't understand how you wanted to sell – or rather undersell according to him – the TEC Group, making several comments which were not very flattering about you…"

"What comments?" the anger began to appear in Pierre's voice. "What did he say?"

"That you were beginning to lose the plot a bit, that you were getting older – I think at that point he must have forgotten just how old I am – that you were losing control of all that you had built up… you didn't trust him, instead you trust strangers, and here I think he meant you Tonio. I let him ramble on a bit putting him at his ease. Then finally he came to the point. He wanted to know from me where your famous personal arms depot was.

"I pretended not to understand and to be dumbfounded, but I don't think he believed me. I was shocked by the fact that he was even aware of the existence of your depot. But how does he know? Very few of us know of the existence of that arsenal."

"I don't know Nadhir. Obviously he's always been aware of this activity of mine and he's frequently tried to become a part of it. As you well know I've always refused, because I don't think that he's up to doing a job which requires special qualities...diplomatic skills, which he totally lacks.

"The only thing which comes to mind, is that a few years ago when I thought that we might work together, I revealed to him that part of my commission was paid for in arms. However, I've never confided to him the place where they're hidden. I think he's fumbling in the dark but, since he's not a complete idiot, I would assume that he's guessed that the depot is in Tunisia, where I enjoy your protection."

"I'm sure you're right," Nadhir said. "In fact, he's been going around asking a lot of questions to everyone. I know this because after his visit, I had him followed; I know who he's spoken to and what he asked. Naturally he didn't find out anything, because nobody knows anything. The people who know the location of the depot can be counted on the fingers of one hand. A toxic waste dump, at the centre of a military base, in the middle of the desert, guarded twenty-four hours a day by uniformed soldiers does not attract much attention. I've also discovered that he goes around with two men, Italians with criminal records."

"That's all we needed," Pierre said. "My son's interference. As the years go by he's showing his true character. He acts in an underhand and twisted way. He can't be trusted. The last time we saw each other he was on the point of attacking me. As he left, he said he'd make me pay. I'd hoped that he'd got over the hatred he's had for me since he was a child. I now think that this hatred was only lying dormant, and that it's reawakened with renewed virulence. We must stop him, get him to see reason, before he does some harm."

"In my view," Tonio interrupted, "sooner or later he'll find out that your arms are officially earmarked for the SPLA in Sudan. I get the impression that our man there, who is responsible not only for the SPLA contact but also for all the countries in that area – Kenya, Tanzania, Zambia, Somalia and so on – and who'll have to be made aware of our real plan, will play a crucial role in its success. He'll be the Merchant's key man, he'll have a certain autonomy in negotiating, and he'll be charged with looking after the delivery details.

"In my view once Rainer knows about the buying and selling that's taking place, he will go to the Sudan and try and find out from our man, all the details of the operation, including the point of departure, the means of transport, and the dates.

"We have to pre-empt him. We need to bring our operation forward if possible. If we have no other choice, we can allow the goods to be dispatched before payment has been made; and then, when they're lost at sea, it'll be considered an accident!"

"Tonio is right," Pierre said. "There isn't a moment to be wasted. We'll go back to Paris tomorrow on the first flight." He got up from the armchair and embraced Nadhir.

"We won't be able to see each other for a while. It's better if I remain in my shell for a time. Give a kiss to that marvellous woman who is the wife you don't deserve."

The following day on the Air France flight which was taking them back to Paris, Tonio said to Pierre, "I was thinking of Samira…how come you've never remarried?"

"I don't know," Pierre replied, shrugging his shoulders, "perhaps out of idleness…or because of cowardice…I don't know…perhaps out of a false sense of loyalty to a photograph, to a phantom."

He remained silent for a while, his eyes closed. Then he said, "How could such a marvellous woman have given birth to such a worm!"

27

They had decided that Tonio would leave for Sudan as soon as possible, as soon as he had obtained a visa and had had the necessary vaccinations.

Bruno had come to Paris and was helping them to get ready. Tonio also had the impression that another reason for his arrival was principally to be near Pierre during Tonio's absence. He slept in one of the bedrooms on the second floor of the building.

A week after their return from Tunis, Pierre and Bruno came into Tonio's office.

"Here's your visa for Sudan," Pierre said, handing him his passport.

Tonio opened it and realised at once that it was not actually *his* passport. This document had been made out in the name of a certain Piero Donati, but it showed his photograph! The one he had given Bruno for the visa. He was open mouthed.

"But...what's the meaning of this?" he was able to stammer.

"The meaning is that it's a perfectly valid passport, only the photo is not that of Piero Donati. It's a precaution which we take when we travel to these countries...for business that is.

"You see, when you're down there you might happen to meet people who live...how shall I put it...in a parallel world. These people often make extensive checks before they'll meet or speak to you. And you certainly don't want them to find out that they're dealing with Dottor Antonio Brignani, Director of the Banca Nazionale dell'Industria. It wouldn't make sense, whereas this Donati character, is a type they can trust. A close collaborator of the Merchant, who's been forced to stay at home because of his heart condition.

"Our friend Nadhir in Tunis, will be able to vouch for who you are to anyone asking anything about you."

Tonio was turning the passport around in his hands. "It seems…it's perfect! Who made it?"

"Don't worry about that…the ways of Bruno are infinite…ah, and there's another thing…" He went out of the room and came back a minute later.

"When we go to these countries, you have to be prepared," he said.

He held a leather belt in his hand. "You've got your visas and you've had your shots, now you only need this," he said, handing him the belt.

Tonio took it in his hand and looked at it with curiosity.

"What about it?" he asked.

"Look at it closely. It isn't a normal belt."

Tonio examined the belt. It was a bit on the old side and it had been well used. A little heavy and about five centimetres wide. A bit wider than usual belts. Tonio noticed a swelling on the inside of the belt, which went from one edge to the other, and ran the whole of its length from the buckle right round to the buckle holes. The end of the belt was normal without any swelling.

"I bought it many years ago in Morocco, and I've had this little adjustment made. Look," Pierre said.

He took the belt from Tonio's hands and starting from the last buckle hole where the swelling began, lifted up a very small part of the leather with his nail, and pulled. Tonio heard the characteristic sound of Velcro being pulled apart. In the interior of the belt, for the whole of its length, there were rows of rolled up dollar bills. Tonio opened his eyes wide in surprise.

"There are three thousand dollars in this belt," Pierre explained to him. "Five rolls, each containing twenty twenty-dollar notes and one roll containing twenty fifty-dollar notes. Three thousand."

"Ingenious!" Tonio said, astonished.

"Of course. You never know what can happen down there. This is a huge sum in those countries. In case of need, these dollars can open up many doors for you. I've had to resort to this more than once. You see, when you're wearing this belt, the internal part is up against your body and you don't notice the swelling. As it's old and well used, the belt doesn't catch the eye. Always wear it when you're there."

Tonio looked admiringly at the work which had gone into that particular belt.

Pierre continued, "Another thing: don't have anything on you which can link you to anybody else in Sudan, or anywhere else. No names, addresses, telephone numbers in diaries or on bits of paper. Learn them by heart before you leave. If they need to search you, and they do so quite often there, you can't then be linked to anybody else who is already under 'observation' by the police or anyone else. You're a tourist. An ordinary tourist travelling around to see the many ancient monuments. Buy yourself a guidebook and carry it with you."

"These precautions seem a bit excessive..." Tonio protested.

"Do as I say. You never know...as the English say: *better safe than sorry*[*]. You'll meet Awad Khalil, he's a lad...a man who's on the ball and who you can trust with your life. All the information you need about him is here in this folder. Learn it by heart. He lives in Wad Madani, a city which is two hundred kilometres from Khartoum. It would be worth your while renting a car through the hotel."

---

[*] In English in the original text

"All right, all right," Tonio cut him short. "Listen, changing the subject, there's something which is niggling me. It's like a worm gnawing at my brain which I can't get out of my mind: the arms which Irene saw in the cellar at her house.

"It's obvious that her shit of a husband is part of or linked to the mafia. Do you think it's possible to find out how he got hold of those arms and where they came from?

"I'm really unhappy that Irene's living among those people. From the way she described them to me, we're dealing not only with pistols or sawn off shotguns, but sub machine-guns. And you can't buy those from your average delinquent..."

"I've thought of that too. It's not that easy. The quantity in those cases is too small to raise suspicion, it's small beer; it might not even be linked to a large shipment of arms. However, with a bit of luck and a few backhanders here and there, we might be able to find out where those automatic weapons came from. To tell the truth, I've already put somebody on to the case who knows his way around."

Tonio left two days later. In the morning he took a British Airways flight to London and still with BA, a direct flight to Khartoum which left the same afternoon.

When the officer at passport control opened his passport and compared the photo with him, Tonio felt butterflies in his stomach, but everything was fine.

During the nine hour flight in business class, he had plenty of time to familiarise himself with Sudan – a country which he probably would never have visited off his own bat – using the two guides which he had bought. A huge country, the largest in Africa, and one of the poorest. Colonised, exploited and eternally torn by local wars.

He also reflected that, for the first time in his life, he was travelling on a false passport and so was committing a crime.

He did not feel entirely at ease, but at the same time he felt an excitement, which he thought might be similar to what Irene had described some time before as 'the prohibited frenzies of sex'.

He arrived at four in the morning the following day. He was not able to see much during the journey in a taxi, apart from the large number of people who were sleeping at the side of the road, covered in rags or cardboard.

The International Hilton – the best hotel in Khartoum – was a large, modern building with an unparalleled view of the White Nile from Ethiopia flowing into the Blue Nile from Uganda, forming one whole mass of water, the Nile itself, which then flowed northwards towards Egypt.

His room was large and comfortable. Tonio stretched out on the bed, waiting for time to pass so as to call Awad Khalil at a more respectable hour.

He soon realised that he could not sleep. A subtle anxiety made him restless. Having tossed and turned for more than an hour, he decided to get up and have a shower. The bathroom was large and extremely clean, with a washbasin and bath in pink granite.

He looked into the mirror thoughtfully. 'What am I doing?' he asked himself. 'What are you doing here?' he said to himself aloud, "what have you landed yourself in?" He rested his hands on the basin and moved his face closer to the mirror. He looked at the reflection of his eyes very closely '*Ssì proprio na capa 'e cazzo*[*]' he said to himself in Neapolitan dialect. For an instant, he felt an impulse to call Pierre and tell him that he wanted to abandon everything. But he did not do so. Instead he ordered a hearty breakfast and dialled Awad's number. There was no reply.

At eight o'clock he had a call from Pierre. "I've got some interesting news. I spoke to Nadhir yesterday evening. He told me that Rainer had visited other 'operators' in the sector telling

---

[*] You are a real dick head

the same story: that I've completely lost it and that I've lost control of my business. To some he said that he'd take over from me, as the Merchant's heir. Nadhir has promised to set the record straight with everyone.

"A little while ago, Irene called. She asked that you call her at this number. It's Nunzia's number at her new house. Ah, I almost forgot, your friend Franco Müller called too. He asked you to ring him back as soon as you can…heh, I'm working for you here. How am I as a secretary?"

"Not at all bad, if you carry on like this I'll give you a pay rise…ciao."

"Ciao. Let me know how things go down there. You know that you can call me any time, day or night."

After finishing with Pierre, he immediately dialled Nunzia's number. After many attempts, Irene replied. "I can't believe it! You've phoned me straight away! And from Africa! This is the first call to be received on this phone!"

"Hello my love, what are you doing there?"

"I'm helping Nunzia sort out the furniture. I'll try and come here as often as I can, so I'll be able to call you or receive your calls. Peppino thinks I'm at *babbone*'s…by the way, he's really ill now, you know. He suffers a lot. I try to stay with him for as long as I can. I know that Peppino's in Calabria today. Tonio, I think he's going to land himself in a lot of trouble. The people he has around him…I'm trying to keep as far away from him as possible."

"You're doing the right thing, darling, hang on in there. All this will be over soon!"

Immediately afterwards he called Franco. "Well then, my friend, the tireless worker, what's the news?"

"No real news as such. Only one thing which seems a bit strange. It appears that the person who tipped off the prosecutor in Zurich about Haber is some business associate of his son, Rainer. I'm a bit stunned. Do you think it's possible? In other words do you think that the son wants to damage his father in some way or other?"

"I don't know, perhaps." This time he decided to tell the truth, even if it was only a half-truth. "The relations between father and son aren't the best. I can say this because I've witnessed a few scenes. I know that Rainer didn't agree to the sale of the TEC Group. He was probably hoping that his father, on retiring for health reasons, would hand over the management of the Group to him. But to the suggestion that it was Rainer who tipped off the attorney even if through a third party…well, *inter nos* knowing his character, now I come to think of it, I can tell you, yes, it is possible."

"I'm under the impression that this Rainer chap doesn't entirely command your respect, or am I wrong?"

"No my friend, you're not at all wrong, in fact, if you want to know the truth, I think he's an emeritus, presumptuous piece of shit."

After having tried once more to call Awad to no avail, he put on a short-sleeved shirt and a pair of jeans, and went down to the lobby of the hotel. He arranged to hire a car. He was going to Wad Madani. Awad knew of his arrival. He would meet him at his house.

28

In the Toyota he had rented, Tonio had to extricate himself from Khartoum's chaotic traffic. There were no lane markings on the roads, and in the piazzas the law of the jungle ruled: if you hesitated it could take ages to travel just a hundred metres.

Fortunately Tonio had learned to drive on the streets of Naples, which were very similar as far as the lack of discipline was concerned.

When he finally left the city the flow of traffic was slow, but constant. He followed the directions they had given him at the hotel and he drove south, skirting the White Nile.

The road was dusty but made-up and followed the railway line. The sprawling suburbs of Khartoum and the countless shanty towns continued kilometre after kilometre.

He saw many women walking along the side of the road, wrapped in their multi-coloured clothes. Many held a child in their arms. He saw other children, dressed in rags, playing near open sewers. Along the road there were stalls selling drinks, cigarettes, and spices. Some were equipped for cooking, what Tonio thought, were fish fritters. There was not a single white person to be seen. The temperature, at eleven in the morning, was nearly forty degrees. The air-conditioning in the car, even on full, could barely cope with the sweltering air impregnated with red dust.

Some thirty kilometres from the city, the traffic flowed more easily. There were fewer cars and more buses, crammed with people beyond belief.

The river flowed gently on his right. Tonio noticed a few barges loaded with rubbish heading south.

It took him nearly three hours to travel the one hundred and fifty kilometres, which separate Khartoum from Wad Madani.

He had learnt Awad's address by heart. His house was located on a side street about four or five hundred metres in length, which sloped down from the main road towards the river, about three kilometres before the town centre. Awad's house was the last on the right, isolated from neighbours by a large uncultivated field about a hundred metres wide. A little further on, the road disappeared behind an embankment, probably the bank of the river on which lush vegetation of bamboo and various shrubs grew, hiding the river itself from view.

The houses along the unmade up-road were low, single-storey buildings, mostly unplastered and painted white, and a few had bare front gardens. By this time it was almost three in the afternoon.

When Tonio got out of the car he was bowled over by a blast of hot air. The road was deserted. He walked the few metres to the house and knocked on the door. He waited a few moments and knocked again. The house seemed empty but he was certain he had got the right one. Awad's house was the only one to have a green door and windows. He got back into the car, with the air-conditioning running, after deciding to wait for a while.

Half an hour later, when he was on the point of leaving, he saw a motorbike, only a little larger than a scooter, coming down the road, ridden by a coloured man.

He rode up to Tonio's window. "Donati?" he asked.

Tonio nodded, opening the window.

"I'm Awad," the man said, in English, smiling. "Come, put the car behind the house, there's a bit of shade there."

Tonio followed him, parked near the bike and followed Awad into the house through a rear door which opened off a tiny patio at the back of the house.

They went straight into the kitchen, a room containing cheap furniture with a table in the middle. It was clean and had been freshly painted. There was a bowl in the sink which had probably been used for breakfast that morning.

"Excuse the mess," he said, offering Tonio a cold beer. He made a sign to follow him into what seemed to be a dining room. An arch separated this room from a small sitting room. "My wife is away with the children looking after her mother in a village about forty kilometres from here."

"Don't worry," Tonio said. "How many children do you have?"

"Two," he replied, pointing to some photos on a shelf. "A boy and a girl, four and two."

"Congratulations," Tonio said, looking at the photos, "what a nice family."

They sipped their beers for a while. Tonio was able to observe Awad.

He had no idea of his age. He could have been thirty just as easily as forty-five. He was tall, well-built. He was very dark skinned, and his head was devoid of any hair and reflected the light coming through the window. He had a soft musical voice, almost like a woman's. What struck Tonio most about him was his neck, which seemed extraordinarily long. He recalled a documentary film about the Watussi which he had seen many years before. Perhaps he had Nubian origins, he wondered, although without really knowing whether Nubians actually had these characteristics.

Awad asked, "What did the Merchant tell you about me?"

"That you're his friend, you're a lawyer and on the ball, and that you have contact with the SPLA."

"Yes, few words, but true. The Merchant is a great friend of mine. I respect him greatly, and I'm very sorry to learn that he's ill. As for the SPLA, they trust me because I've seen several transactions through with them, without any problems. Now they're all very excited because they think they're going to get a large quantity of arms at a knockdown price.

"One of their representatives will come here this evening, to finalise the details of the deal. But I'd like you to clear up something for me, which I haven't quite understood. Why are you here and why all the urgency to complete this operation."

Tonio remained silent for an instant. He wanted to choose his words carefully while revealing the plan which had been devised.

"I'm here on the Merchant's behalf, to ask for your help. Yes, the Merchant is unwell and has decided to wind things up. His illness, and a road accident which nearly killed him, have produced...what shall I call it...a crisis of conscience. He's realised that times are changing and this activity of...military supplies is now part of a game which is too complicated, and in which the players no longer keep to the unwritten rules, which everybody used to play by until recently. Nowadays there are times when you don't even know who the players are, and even more frequently, the actual 'end users' aren't those declared.

"He's convinced, and with good reason, that he's caused more harm than good, even if it's difficult to see *any* good when talking about arms...

"Now, your help will consist of convincing our buyers that we'll accept all their conditions, so long as they do things quickly. I have 'carte blanche' in the negotiations, and I'll go as far as proposing that we will send the goods even before payment – something completely unheard of in this business. You and I are here together to guarantee that this is what happens – but the goods won't actually arrive at their destination."

Awad opened his eyes wide and leaned forward. "You're joking!" It was more an affirmation than a question.

"Not at all!" Tonio said. "The Merchant intends to destroy those arms!" He said this in a quiet voice, almost in a whisper, which gave a sense of authenticity to his statement.

In a few words he explained the plan they had hatched in Paris: "The SPLA will be disappointed, but will understand that the Merchant would have kept his promise, as always, were it not for the accident with the ship, which will be transporting the arms. And you too will keep your reputation intact.

"Awad, I'm authorised to tell you that for this final service you'll be well rewarded, so that if you wish, and the Merchant hopes that you decide to do so, you too will be able to leave this business for ever."

"I understand," Awad said, after a moment's silence. "But why do all this?"

"Because ever since news spread that the Merchant is retiring, there are too many people about who have shown an interest in those arms. The sooner we can get rid of them, the better. After we've met the emissary from the SPLA, we'll call Pierre in Paris to let him know the result of the meeting."

"OK," Awad said. "Let's hope that the phone works this evening. You know the connections here come and go all the time. And…another thing, we might be up very late. It's best if you sleep here tonight. The roads aren't too safe after a certain hour."

They carried on talking for a long time, going over the plan and all its various stages, finally agreeing that there was no reason why it shouldn't work.

At one point, Awad prepared a salad of spinach with beans and onions, and dressed it with what he called 'Shata' which was nothing more than a tangy sauce made with lemon juice, chopped garlic, salt and ground red and black pepper.

About ten that night, they heard a car pulling up in front of the house. Awad went to open the door and let in a middle-aged man, with greying hair, not very tall and with a lighter complexion than Awad's. He seemed to be more Middle Eastern than Sudanese. He was wearing a brown crumpled suit. He resembled a civil servant more than a guerrilla.

Awad introduced him as Morgan, clearly a false name or his 'nom de combat'. The meeting was unexpectedly short, lasting perhaps twenty minutes.

Awad, following his brief from Pierre, confirmed the quantity of goods involved in the transaction. In the list, the most significant articles were the sixty thousand AK-47s, ten thousand mortars, ten thousand flame-throwers and three tons of ammunition. Then there were spare parts, and a thousand or so pistols and other small arms.

The Merchant had given instructions on the money to ask for – twelve million dollars – but he had left it to Tonio to finalise the contract. Morgan, while accepting that it was a considerable quantity of arms, said that the sum exceeded their budget, at least at that time. Tonio had his doubts about this because he knew that if they wanted to, they could demand payment from the CIA, and it couldn't be ruled out that they'd already done just that.

In the end, it was agreed that the price of a single AK-47, the item which interested the SPLA the most, would be reduced from ninety to seventy-five dollars, which together with a few other minor adjustments, would bring the price down to ten million. The only condition which the Merchant imposed was that delivery had to take place within a week. This haste was because of his illness; this was to be his final transaction and he wanted to get rid of the arms as soon as possible, before going into hospital.

"One week!" Morgan exclaimed. "But that's impossible! We need more time, much more time to get the money together."

"That's not a problem," Tonio said, to Morgan's great surprise. "We'll deliver the goods the week after next anyway; you can pay us when you're ready. We trust you. And don't forget Nadhir who looks favourably on this operation and guarantees it; not to mention our American friends."

They agreed that the ship coming from Tunisia, and sailing down the Red Sea, would arrive in two weeks time at an inlet near the village of Trinkitat on the East Coast, about thirty kilometres North of Tawkar where the SPLA had a base.

Morgan left, clearly satisfied, after shaking Awad and Tonio vigorously by the hand.

Then they called Pierre. After many attempts they finally got through. Tonio told him the outcome of the meeting without mentioning any names, referring to the arms as 'chickens' and the ammunition as 'chicken feed'.

Tonio went to bed around midnight, satisfied with the way he had concluded this first stage of the plan. He felt optimistic. His latent worries had disappeared. He thought his role in this matter would soon come to an end.

He would go back home and concentrate on his future life with Irene and his son. He had to help her free herself from her husband. She would come to live with him, she would ask for a divorce…he was extremely tired, not having slept much since leaving Paris the previous day. He was sure that he would sleep well, now that he was beginning to relax. He could not have been more wrong.

29

He woke up all of a sudden, unable to breathe. A great weight was obstructing his nose and mouth, preventing him from getting air into his lungs. A growing panic paralysed his mind.

He began to struggle violently. He could not move his arms as they were immobilised behind his back. He could not understand what was happening.

In the dark his eyes, now wide open, were not able to register anything to tell him what was happening. The panic transformed itself into an intense, visceral, fear.

He thought he was going to die. His convulsive movements became uncontrollable, like those of an epileptic fit.

His desperation gave him the energy to kick out violently as if he were drowning. This provoked a hoarse cry in his ear, and at the same time a relaxation of the grip on his face. He was able to open his mouth and get some air into his screaming lungs, which gave him the energy needed to kick out again even more vigorously.

He heard a voice behind his shoulders, a curse. There was somebody else on his bed, a man!

Without stopping his convulsive contortions, he succeeded in creating a little space between himself and the individual behind him. A violent tug freed his arms. With another sudden movement, dictated purely out of fear, he rolled to one side and fell off the edge of the bed. His attacker landed on top of him. In an attempt to pick himself up, he hit the individual's head violently, and there was a scream. Tonio managed to get up again and began to move quickly towards the door, whose dark outline he could now make out from the bottom of the bed. However, an indistinct figure appeared at the door and tried to grab him. Tonio defended himself by flailing his arms.

At that moment he felt something explode in his head. A deafening sound, accompanied by a searing pain and multicoloured flashes in his eyes. He was vaguely aware that the floor was coming up towards him.

When he came to it was the pain in his head which he noticed first. A deep, dull pain which seemed to grip his brain in waves and which prevented him from opening his eyes.

When he finally managed to half open them, at first he did not recognise the room; then he saw a small pile of toys in a corner and realised that he was in Awad's sitting room.

He tried to move, but this caused a searing pain in his head. He remained immobile for a minute and then he tried moving once more, slowly. He realised that he was on the floor, with his wrists and feet bound in a foetal position.

With a superhuman effort, he succeeded in straightening his legs and lying on his back. Another wave of pain went through him, which made him close his eyes. He felt two tears trickle down his face.

He heard a noise on his right. He turned his head gently and to his surprise saw Awad, who was also tied up and whose face was completely swollen. His T-shirt and his short trousers were stained with blood. One of his eyes was closed and puffed up; the other was streaked with red and was looking at him, trying to tell him something.

Tonio opened his mouth to speak, but Awad stopped him, shaking his head and looking towards the kitchen. Tonio looked back at him with a questioning expression on his face. Awad turned to look towards the kitchen, from where Tonio could now hear sounds. Then he heard some footsteps crossing the dining room, coming towards the sitting room. He saw Awad close his eyes and he did the same. The footsteps stopped for a moment in the room and then turned back.

He opened his eyes again and saw that Awad was trying to tell him something. Pushing with his heels, Tonio was able to move a few centimetres closer.

"The arms," he said, in a whisper which Tonio could hardly make out.

Tonio looked at him without understanding.

"They want to know where the Merchant's arms are…there's three of them."

"Who are they?" Tonio whispered back.

"I don't know. I've never seen them before."

They heard the steps once more, getting closer. The two men closed their eyes as they had done before. Then, unexpectedly, somebody poured a stream of water onto Tonio's face. He reacted with a start, and opened his eyes.

"He's awake!" the man who was standing over him said. More steps could be heard approaching.

It was like a punch in the stomach for Tonio. One of the men was Rainer!

Having recovered from the shock, Tonio said, "Rainer…but…but what's going on?"

He did not reply. He continued looking at him with a thoughtful expression on his face.

"Rainer, please…can you tell me what's going on?"

"I'll tell you what's going on, I need some information, that's all. I need information which only you and your friend can give me…but he's pretending he doesn't understand me."

"What information?" Tonio asked, suddenly assuming an interested tone.

"What information do you think? You know very well what I'm talking about. I want to know where my father has been storing all his material. I've found out that this gentleman here is organising a sale to the Sudanese rebels, so he must know where they're coming from and where they're going to – there's no two ways about it. I want that material, because it's mine and I need it. I didn't expect to find you here. But it's better like this. Now I know, I'm certain that I can get what I want, because if he doesn't tell me, I'm sure you will."

"Listen, Rainer, let's try and be reasonable…civilised people…why do you keep me tied me up like this? And him!" he said turning his eyes towards Awad, "was it necessary to reduce him to that state?"

"Listen," Rainer said, "everything can be sorted out immediately. I haven't got time to waste. As soon as you've told me where the arms are, we'll go."

Tonio looked at the other two men carefully for the first time. One was coloured, on the youngish side, with a scar all along his right cheek and stringy yellowish hair. The other could have been Arabian, perhaps Egyptian or Greek, around forty or fifty with greying hair. He was wearing an open-necked shirt with rolled-up sleeves. He was very muscular and was sweating profusely.

"We don't know, Rainer. We really don't know," Tonio said.

"I don't believe you. And I've got a way of getting this young gentleman to talk. He went out of the room and came back almost straight away with a black bag in his hand. He put his hand in it and pulled out a gun.

"Rainer, for heaven's sake, what are you doing? Put that gun away…please!"

"I'll show you what I'm doing."

With help from the other two, he raised Awad up, propped him against the sofa, and pointed the gun at his chest. "Well where is the material? In Tunisia? In Algeria? In Morocco? Where's it leaving from? Where *exactly*?"

Awad shook his head. "I don't know, so how can I tell you?"

"Look, you ugly son of a black whore, haven't you got it into your head that I'm not leaving here until one of you has told me? I mean it. You must know, otherwise how else could you negotiate with those other shits of friends of yours?" He began to press the barrel of the gun against Awad's swollen eye, making him scream from the pain.

"I don't know, I don't know! The only thing I can tell you is where the arms are due to arrive...they will arrive at Trinkitat..." He said this with a tone of desperation in his voice.

"You ugly turd, do you really think I'm that stupid?" Rainer shouted, his face contorted. With his left hand he squeezed Awad's jaw, forcing him to open his mouth. He put the barrel of the gun in it and began shouting again. They could hear the sound of the barrel against Awad's teeth.

"I don't give a damn where they're arriving, you have to tell me where they're coming from, fuck it!"

As he said this he pushed the barrel of the gun even further into poor Awad's mouth, twisting it upwards, causing him to cough and jerk his head forward.

And the gun went off.

Rainer remained there looking incredulous, his hand spattered with blood, still holding the gun in Awad's mouth. The body, after having first leapt upwards, slipped down sideways towards where Tonio was still lying.

They all remained motionless, looking at Awad's lifeless body which slowly crumpled down on the floor, leaving a streak of blood and grey matter on the front of the sofa.

The sound of the shot was still ringing in everyone's ears.

Awad's head gently came to rest on the floor, half a metre from Tonio's face. Blood flowed copiously from an enormous hole in the top of his head.

Tonio turned his face the other way and threw up. Waves of fear overcame him, paralysing his brain and immobilising his body.

Then Rainer moved, still with the gun in his hand. He was pale. His lips were bloodless. He took his gaze off Awad's body and looked around him; he seemed to be asking the others to explain what had happened.

The first to come to his senses was the big man, who went to the window and glanced outside to see whether anyone had heard the shot. It was almost dawn.

"All OK," he said, "but its better that we clear out as soon as possible."

"Yes," the other agreed. "But what are we going to do with him?"

Rainer went up to Tonio with the gun still in his hand.

'This is it,' Tonio thought, 'what a shitty end. In a shitty country at the hands of a shitty man!' For a fraction of a second he thought that he should pray, but he was too paralysed with fear to do so.

Rainer knelt down next to him. He looked with contempt at the vomit on the floor and Tonio's face. "Well then, Tonio, are you going to tell me?"

Tonio was terrified and started to tremble slightly. He was unable to speak, his mind overcome by the thought that he was about to die. Then with an enormous effort, trying to control his breathing, since he was breathless as if finishing a long race, he said, "You're…stupid…Rainer. You're…an idiot. We don't …we can't…know it. You should know how…how your father works. He's always used it…the need to know principle of…of watertight doors…he protects himself."

"Um…perhaps…" Then, looking at Awad's lifeless body, "Do you want to know something? That fool there told me that the goods are to be delivered in Trinkitat, which is a village on the coast, if I'm not mistaken. So I've worked out that the goods will arrive by sea. I was convinced they would be coming by air, but perhaps there's too much stuff to carry on one of the planes which my father usually uses. That, my friend, will narrow down our search…there aren't too many ports from which this kind of export can pass unnoticed…"

He turned to the other two and said, "Turn him over!"

"Rainer, for pity's sake, what are you doing?" Tonio's terror affected his voice.

"Don't worry," the other said, "don't carry on like a little girl."

The two turned him over and Tonio sensed Rainer wielding the gun. He felt Rainer pressing the weapon into his right hand, and forcing his index finger onto the trigger. Then he took the gun back.

"That's done it," he said. "Now you're the murderer. I've even got your passport. Or even better still, Piero Donati's. I only need to make one call to the police to get them here to arrest you. You're in my hands. Do as I tell you and everything'll be fine."

"What do you want me to do?" Tonio asked.

"You know what? We're going to call Pierre and get him to tell you where the merchandise is."

"And you think that your father will tell you?"

"Not me, but he will tell you. You'll speak to him. Tell him what's happened here today, if you want, so he'll understand that I'm not joking."

"Christ, Rainer, why don't you forget it…if you need money I'm sure your father would give you some, to help you…he's done it before and…"

"You haven't understood anything. If you really want to know, I've already sold the merchandise! Yes I've really sold it, I've even received the money; all I have to do now is deliver it, and I don't have much time to do it. And stop calling him my father. That old man in his dotage isn't my father. He married my mother, exploiting her weakness…getting her all mixed up and then leaving her to die in hospital!" Then turning to the other two, he ordered, "Untie him!"

While they were untying him, he got the man with the scar to explain how to get an international line, and he dialled Pierre's number. He had to repeat the operation several times, cursing, before the telephone began ringing at the other end.

Rainer passed the phone to Tonio. Pierre answered the phone almost immediately, in a drowsy voice.

Tonio did not waste time in small talk. In an expressionless voice he told him that he was with Rainer, that Awad was dead, and that Rainer wanted to know at all costs where the precious arms were.

Pierre listened in silence. Then he asked, "How did Awad die?"

"A shot went off…"

"Rainer?"

"Yes."

"And you? How are you?"

"OK, but…not too free."

There was a further silence, then Pierre said, "I think I understand the situation…can Rainer hear me?"

"No."

"Good, then listen. I'll speak quickly. I'll try to gain time. Rainer is serious…he wants this information desperately. I won't give it to him unless he assures me of your freedom in exchange. I'll think of something here at this end. In the meantime, be on your guard. He's mad…pass him over to me."

Tonio signalled to Rainer that Pierre wanted to speak to him, and handed over the phone.

Rainer listened attentively and then said, "No deal, I won't even consider it. Do you really think I'm stupid? *First* you tell me where they are and *then* I'll let him go."

Rainer remained silent for a long time, while Pierre proposed the terms of an eventual exchange to him.

At the end he said, "Um, well yes, OK. It's complicated, but I think that it can be done." Then he passed the telephone to Tonio again.

At the other end Pierre said, "Listen, we've agreed that I'll feed him information a bit at a time, so I can be sure that nothing will happen to you. For now, I've told him to take a plane, with you, to Cairo. It's not difficult from Khartoum, there are several flights a day. Once there, you'll have to call me again. I'd like to speak to you often, to ensure that you're OK. In the meantime, I'll organise something with Bruno from this end. Tonio?"

"Yes?"

"I'm sorry."

At the end of the call, Rainer looked at Tonio and said sarcastically, "Well, well, I see that daddy-boy is concerned about your safety. He's succeeded in pulling the wool over your eyes too."

Tonio did not reply. After a while he said, "I have to go to the bathroom." He was still wearing the shorts he had slept in. Passing by his bedroom he went in for a moment to get his jeans, which he had left on a chair. The belt was still in place.

In the bathroom, which had only one small window set high up, he washed and dressed himself as best he could.

When he came out they were all ready to leave. Tonio gave a last glance at Awad. This time he found the strength to say a brief prayer to himself.

Before opening the door, Rainer said with a smile on his lips, "You're intelligent, and you've certainly understood that you shouldn't try any tricks. That gun on the floor and the car in which you arrived are my insurance policy. The irrefutable evidence that you're a murderer. Once I've got the information and we've left this country, I'll send someone to get rid of the gun and to take the car back to your hotel. I'm sure it'll take a few days before anyone discovers the body. We have plenty of time to get away. Let's go."

30

For the first half an hour nobody spoke. Tonio was sitting in the back, beside the man with greying hair. He had heard the coloured man call him Ali. From the time they had left, this man had already smoked three cigarettes, fouling the air. The black man was driving the car: also a Toyota, but an older model than the one which Tonio had hired the previous day. Before getting into the car, in front of Awad's house, Rainer had child-locked the door on Tonio's side so that he could not open it.

He thought back to the moments when he had believed he was close to death. He was ashamed of his behaviour. He saw himself once more, lying on the floor, impotent, paralysed, with tears running down his face. And he saw himself once more, vomiting and shaking with fear. Then Awad's death, his head split, the red stain which had soaked into the fabric of the sofa. In all his life the only violent death he had witnessed had been when a slaughter man's gun was used against the head of a cow by a farmer during a summer holiday with his uncle in the Abruzzo. An unpleasant memory of his childhood.

He also visualised once more the photographs on the shelf in Awad's living-room…

He stopped staring at the road and looked at Rainer's profile, which he could see next to the driver.

"What does it feel like killing a man, Rainer?" he asked, but did not receive a reply.

The nearer they got to the city, the more the traffic increased.

Tonio saw a train, overcrowded with people as usual, which was travelling in the opposite direction, towards Wad Madani. He tried to summarise his situation and he realised with alarm that he was in a difficult position: he was in effect the prisoner of a mad murderer. Even if he managed to escape, he would not get very far without a passport. He could not go to the Italian Consulate to ask for another one, because the one with which he had entered Sudan had been false; he could not ask for one in his real name because there would be no trace of his entry into the country.

More to the point, there were his fingerprints on the gun which had been used to kill Awad, and the police – once having discovered the body – could easily trace him after checking the car parked next to the house. He had to get out of the country as soon as possible, and hope that the police at some later stage would not circulate his photograph, as there was always a remote possibility that somebody would recognise Antonio Brignani. He was also convinced that Rainer would not send anybody to get the gun and the car as he had promised.

They arrived at Khartoum Airport in the early afternoon. In the large square in front of the terminal, absolute chaos reigned: foot passengers, cars, buses and taxis were going in all directions. People were abandoning their cars wherever there was a space.

After driving around for ten minutes without success, Rainer double-parked the car in front of the entrance to the departure lounge.

"I'll go and check the first flight for Cairo," he said. "Wait for me here."

The heat in the car was unbearable. Ali, sitting next to Tonio, was bathed in a sea of sweat and was still chain-smoking.

Tonio noticed a group of policemen chatting and smoking about twenty metres away, armed with sub-machine guns, and probably there to guard the large square. Every now and then the one facing their car cast a casual glance in their direction.

Little by little, an idea began to form in his mind. A mad idea. He decided to risk a manoeuvre which might create a means of escape. A true leap in the dark, he thought, but after all…it can't get any worse than this…

He asked Ali for a cigarette. Ali pulled one from his packet and lit it for him.

Tonio had never been a real smoker. He had stopped smoking a few cigarettes a day many years earlier, when a surgeon friend of his in Italy had shown him the x-ray of the lungs of a seasoned smoker who had died of cancer.

The car window on Ali's side was half-open so that he could drop ash from his cigarette outside the car. Tonio also half-opened the window on his side.

When he wanted to shake the ash off, he stuck his hand out with the cigarette between his thumb and his index finger. At the same time he completely folded his ring finger and his little finger until they touched the palm of his hand. The middle finger remained straight and extended.

Whoever saw his hand at that moment would have recognised an unequivocally obscene and offensive gesture. The next time the policemen looked in his direction, Tonio gently raised his hand upwards. The man appeared not to notice.

Tonio carried on smoking. A minute later he repeated the gesture. This time the policeman looked hard at him.

Tonio drew on the cigarette again, he put his hand out of the window and he repeated the gesticulation quite boldly. The policeman said something to the other two and they all approached the car.

Ali and his black companion, who were not aware of what was happening, were taken by surprise when the policemen came up to the side of the car and began to speak in Arabic.

They signalled to all of them to get out of the car and to show their papers. Tonio, with an innocent smile, shrugged his shoulders as if to say he had not understood.

One of the three, who seemed to be the one with the highest rank, asked him in broken English to show him his passport. Tonio, still smiling, replied that one of his friends had it with him, inside the airport, where he was booking a flight.

The policeman, who was becoming increasingly irritated, told Tonio to go with one of his men to fetch the passport to show it to him. Tonio entered the crowded airport hall with the young policeman, and after a while he spotted Rainer talking to a clerk at one of the ticket desks.

Behind Rainer there were at least thirty people who were pushing and jostling in an attempt to speak with one of the clerks. Tonio pointed out Rainer to the policeman who, after a moment's uncertainty, signalled to Tonio to stay where he was, while he forced a way through the crowd in order to reach Rainer. Tonio nodded, smiling politely.

"It's now or never," he said to himself. He watched the policeman for a moment as he pushed towards Rainer through the crowd.

Then Tonio turned, and briskly headed for a side exit from the ticket hall, mingling with the crowd.

31

As soon as he was out of the terminal building, he was approached by two or three taxi drivers who all invited him to get into their vehicles. He quickly climbed into the nearest one and told the driver to take him to the Hilton.

He could hardly believe his luck. He was still in trouble, and the feeling of anxiety had not yet left him, but at least I've freed myself from that madman Rainer, he said to himself.

He began to think furiously about how he could extricate himself from his situation.

The first thing to do, he decided, was to call Pierre; tell him that he was free, and that he was returning to Wad Madani in order to remove the gun and to collect the hire car.

But how he asked himself? He would have to catch a train. He had noted that they were quite frequent on the route heading south.

But he had to hurry. Rainer, once he had freed himself from the policemen at the airport, would immediately start looking for him. And the first thing he would do would be to go to the Hilton to see whether he had returned or called in there. Perhaps it wasn't a good idea to go to the hotel after all.

'Let's see...' Tonio thought. 'If I were Rainer, what would I do once I'd found out that I hadn't been back to the hotel...?'

The man isn't stupid, he thought, he'll probably work out that I'll go back to Wad Madani in order to make the pistol disappear and retrieve the car, both apparent proof of my guilt.

The optimism which had pervaded him a little while before began to fade. He thought that he might not get to Wad Madani in time. Rainer would be able to get there more quickly, and might be waiting for him there. All of a sudden he felt terribly alone. He desperately needed help. He must call Pierre as soon as possible. Perhaps his friend could give him a few ideas.

Then a thought struck him, like a hammer blow: the Salesian missionaries! Yes, he thought excitedly, he could ask them for help…what was the name of that missionary to whom Oreste had sent some of the fifty thousand dollars? He had mentioned two names. What was the name of the one who was in the Sudan…Tonio thought back to that conversation…Savino! That's the name: Don Savino! But how am I going to find him? Perhaps Pierre could help him with that too…

By now the taxi was quite near the centre of Khartoum. Tonio saw the sign of a large hotel: the Khartoum Meridien, and he told the driver to take him there instead.

Without letting on what he was doing, he undid his belt, gently lifted off the strip of Velcro, and pulled out a twenty-dollar bill from the first roll of dollars. He mentally blessed Pierre's foresight.

They stopped in front of the Meridien, where a coach was unloading a group of tourists who had just arrived.

The driver looked at the twenty dollars which Tonio offered him with eager eyes. Naturally he said that he didn't have any change. Tonio did not have the time to argue. He gave him the dollars and went into the large lobby of the hotel.

Considerable confusion reigned there. Tonio noticed from the luggage labels that the new arrivals were actually part of a French humanitarian delegation, Action Contre La Faim, which had just flown in from France.

Pretending to be part of the group, he approached one of the girls at reception and told her that he needed to use the telephone urgently, even before his room had been assigned; he would pay for the call in cash. He also asked her to change some dollars into dinars, the local currency. The girl indicated a telephone kiosk near the desk and told him that she would try and connect him as soon as possible.

Tonio had another idea. He asked the girl to find the number of the Italian Embassy; he would ask them how he could get in touch with Don Savino. He was sure that they would know him.

Tonio had to wait ten minutes before the girl informed him that she had managed to get an international line for the kiosk.

Tonio entered it and dialled Pierre's number. To his great relief he answered almost immediately. It went without saying that Pierre was very happy that he had been able to escape. But there was still the problem at Wad Madani.

"Don't worry," Pierre said. "I still have a few friends in Sudan who should be able to help. Try and find a place to hide. The idea of the Salesian Mission is a good one. I'll try and arrange from here in Paris for the car to be picked up at Wad Madani, and for the gun to be removed. If Rainer decides to go back down there, and if he should meet my men, he'll find that his work will be cut out for him. The idiot still hasn't realised who he's dealing with."

"One last thing," Tonio said, before saying goodbye to his friend. "Rainer has said that he's already sold the arms and now he just needs to deliver them. That explains why he's so desperate to find them. It should be possible for you to ask around and find out who's bought them. Perhaps your friends at the CIA are playing a double game with someone…"

"Improbable in this case," Pierre replied. "It's more likely that he's got in touch with one of those small groups of terrorists, or perhaps with the organised crime. I'll widen my enquiries. Call me when you're safe."

His next call was to the Italian Embassy. Their switchboard put him through to the Cultural Attaché.

"Don Savino Lanfranchi? Who doesn't know him here!" the latter said. "The most likeable ball-breaker in the whole of

Africa! I'm joking, of course. He calls us quite often to ask for our intervention when the money he's due to receive from Italy gets held up by some bank or other. What's your connection with him, Mister…?"

Tonio did not let him finish. "Sabatini. My name's Sabatini and I'm here with the French Delegation from Action Contre La Faim, and I've brought a little present to give him on behalf of a mutual friend. Could you give me his address?"

"Certainly…and if you go to meet him…give him my regards when you see him."

Tonio came out of the kiosk and paid for the calls. He looked at his watch. It was a little over an hour since he had left the airport. Before leaving the hotel he asked the girl for the times of trains to Wad Madani and where the railway station was. She answered that, in theory at least, there should be a train every hour and that the station was quite near.

Before going to see Don Savino, he decided to give Rainer some evidence, should he check, that he had taken a train to Wad Madani. He calculated that he had enough time, before Rainer and his friends could free themselves from the police at the airport, and go to check for him at the Hilton or the station. It might be a mistake to try and anticipate Rainer's actions, but it was worth trying.

He went out into the road and saw the same cab driver offering his services to other guests outside the hotel. Tonio went up to him and asked him to take him to the station. The latter was only too happy to accept, hoping to make another financial killing.

In fact, the station was not very far away. They got there in ten minutes. An even greater chaos than that at the airport, if that were possible, reigned at the station. He was forced to get out of the cab about a hundred metres from the entrance. This time he paid the protesting driver the equivalent of two dollars, in Sudanese dinars. Right, now we're even he said to himself.

He entered the station, worked out where the ticket office was, and waited patiently in line.

He was the only white man. People looked at him curiously; western tourists rarely travelled by train. They usually travelled by car, or in mini-buses laid on by their hotels.

When his turn came Tonio asked, speaking in incomprehensible English, what time the next train for Wad Madani would leave.

The man at the ticket office did not understand. Tonio repeated the question. The man looked around him, to ask for help, and said something in Arabic.

Tonio pretended to get angry. He raised his voice. The other man did the same, still speaking in Arabic.

By now a small knot of curious people had gathered around Tonio. Some were laughing scornfully. Out of the corner of his eye he saw a policeman approaching, with the customary sub-machine gun under his arm. Tonio continued to shout, "Surely I can buy a train ticket? I want to know at what time the train for Wad Madani leaves. It's not that difficult!" Then pretending that he had only just noticed the policeman, "Ah! Perhaps you can help me. Do you speak English?"

"Yes, a little," the other said.

"Would you ask this gentleman here why he won't sell me a ticket for Wad Madani?"

The policeman turned to the clerk brusquely and asked for an explanation.

The clerk explained that he had not understood the question. There wasn't a problem. The next train would leave in ten minutes. Then he added something which provoked general laughter. When he had to pay, Tonio pretended to get confused with his dinars, causing all those nearby to help him count out the money.

The policeman, still laughing, escorted him to the train – three platforms further on. At this point, he was certain that the policeman and the ticket clerk would remember him.

By now it was evening and the train was very crowded. He was able to clamber into the penultimate carriage and find a small space to stand near the door, on the opposite side to where he had boarded. The smell of sweat, mixed with other odours emanating from the bodies which thronged around him, made him feel nauseous.

After a few minutes, he heard a series of whistles and sirens, and saw people running alongside the train. With a violent jerk the train began to move.

All of a sudden, pretending to remember that he had left his wallet or his passport somewhere, he began cursing in a loud voice, feeling in the pockets of his jeans. The people around him looked at him, their curiosity aroused. Then he boldly opened the door against which he had been leaning and jumped down from the train which was just beginning to pick up speed.

He crossed the tracks to another platform and from there he found a side exit from the station.

This time it took him longer to find a taxi; nobody wanted to go to the address, given to him by the Italian Embassy, which the girl at the Meridien had written down on a piece of paper in Arabic.

Finally, an elderly man driving a battered Peugeot, and who did not speak a word of English, agreed to take him to the Salesian Mission. He wrote the price of the fare he was asking on a piece of paper: fifty dollars. Tonio made a sign to him that he was mad and pretended to walk away. The man called him back. In the end they agreed on a price of thirty dollars.

As soon as he sat down in the car, Tonio felt a wave of tiredness engulf him. He had lost count of the hours that had passed since he last slept.

After less than ten minutes, rocked by the undulating motion of the car and by the Arabian music coming from the radio, he fell into a deep sleep.

32

Tonio found it difficult to wake up. The old taxi driver was shaking him vigorously by the leg. When he opened his eyes he realised it was night-time, although it seemed to him that he had only been asleep for five minutes. He looked at his watch: more than an hour had passed since they had left the railway station.

While he got out some money to pay the taxi, he looked around him. They had stopped in a large dark square which consisted of bare-beaten earth, lit only by a solitary light-bulb above a wooden door. Over the door there was an arch bearing the words: CATHOLIC MISSION DON BOSCO. In the lower part of the arch, at the centre, there was a cross. On each side of the door there was a long wall stretching for about a hundred metres. On the other side of the large square there were a few small huts with flickering light coming from their interiors. Apart from somebody calling out every now and then, the area was silent.

When the taxi had left, Tonio approached and tried the door, but it was locked. He looked around and saw a small rope hanging at one side. He pulled it and heard the tinkling of a small bell in the distance.

A large black boy opened the door. He wore glasses, did not have much hair, was wearing shorts and had sandals on his feet.

Tonio asked for Don Savino. The boy beckoned to him to follow. After having closed the door behind him, they crossed an internal courtyard which was also of beaten earth, and went towards a long, low wooden building. The boy pointed out some chairs in what appeared to be a kind of waiting room, and went out.

Tonio looked about him. Apart from the chairs, there was a table and a pair of metal shelves. In a corner there was a small low stand on which stood a little statue of Our Lady. In front of him there was a portrait of Don Bosco hanging on the wall.

A few minutes later, a tall thickset man with a beard and whiskers, which were almost white, entered the room. Tonio thought he was probably in his sixties. He was wearing a light-blue, open-neck shirt with the same words he had noticed on the arch over the door, stitched on the pocket. He was wearing a leather cord around his neck from which hung a small crucifix.

He stretched out his hand to Tonio and said in English, "I'm Savino, what can I do for you?"

"I'm Italian," Tonio said, "and my name is Antonio Brignani. I need your help."

"Italian? Good. Speak to me with the 'Tu' form as we don't stand on ceremony here. Have you eaten?"

"Well…not really…I…"

"Then come with me. We're at table…goat's meat with salad…it's good," Don Savino said, smiling.

Tonio followed him into a building which flanked the main one. He felt an immediate warmth for the priest, who had put him at his ease at once.

They went into a room where about ten people, both men and women, were seated at a long table. Don Savino introduced him to them – Tonio immediately forgot their names – and then asked the boy he had already met to prepare another place. The conversation round the table was mostly in English.

When Tonio said he lived in Paris they assailed him with questions about the French capital, which none of them had ever seen. Tonio noticed that they were all younger than him, with the exception of a coloured man with greying hair, who had difficulty in understanding English. Most of them were wearing the same light-blue shirt as Don Savino, with the same writing on the pocket.

Dinner was soon over, and everyone got up to take their plates and cutlery into the adjacent kitchen. Tonio did the same but was stopped by Don Savino.

"Not today. The first day our guests don't work, but from the second day they begin to wash the dishes," he said laughing. "Let's go over there and talk."

Tonio followed him into what seemed to be his office, after crossing a small room which contained a radio-transmitter and receiver.

"Well now, tell me what it's about, and call me Savino, forget about the Don," the priest said, after they had sat down on two small leather armchairs.

"Well…I'm in trouble. But before anything else, let me tell you that your name has already been mentioned to me some time ago by Don Oreste in the Church of the Sacro Cuore in Rome…"

"You know Oreste?" the other interrupted him, smiling.

"Yes, I met him a couple of months ago, a mutual girlfriend introduced us."

"OK. Carry on. Tell me everything."

Tonio told him everything. Absolutely everything, starting with Pierre's decision to change his life. While he spoke, he saw the expression on Don Savino's face change several times. When he told him about Awad's death the priest seemed to be truly saddened. Tonio told him that he didn't have any documents, and that if it were possible, he would like to stay at the Mission for a few days, giving him enough time to get his real passport. In order to do this, he needed to contact his friend Pierre in Paris. He asked whether he could use the phone.

"Oh," the priest said with a downhearted expression, "what you see on the table is a phone, but it hardly ever works. This is because the wires are regularly stolen and sold in the markets of

Khartoum. They're valuable because of the copper they contain. When we want to communicate abroad we use the radio which you saw next door. We contact our brothers in Khartoum and they, using some technical gadget, get us connected. In effect, we use their phone. It's a tedious system, but it's better than nothing, not least because they too, like everyone else in this country, have difficulty in getting a line. It's too late now, so we'll call tomorrow. Go to bed, you must be very tired. Mohamed – we call him Mo – the boy who opened the door to you, will have prepared a bed for you in the room next to his. I'll also tell him to bring you some clean clothes."

Tonio's sleep was disturbed. He woke up several times, only to fall back into a fitful doze but without dreaming. At one point near daybreak he reflected on the fact that a mere twenty-four hours had passed since he had witnessed Awad's murder. He remembered seeing a flicker of interest in Awad's eyes when he had told him of Pierre's proposal to help him financially to start a new life, provided he decided to abandon his present activities.

Instead, he had died at the hands of a mad imbecile who liked playing with guns, even though he didn't know how to handle them.

Thinking back to that moment, Tonio saw once more the shock on Rainer's face when the gun went off, replaced immediately afterwards by a total indifference for what he had done. He had not shown the slightest remorse at having caused the death of another human being.

He would like to avenge Awad's death. He would like Rainer to pay dearly for what he'd done. He would make him pay! He hoped that Rainer would be given the lesson he truly deserved by Pierre's men at Wad Madani, if he went there as a result of Tonio's tricks at Khartoum station.

The only thoughts which calmed him, were those about Irene, and Nanni. He wondered if he would ever see her again.

Before going back to sleep, he had a brief vision of his previous life. Paris, Rome, the bank…seemed light years away from the planet on which he now found himself.

33

Mo came to wake him early. "Telephone," he said, "it's working, come."

Don Savino was in the small room containing the radio equipment.

"Yes, yes," he was saying into the microphone, "when you see him, also tell him that there's a friend of his here, Tonio Brignani. Do you understand?"

"Yes, OK Ciao." The remote voice was distant but reasonably clear. Tonio heard a click, and Don Savino began speaking again into the microphone. "Andrea, now you have to call another number, in France, wait a minute…" He handed the microphone to Tonio and went out.

After a couple of minutes, Pierre was on the phone. "Things are a bit more complicated than we expected, Tonio. Apart from the short time we have to get a visa for your passport, in reality in order to leave Sudan, you would need an entry stamp in it. We'll have to get you out another way. Bruno and I are wondering whether you can get to North Sudan, near the Egyptian border. In that area, in the past, we've used a couple of disused airstrips to deliver some merchandise. I could get one of my men to land and pick you up. Do you think that would be possible?"

"I don't know. I'll have to ask Savino here."

Don Savino, who was nearby, entered the small room and took over the microphone.

"It's possible but risky. It's a terrible region, desert for hundreds of kilometres, often plagued by rebels, but with a bit of luck and God's help, it can be done…we did it a couple of times last year in order to help some villages which had been attacked by guerrillas."

"Thanks Don Savino," said Pierre. "It goes without saying that any expenses incurred are down to us…"

"Fine, but it's something that will have to be well prepared and organised. We'll have to find someone who's prepared to go to that area…I'll need a couple of days."

"OK, let me know when you're ready…Tonio, another thing: making enquiries into the source of that cache of arms in Irene's cellar, I've been told that the underworld in Sicily and Calabria is excited by an exceptional consignment of arms which they expect to arrive there soon. It can't be a mere coincidence. My suspicion that Rainer is involved is becoming more of a reality day by day. Another reason why he has to be stopped. The operation to transfer the goods from the warehouse to the coast in Tunisia has begun. It will take a few days to complete the loading of the ship; it will leave from the Port of Biserta."

At the end of the call, Tonio remained seated in front of the radio, reflecting on Pierre's arsenal thoughtfully. Had Rainer really sold the arms to the mafia, to the N'drangheta or to the Camorra, before actually getting hold of them? Thoughts and questions put his mind in a turmoil.

Because, if this were the case…no! It wasn't possible! If Rainer had offered the arms to those people, it was also probable that he'd had dealings with Peppino Cantera!

By now it was quite clear that Peppino had links with the mafia. The arms in the cellar…the boss hidden in his house…the more he thought about it, the more he was convinced that this was more than a theory. He had to warn Irene. That man was a lot more dangerous than anyone imagined. He had to convince her to leave with Nanni.

"What's up, Tonio?" It was the voice of Savino behind his back. "You seem to be worried."

"Complications. I have to leave as soon as possible. What can we do to…?"

"Nothing for the time being. Or to be more correct, there is something which I can do. Today I have to go to Omdurman, on the other bank of the Nile, west of Khartoum.

"A Combonian* Missionary has found the three missing children of a woman who is our guest here with her two youngest children. I'm going to fetch them. At the same time, I'll ask the missionaries if they can take you in one of their cars which each week travel up north to Atbara and then on to Berber.

"They know the area well. They have Missions up there too. And they could advise us on how to get to the Egyptian border. You stay here. It's better if you don't show yourself too much. And anyway as I've got to bring back the children, there wouldn't be enough room for everyone on the return journey. While you're waiting for me, you could give a hand to one of our volunteers. They'll be very happy to have some help. There's always a lot that has to be done here. We'll see each other this evening."

When Don Savino had left, Tonio went to wash. Looking at himself in the mirror in the small bathroom he shared with other members of the Mission, he saw that he had a beard which was three days old. He decided to keep it.

Mo acted as his guide around the Mission. All the buildings were low: some were built of bricks and others of wood. The school consisted of two large wooden huts with sloping roofs, supported by poles, and with no walls. In both of the large huts there were four classes, each of about sixty children of various ages seated at long tables.

---

* A religious order named after Daniele Comboni, a missionary to the heart of Africa, who was beatified in 1996 and canonized by John Paul II in Rome on October 5, 2003.

Tonio was particularly struck by the nutritional centre, created in order to overcome malnutrition, which held about eighty children. Kayla, a Sudanese nun, explained to him that they were all children who had lost one or both parents. They were brought to the centre by aunts or grandmothers, with barely any strength left in them. When they arrived food was provided for them, and they were weighed and periodically examined. When they began to gain weight they were moved from this centre and transferred to another part of the Mission.

What struck Tonio more than anything else, was the seriousness and the slow pace, at which the children were eating from their bowls with their fingers. They're not unhappy, Tonio thought, they're eating with dignity. As he walked past them, some smiled at him, waving their hands.

Still accompanied by Mo, Tonio visited the centre where the street children were received.

They were children who had been literally picked up from the streets by the members of the Mission, who went out at night to try and persuade these youngsters, who were sleeping rough in their hundreds in the streets of Khartoum, to come to the centre to eat something, to put on clothes, and eventually to go to school.

Not an easy task, because often the boys were members of gangs, dedicated to petty crime. This centre also housed about a hundred children, from the age of nine to sixteen. Mo explained to him that he was one of those who had been picked up, two years earlier. Now he was working and attending school in the Mission.

Then Tonio came to a kind of infirmary, where about twenty beds were occupied by coloured women.

A white woman, about thirty years of age, approached him, smiling. Tonio recognised her as one of the people sitting at the table the previous evening.

"Hi there!" the woman said, "...Antonio, isn't it?"

"Yes…Tonio…"

"I'm Elisabeth…Sister Eli is what they call me here. I'm English." She was a petite woman with delicate features. She was wearing a wide pair of shorts which came down as far as her knees, and the usual shirt displaying the name of the Mission. Her blonde hair was tied together in a ponytail.

"Come, I'll show you round," she said. "We have a small clinic here where these poor women are looked after. We try and do our best to get them back on their feet again. Some of them have come to us after walking for days on end from some remote village, completely exhausted, malnourished, desperate. Often they have children with them, some of which are very young. We have a doctor who comes every two days. We keep the very worst cases over there in a room at the back. Many have AIDs. For some there is very little we can do…"

"I'll be here for a couple of days, I think. I'd like to do something to help," Tonio said.

Sister Eli's eyes lit up. "Can you play football?"

"Football?" Tonio wasn't expecting such a question, "Yes of course, but…"

"Come with me," Sister Eli said, moving off in a determined fashion towards the back of the building. "You see, many of our women with babies also have children who are getting bored in class now. In the coming lunch break, they won't know what to do with themselves, and they'll turn up here trying to be near their mothers. I think if you could organise a football match, that would keep them occupied and they'd enjoy it. At the same time it would help us work in peace. What do you think?"

Tonio did not only organise a football match, but a real and proper mini-tournament, in which all the boys took part. They all played in bare feet. The oldest, in well-organised teams, entered eagerly into the spirit of the competition. On more than one occasion Tonio, who also refereed, had to calm down some of the more serious disputes. The smaller boys amused everyone by all running after the ball.

After a light lunch the children went back to their classrooms to escape the oppressive heat. In the late afternoon, Tonio organised other matches. At one point even three of the nuns joined in the game, provoking much laughter.

A little before dinner time, Don Savino returned with the three children. Tonio saw him take them directly to the reception centre.

"Tonio," he said. "I looked in on Andrea – you know, the one who lets us use the phone. I've spoken to Oreste in Rome. Why didn't you tell me it was you and your friend who sent the twenty-five thousand dollars? It's not that your welcome would have been any different on our part, but we like to know some of our benefactors personally, so we can show them how we use their money."

"Well…I don't know…it didn't seem to be relevant…and it's only an unfortunate coincidence that I'm here…and please, you don't have to show me anything. What you're doing here is fantastic! I'm the one who's grateful to you for the help you're giving me."

"Anyway, I'd like to thank you, on behalf of everyone. And I'd also like to thank you for organising the games today. A great success I've been told. Now listen, you'll be able to leave tomorrow. Come, I'll show you the plan."

Tonio followed him into his office, where Don Savino took a map of the Sudan from a cupboard, and spread it out on the table.

"Tomorrow I'll arrange to have you escorted by Ahmed to Khartoum North, which is a separate city from Khartoum itself. It's near the confluence of the White and Blue Niles, but is further north. There are bridges linking it to Khartoum. Unfortunately the car going north with our fellow brothers left yesterday. I'd advise you to catch the train which will take you as far as Atbara.

"It's a long and uncertain journey. It could take you as much as twelve hours to cover the three or four hundred kilometres. Once there you can spend the night with the Combonian Fathers, who are now expecting you.

"The following morning, there'll be a car which will take you as far as Abu Hamed. That's here, look," he said, pointing to the map with his finger. "It's another two hundred and fifty kilometres. After Berber, about fifty kilometres north of Atbara, the road carries on in a straight line, passing through little towns which are not much more than villages. This too could be a journey full of surprises.

"It goes without saying that the road is just a track. At some points it's very narrow. It's the only road linking the Sudan with the north of the country, and with Egypt. It carries a lot of traffic, so that if there's an accident, you run the risk of having to wait up to four hours, before the traffic can get going again. I'm not exaggerating.

"You're lucky this time, because the Combonians don't usually take the car that far north. Up to Abu Hamed the road follows the course of the Nile and the railway. At Abu Hamed, the river turns southwest to form a wide semi-circle of several hundred kilometres, before turning north again. It's here at Abu Hamed that your possible route divides into two. One road follows the Nile, first to the southwest, and then north up to Wadi Halfa on Lake Nasser and the Egyptian border. That's a good nine hundred kilometres, and it can take two whole days to cover the distance. The other shorter road carries straight on across the desert, direct to Wadi Halfa. Do you see?

"If someone's in a hurry to get to Wadi Halfa as soon as possible, as you are, then the direct road is the one to take. But it's also the more dangerous route. From Abu Hamed it carries on northwards, leaving the river, and follows the other branch of the railway. On this stretch the trains are pretty much hit and miss. There should be one a day, but it's not unusual for five days to go by before seeing one. Not surprisingly, only a few venture out on this road. It's 'only' three hundred and fifty kilometres to Wadi Halfa on this side of the border. But they are three hundred and fifty kilometres of pure desert. There's nothing there. Absolutely nothing but an occasional camel caravan and perhaps the odd nomad camp.

"About halfway – here, do you see – to the right of the road there's the Mount Nahoganet range, a thousand metres high. One of the most inhospitable places on this planet.

"The road winds along the bottom of some valleys for about fifty kilometres. This is the most dangerous stretch. It's here that attacks by rebels or bandits have taken place in the past. Our Combonian friends have told me that at Abu Hamed, where they'll leave you, there are some men who'll take you as far as Wadi Halfa by jeep, for three or four hundred dollars. They offer this service to those who want to save time and who are prepared to accept the risk. That's why the owners of the vehicles, although they're tough characters, prefer to leave in a group. All being well, you could be at Wadi Halfa in six or seven hours. If you're lucky you'll find a group of cars about to leave when you get there. Once you've arrived at Wadi Halfa, you can call your friend. I believe there's an airstrip there with little or no security…well, I assume from then on, you and Pierre will know what to do. Well, what do you think?"

"It's fine by me…there's no doubt about it, the distances are enormous…"

"Yes this isn't a stroll in the park, believe me! If you decide to go I can't give you any documents, but I can pin one of these plastic name badges onto your shirt with the name of The Mission, giving you the appearance of a travelling missionary, and provide a couple of rubber stamps. They're not worth a bean but they do have quite an official look. If you agree, we can try and call your friend Pierre to explain the plan to him. But we'll do this after supper, my son. I'm so hungry that if I don't eat something soon you'll have to take me to Sister Eli on a stretcher!"

34

Apart from the countless stops, the heat, the dust and the pungent smell of poverty, the journey was undertaken without any problems.

They arrived at Atbara about five in the afternoon. Shortly before entering the railway station, Tonio noticed a siding which led to a building about a hundred metres away, behind which large black and green railway locomotives were visible: this must be the locomotive cemetery, fulsomely praised in the tourist guide. Perhaps the only thing worthy of note in that chaotic city.

Outside the station, Tonio took a taxi straight to the Combonian Fathers' Mission on the outskirts of the city.

Father Marcel, the Head of the Missionaries, was waiting for him. He was tall and slender, had sunken cheeks and a hooked nose. He was wearing a white soutane. He reminded Tonio of the Headmaster at his school in Naples who the boys had nicknamed '*L'auciello do' malagurio*[*].'

"I've spoken to Savino," he said, after they had introduced themselves. "I've delayed the departure of our car to Abu Hamed by a day. He told me that it's very urgent that you reach the Egyptian border as soon as possible. You know, we're used to doing favours for each other…however, from Abu Hamed you're on your own. Right now, I can't risk going any further north, especially since the presence of rebel bands have been reported."

---

[*] The bird of ill omen

He said this while staring at the writing on Tonio's shirt pocket. Tonio got the impression that Father Marcel did not approve of the subterfuge which they had resorted to in order to help him travel.

At supper the atmosphere was quite different to that of the Don Bosco Mission. The two priests and their helpers, all French, were less noisy. They were very composed, more formal, even among themselves. Tonio could not help noticing that nobody wanted to know where he came from, why he was there, nor where he was going. Perhaps they had been instructed by Father Marcel not to get involved.

They tried to contact Pierre several times, but without success. A couple of hours later, lying on the bed in the room he was sharing with a helper, Tonio thought back to his call to Pierre the previous evening. They had agreed on a plan of action to get Tonio out of the country.

They would use an aircraft, which the Merchant's organisation had used many times, to deliver merchandise to remote places far from civilisation. It would have a flight plan drawn up to land in Egypt at Abu Simbel, close to the Sudanese border, about fifty kilometres to the North of Wadi Halfa. Apart from the pilot, it would have a wealthy tourist on board who wanted to visit the famous temples on the shore of Lake Nasser. Bruno was to play the role of the tourist. The pilot, claiming a technical fault, would make a 'mistake' and would land at Wadi Halfa, instead of Abu Simbel, some fifty kilometres away.

If he got there before them, Tonio would wait for them. If in fact the plane arrived first, then on the pretext of making a difficult repair to the engine or to the navigation instrumentation, they would wait for him, if necessary for two or three days. Tonio would try and call from Atbara and, if possible, from Abu Hamed, before crossing the desert to reach Wadi Halfa.

"As for your worries in Sudan," Pierre said, "you can relax. The car has been taken back to the hotel and the gun has been recovered. In a few months' time when the visa has expired, it will appear that Piero Donati entered the country but never left it. No sign of Rainer, we've lost all trace of him. And that worries me."

Tonio's last thought, as was almost customary every evening by now, was of Irene. The vision of a future with her and Nanni, like a soothing and comforting drug, helped him fall asleep.

They woke him at dawn. Before leaving, Tonio tried to call Pierre once more but it was impossible. He urged Father Marcel to try again during the day to get in touch with his friend in Paris, and to tell him that he was heading for Abu Hamed, and that he would try to contact him from there. In case he wasn't able to reach him then, he would certainly call him from Wadi Halfa, where he was hoping to arrive in two or three days' time. Tonio left twenty dollars with Father Marcel to cover the cost of the call.

They left at seven in the morning. In the car, an old Land Rover driven by a young Father Bernard, there were two other people heading for the Mission at Abu Hamed which had been founded by the Combonian Fathers only a few years earlier. A doctor and nurse were going to help the missionaries up there, as they had severe problems with the exceptional number of refugees who had turned up at the Mission in the last few weeks. Father Marcel attributed this to renewed attacks by the rebels against isolated villages.

"It's a terrible state of affairs," Father Bernard said, replying to a question from Tonio. "They arrive in gangs of twenty or thirty, on horseback or on camels, armed to the teeth, and they raze the villages of these poor souls who own so little as it is. Sometimes they take away the only cow or the few goats which provide milk for the babies. The women, or should I say any girls older than ten, are regularly raped. Each day we hear dreadful stories. It's difficult to comprehend. This also happens in other African countries like Kenya, Somalia or Malawi. Everywhere seems to be resigned to this violence which goes hand in hand with the direst poverty, engrained into the very beings of the people. They've lived like this for years. I admire them greatly."

The road, although crowded as usual, was reasonably good, so that in less than half an hour they arrived at Berber, about fifty kilometres north of Atbara. It was market day and the little town, scarcely larger than a village, was very busy. While they were queuing to fill up at the only petrol pump, everybody got out of the car to stretch their legs. Tonio was twice offered a camel to buy.

While they were waiting, Father Bernard explained to Tonio that Berber had for centuries, been the departure point for the camel caravans, which crossed the Nubian Desert to reach Suakin on the Red Sea. It was a journey of more than three hundred kilometres across one of the most arid regions on the planet.

"It's difficult to believe," the priest said. "But even today, despite the roads and the railway which leave from Atbara, there are nomads who still prefer to join the caravans which go eastwards."

They stopped again three hours later at Abu Hashim, a dusty village of a few houses with peeling and crumbling walls. They bought a few ring-shaped pies filled with goat's meat and cheese, and drank hot tea.

After having set out on their journey northwards once more, they were stopped by some soldiers at a temporary roadblock on the outskirts of a village called Abu Dis. They were examining the documents of all the occupants of every car.

When it was their turn, a young soldier with a machine-gun round his neck, inspected Tonio's false name-badge for a few seconds, then said something while pointing to the passports of the others. Tonio tried to explain that he had left his behind in Khartoum, and that he was a member of the Catholic Mission. He said this while pointing to the badge and the writing on his shirt. The soldier shook his head and pointed to the photographs in the passports of the others. Tonio understood that he hadn't been taken in by the badges he was wearing.

After a few minutes' discussion, the soldier's voice began to change. Tonio realised that he was in trouble when the latter ordered him to get out of the car. Another soldier approached, but he carried on past the Land Rover, signalling to another car to stop behind it. Tonio, taking advantage of the fact that the two men were exchanging a few words, put his hand quickly into his pocket and pulled out twenty dollars. He took a step forward and, turning his back on the second soldier who was still behind the car, put the twenty dollars into the hand of the one who was carrying the machine-gun.

The soldier gave a quick glance both at the money and at his colleague, but he imperceptibly shook his head. Tonio cottoned on straight away, and pulled out another twenty-dollar note. The man seemed satisfied. With the point of his weapon, he indicated to Tonio that he could get back into the car. He then shouted something at the man in front, who was guarding the temporary barrier, and he let them through.

After travelling for a further five minutes, during which nobody said a word, the doctor who was sitting at the back next to Tonio asked, "How much?"

"Forty dollars," Tonio replied.

After another silence, interrupted only by the noise of the car's engine, Tonio heard Father Bernard say, "That's the equivalent of at least three months of his salary, a good day for him."

'Yes, a good day', Tonio thought, looking out of the window. 'I got off the hook with a mere forty dollars, a paltry price for another chance of freedom.'

Despite the fact that the traffic had noticeably decreased, they had to slow down often because of the condition of the road, as some stretches had disappeared altogether under wind driven piles of sand.

Tonio looked to his left, trying to see the railway line and the Nile, but at that point they were at least five kilometres from the river. Then he looked to his right – only sand and stones were visible, under a clear sky of such an intense blue that Tonio had never seen anything like it before.

They arrived at Abu Hamed before nightfall. Although the heat had dropped by a few degrees. When Tonio got out of the car in front of the railway station, he felt the sweat pouring off him, even down his legs.

Father Bernard pointed out a small hotel near the station. "You can find a phone there, we don't have one at the Mission yet, and the cars which cross the desert to Wadi Halfa are normally parked in front of it. If you have any difficulty in continuing your journey, take one of those taxis and come to us. We'll find a place for you to sleep. Good luck."

Tonio crossed the road and went into the hotel. The clerk, an old man with a completely toothless mouth, only knew a few words of English. When he asked him for identification Tonio showed him the name badge and the stamp, and smiling said, "Mission," making a vague gesture in the direction in which Father Bernard had gone. It seemed to be enough, because the man gave him a key with the number nine on it, and pointed to the stairs.

Before going up, Tonio asked to use the phone. The man gesticulated and raised his eyes to heaven in a universal language – there was no phone connection. He lifted the receiver, put it to his ear and then handed it to Tonio – nothing.

"When?" he asked him, hopefully.

"Insha'Allah," the other replied. "If it is God's will." He should have expected this. However, he made the clerk understand that he must carry on trying, and to call him if he managed to get a line.

The room assigned to him was small but clean: a single bed, a tiny table and a small cupboard. The bathroom was outside down the corridor.

Tonio looked out of the window. Apart from the usual bustle, which by now he had noted in all the cities in the vicinity of their railway stations, he saw a shop in front of the hotel which sold a bit of everything, from cooking pots hanging outside the door, to clothing for both men and women displayed in the shop window. He decided to go and buy a change of underwear, and to have a wash. A decent meal also wouldn't go amiss. He took about a hundred dollars from the belt and went downstairs.

As soon as he saw him, the clerk rushed to the phone to see if there was a line – nothing.

Tonio bought two white short-sleeved shirts, two sets of underwear and a plastic bag.

Before going back to his room, he approached a group of men who were resting next to their heavy 4x4 vehicles in front of the hotel.

"Do you speak English?" he asked. They all nodded. "I'd like to go to Wadi Halfa tomorrow. Can any of you take me there?"

The men exchanged glances, then one of them asked, "How many people?"

"Just me," Tonio replied.

"One person, no," said the other. "I have to fill the car, I need at least two."

"How much?" Tonio then asked.

"Six hundred dollars," the other said without hesitation.

Tonio began laughing. "Six hundred dollars? You're joking! My friends in Khartoum told me that they paid only two hundred dollars some time ago."

"That's right, we charged two hundred four years ago. Times have changed. Six hundred dollars."

"Listen, let me make you an offer. I'll give you four hundred dollars provided we leave tomorrow, even if you haven't found another passenger. If you do find someone else, this evening or tomorrow morning, I'll still give you the four hundred. What do you say to that?"

"Five hundred and fifty dollars!"

"Four hundred and fifty!" The other shook his head. Tonio shrugged his shoulders and started walking towards the hotel entrance. As expected, he heard the voice of the man. "Wait!"

Tonio turned around. The man was coming towards him, offering his hand to him. "Five hundred dollars."

Tonio looked at him and exchanged a smile. "You've got a deal!" he said.

At that moment the clerk from the hotel burst out of the door to call him; evidently the telephone was now working.

Before going in, he heard the voice of the driver shouting at him, "Tomorrow morning at five!"

After a few failed attempts, Tonio finally heard Pierre's voice.

"You're at Abu Hamed! Good! You're almost at the end of your journey!"

"Don't say that Pierre. I've a feeling that the most difficult part will be tomorrow. There's almost four hundred kilometres of desert to cover. And today I've been told that the rebels in that area are keeping themselves quite busy."

"Yes, I know it won't be like taking a stroll along the Champs Elysées. I know what it's like down there. A couple of years ago we delivered two consignments in the middle of the desert, using an airfield built by the British in the fifties and which hadn't been used for many years. The rebel bands are under the protection of the SPLA and I personally negotiated the deal at Port Sudan. Together with Morgan, the SPLA representative you met at Wad Medani, I dealt personally with the head of those rebels. I remember him because he was known as Banga, and whether that was his real name or not, it means 'Sword'. He was very proud of it: a man so dedicated to the cause that he was bordering on the fanatical."

"Well, that's as maybe, but I hope I don't run into them. If all goes well I hope to be at Wadi Halfa in the afternoon..."

"You'll be pleased to know that Bruno is flying to Egypt. He'll arrive at Aswan tomorrow morning. Then three hundred kilometres to Wadi Halfa, a little over an hour's flight."

"Good, I'll do my best to be there. By the way what plane is it?"

"It's a STOL* 'Twin Otter', a Canadian twin-engine by De Havilland which we've used many times in the past. Great range and extremely reliable. But now, I have to tell you something very sad...Nadhir is dead. He's been assassinated. The Tunisian authorities don't believe the scenario that there was a burglary at his house, and neither do I.

"Samira's still in hospital suffering from shock. I have a nasty suspicion that it has something to do with the arms warehouse."

"I'm really sorry. I know he was one of your best friends."

"Yes...one last thing, Tonio. Irene called me. She's left with her son and has taken refuge in Nunzia's house. It seems that her husband has really gone mad. Call her there, when you can."

"In some ways that's good news! I don't know whether I can call her though. The phone lines are so unreliable here. Please call her for me and tell her that I'll give her a ring as soon as I'm out of trouble."

After washing and changing, Tonio went out again and into the first restaurant he found. It was a bit of a dump, with a floor

---

* Short Take-Off and Landing

of beaten earth, metal tables and chairs, and an enormous fan hanging from the ceiling whose movement appeared to have no effect on the heat. However, by way of compensation he ate the best couscous – with vegetables and mutton – that he had ever tasted.

Returning, he asked the hotel clerk to wake him in time for his departure. When he threw himself down on his bed, dead tired, he thought of Irene and of the battle she was waging to free herself from her husband. More than ever, he yearned to rescue her and take her away with him.

Then the thought of Nadhir crept back into his mind and spoiled that pleasurable thought. He remembered Nadhir's speech at his house and all the countries he was hoping to visit with his wife Samira, and all the secrets which he would no longer be able to reveal in his memoirs. His sleep was restless, and not only because the bed was uncomfortable. He was worried about the last part of his journey. The darkness and the silence increased his apprehension. He felt like a pawn in a game over which he had no control. The fact that the success of the plan was at the mercy of others irritated him, and made his stomach turn over with apprehension.

35

"Are you a priest?"

"No."

"The shirt you were wearing yesterday is worn by the priests at the Mission."

"I know. They lent it to me."

"Um."

They were the first words exchanged in the car, about twenty minutes after their departure.

It had still been dark when the hotel clerk had come to wake him. He had dressed quickly and gone down into the street.

There were two vehicles outside getting ready to leave. Both were Land Rovers, sandy in colour, and more recent models than the one owned by the Combonian Fathers.

On the roof of each vehicle, there were fuel cans and some luggage. At the back there were two spare wheels. There were two large twenty-litre water bottles inside the luggage compartments.

The driver Tonio had negotiated with the previous evening, had asked him for the money before they left. Tonio had paid. The passengers in the other vehicle had done the same. Then all the money had been handed over to a small boy who went off with it, running.

"Why?" Tonio asked the man.

"Just a precaution the latter replied, winking. "If we are robbed in the desert, at least they won't get their hands on this money. My wife would never forgive me. What's your name?"

"Luigi, in English Louis, and what's yours?"

"Yussuf. We're ready, let's go."

Tonio thought about the other five hundred dollars which he had taken out of the belt and put in his pocket. He could lose it.

He had got into the vehicle and found a man sitting behind him, smoking a cigarette. His body occupied almost two seats. His polished bald head reflected the lights on the road.

"Hi there!" Tonio said. The latter acknowledged with a nod of his head.

Less than a kilometre from the railway station, the two vehicles plunged into the murky surroundings of the desert. To the right, a growing luminescence heralded sunrise. To the left, the railway line, like the road, disappeared beyond the range of their headlights.

Progress was steady. The Land Rover in front, which seemed to Tonio to be identical to the one he was travelling in, was throwing up a lot of dust. Yussuf slowed down, leaving a bigger gap between the two vehicles to improve visibility. At a certain point the crackle of a radio broke the silence. Yussuf plunged his hand under the steering wheel and took out a microphone attached to a spiral cable. He said something in Arabic, and laughed.

"The car in front?" Tonio asked.

"Of course," the other replied. "He says the two women with him haven't stopped chattering for a minute. He says that Allah hasn't been too kind to him today."

An hour later, the sun had risen in all its glory, illuminating a surreal landscape where even the smallest pebble cast a very long shadow.

Tonio had never before seen a landscape as flat as this, extending all the way to the horizon. There was not a single tree or hill to be seen, only a sea of stones and sand. He felt intimidated, but at the same time excited. 'I'm crossing the famous Nubian Desert', he thought, 'believe it or not.' Little by little however, he recognised the tell-tale signs of anxiety welling up inside him.

The large man behind had begun to snore.

At one point, without any apparent reason, the road crossed the railway line so it was now on their right.

There was a fresh crackle from the radio, and Tonio saw the vehicle in front of them slow down slightly and move over to the right-hand side of the road. While Yussuf was overtaking it, Tonio took a look at the passengers in the other vehicle: a man and two women, as well as the driver.

The driver nodded his head, smiling. He seemed younger than Yussuf, but there was something familiar about him.

"Is he your brother?" Tonio asked.

"You've guessed it!" Yussuf replied, pleased. "He's called Rashid, which means 'wise'. Wise my foot! He's a hothead. I've got to keep an eye on him because he has a tendency to get into trouble. Especially with women. He's twenty-five, it's about time he got married and settled down!"

"You're not from around here, are you? I mean, you don't seem to be Sudanese," Tonio asked. In fact, he had noticed their paler skin and North African features.

"Oh, no, we're Egyptian. My family originally comes from Luxor, a lovely place on the banks of the Nile with the famous temples. My father moved to Atbara to work on the railway. I grew up with my uncle in Luxor, he even loaned me some money to buy these two vehicles. If all goes well, I'll finish paying him back in a year's time. Even the fat chap behind us is Egyptian."

"How's business?"

"Well…ups and downs. Backwards and forwards along this road…it's not too bad generally. I can't afford not to keep my cars on the road. I have to pay off the debt, keep the vehicles serviced, pay Sudanese officials so I can carry on working, and twelve people have to live on what's left over."

Tonio began to warm to the man. He had wavy hair which was beginning to turn grey, and a moustache over a wide mouth. On their departure, Yussuf had put on a pair of glasses, which made him look like a schoolmaster.

Now that they were in front of the other vehicle, without the dust to restrict their vision, Tonio noticed piles of stones on both sides of the road, at least half a metre high, at two or three hundred metre intervals.

"They're for marking the road at night, or during sandstorms," Yussuf explained to him.

During another hour of travel, in which Tonio lost his battle against sleep a couple of times, they stopped near some ruins, which appeared unexpectedly at the side of the road. The two women rushed off behind a wall to re-appear after a few minutes with a more relaxed look. Then it was the turn of the others to relieve themselves.

They ate some rolls, which Yussuf and Rashid, had prepared for the passengers, washed down with warm tea from two enormous thermos flasks.

The women introduced themselves as two English free-lance journalists who were researching for a series of articles on the life of women in Africa, which they hoped to sell to some feminist magazines in Europe. The young man with them was Kenyan and was their guide and interpreter, as he spoke several African dialects.

The large man who was travelling with Tonio, had remained seated in the vehicle with his legs dangling outside. He had hardly said a word since leaving.

Tonio discovered that on arrival at Wadi Halfa, they were all due to take the weekly ferry across Lake Nasser, which would take them to Aswan in Egypt.

"By the way," Yussuf asked him, "you've got your ticket haven't you?"

"What ticket?" Tonio asked in his turn.

"A ferry ticket. Excuse me, aren't you going to Aswan too?"

"Well…to tell the truth no. I'm going to Wadi Halfa to meet a friend."

"And then what are you going to do? Are you going to come back?"

"Well…I don't know…it depends on my friend."

Yussuf looked at him for a while, a little perplexed, but didn't ask any more questions.

After about twenty minutes they set off again.

Ahead, an hour later, Tonio began to see a chain of low mountains in the distance.

"Jebel Nahoganet, Mount Nahoganet," Yussuf said, pointing to the mountains.

Two Jeeps, which were travelling in the opposite direction, stopped after Yussuf had flashed at them. The drivers exchanged a few phrases in Arabic and set off again.

Tonio noticed a slight change in Yussuf's expression.

"Everything OK?" Tonio asked. "What did they say?"

"Nothing in particular…only that they haven't seen a soul since they left Wadi Halfa…strange…"

As they approached the mountains, Tonio began to make out their pale grey outlines. The mountains, which were at least a thousand metres high, were formed of humps rather than peaks, with deep valleys, and were devoid of any vegetation whatsoever. In the distance, on the left, he saw the road and the railway line disappear down one of those valleys.

Yussuf reduced his speed noticeably. Rashid drove up next to him and began to speak quickly. Then Yussuf took out a pair of binoculars from their case in the side pocket of the car and, stopping on the side of the road, began to scrutinise the mountains. Rashid got out to check the tyres of the other vehicle.

"Something wrong?" Tonio asked.

"No, no…everything's OK…it's only that I try to avoid surprises as much as I can."

An unnatural silence descended on the group. Yussuf carried on looking through the binoculars in the direction of the mountains.

Tonio noticed that Rashid was bent over one of his Land Rover's rear wheels, but was not doing anything, he was merely crouching down near the tyre.

While he was observing him, he saw a small stone roll into a depression in the sand. Tonio looked carefully. There, immobile, was a scorpion, brownish in colour with its sting arched forwards.

After a few minutes, they set off again, and Tonio asked Yussuf what he had been looking for in the mountains.

"At times the rebels wait for cars at the entrance to the valley. But I didn't see anyone. Rashid pretended to be checking a wheel to give me enough time to scan the mountains…in case we were being observed. In the past they've even attacked the train. But that hasn't happened for a long time."

"But what do they want?"

"Money, arms…women…but not those who are travelling with us, who are European. They're careful not to spark off an international incident!"

They arrived at the entrance to the valley, it was like a canyon. The sides at first formed a gentle slope getting ever steeper and closer together as they progressed, until there were only about a hundred metres separating them. The railway and the road were now very near to each other. The road seemed to be clear. Yussuf lit a cigarette, despite the fact that there was one already burning in the ashtray from which he had only drawn a couple of puffs.

The road began to climb gradually. All of a sudden the railway line broke off from the valley to plunge into another narrower one, to the left. Seeing the railway line disappear caused Tonio's fears to increase.

It was like a lunar landscape, and Tonio felt as if he was on the dry bed of a giant river, with the rounded mountains taking the place of smooth water-eroded pebbles, with their cars like two tiny ants running around on the bottom, looking for a way out.

The men appeared from nowhere. They were surrounded by them, there were about ten of them. They were all in Arab dress, their faces and heads covered by turbans. Only their eyes were visible. All had machine-guns in their hands.

A man on horseback, in the middle of the road, signalled to them to stop. He approached them and, after scrutinising the interior of the vehicles, ordered them to get out.

One glance at Yussuf was sufficient for Tonio to realise that they were in serious trouble.

36

The rebels made them sit on the ground, away from the vehicles, against some boulders at the base of the rock walls. They were searched while some of the other men threw the passengers' luggage onto the ground.

The man who found five hundred dollars in Tonio's pocket smiled, revealing at least three gold teeth, and shook the money in the direction of the man on horseback who, in the meantime, had moved off.

They found more money in the pockets and bags of the other captives.

When they emptied out the large Egyptian's bag onto the ground, only a pile of documents in folders held together with elastic bands fell out. The man charged with this operation looked at them, gathered some up, and went to show them to the man on horseback, who seemed to be the leader.

Tonio noted that there were two other men high up on the rocks, who were scouring the entrance to the valley with binoculars.

The man dismounted, went to examine the other papers spread on the ground and, crouching over them, began to study them closely.

After about ten minutes he approached the large man and interrogated him.

Tonio, looking puzzled, turned towards Yussuf, who was sitting next to him. The other shook his head, shrugging his shoulders, he too not knowing what was going on.

The leader of the rebels began shaking the papers under the Egyptian's nose, shouting. The walls of the canyon echoed his voice clearly. The other remained silent.

The leader looked at other papers taken from the pile. At one point he showed a sheet to one of his comrades, and once again approached the man sitting on the ground. This time he had a gun in his hand.

"Hey," Tonio shouted at him in English. "What's going on here? What are you doing?"

The man took a few steps towards him, and shaking the gun, said something to Yussuf.

"He said to keep quiet, and not to meddle if you don't want to finish up with a bullet in your head," Yussuf translated.

The two women began crying.

The leader returned to the Egyptian again, who remained silent. He showed him the paper which he had in his hand, but the other turned his head away, murmuring something.

This continued for some time without producing any further result.

Eventually the leader said something to his men. Two of them came and lifted the Egyptian up and then pushed him into a gap in the rocks which seemed like the entrance to a cave. After a moment, the men came out with three horses. The large man had an idea of what was about to happen and began shouting. The others pushed him further into the cave by kicking and shoving him until he disappeared from view.

A few seconds later Tonio heard a gunshot, followed immediately by another. The sound of the shots echoed around the walls for a long time before fading. Tonio, Yussuf and Rashid leapt up straight away, while the women screamed hysterically. The young Kenyan hid his head between his knees. Tonio's mouth had dried out completely. He found it difficult to swallow.

The rebel leader came out of the cave with the gun still in his hand. He turned to the group and Yussuf translated for Tonio and the women.

"He says that the man was a spy and deserved an even worse death. He says that he and his men are fighting for the independence of Sudan, and that those who steal from the people, and who are spies like him, have to be eliminated like poisonous snakes. He says to keep calm, and that they're now going away."

Having said this, the man gave the reins of his horse to one of his comrades and moved towards Yussuf's Land Rover. Another man got into the driver's seat of the second vehicle.

Yussuf understood immediately what was happening. They were trying to steal the two Land Rovers! He ran towards the rebel leader, shouting and imploring him to stop. As the leader was about to get into the vehicle, Yussuf reached him and grabbed him. The latter turned round but, at the same time, another rebel approached Yussuf from behind, spun him round, and dealt him a vicious blow to his face with the butt of the gun he had in his hand.

Yussuf fell heavily to the ground, putting his hands to his mouth which was bleeding profusely. His glasses were smashed to smithereens.

Tonio and Rashid rushed to help Yussuf.

The rebel leader spoke again, turning to Yussuf and Rashid in an angry voice, but the latter appeared not to hear him. He was trying to staunch his brother's flow of blood with his hand while calling him by name.

Tonio wanted to know what the rebel leader was saying. He got up and called to the young Kenyan to join him. He came up to Tonio and told him that the rebels were going to leave them there with their bags, and the water which they had in the vehicles. They needed the Land Rovers to serve their cause.

Sooner or later somebody would pass by and would help them to get to Wadi Halfa.

'Abandoned in the middle of the desert!' Tonio thought 'I'm running the risk of being here for days on end before anyone comes along…' He decided to take a risk.

He took the Kenyan by the arm and pulled him over to the leader, who had not yet got into the vehicle. He met the Arab's eyes and said to the Kenyan without turning, "Now you translate to him exactly what I say to you. Tell him that I have something important to say to him and that he must listen to me very carefully."

The Kenyan spoke to the man who, in turn, returned Tonio's firm gaze.

"Tell him," Tonio continued, "that I'm the son of the Merchant." The Kenyan translated this, but the other did not seem to understand.

Tonio spoke again through the Kenyan. "The son of the Merchant, the Swiss." The leader seemed to screw up his eyes, but still said nothing.

"Tell him that only a few days ago, I met Morgan at Wad Madani."

The young man translated. This time there was a reaction: "Morgan?" the Arab said.

"Yes, Morgan. At Wad Madani. SPLA." After the translation, the man remained silent for a moment and then asked, "Why?"

"That's none of your business," Tonio said, beginning to enter into his role, and forgetting the fear which had gripped him up to that moment. "But you'd better realise that without my father…you see these," indicating the sub-machine gun held by the man next to him, "you won't get any of these ever again."

The man leaned on the bonnet of the vehicle. His glance went from Tonio to the Kenyan, then to his men, then back to

Tonio. It was clear that he was weighing up the situation and thinking hard.

Tonio decided to play his last card, perhaps the riskiest, because in reality he did not know all the players in the game.

He turned to the Kenyan and said in a quiet voice, but loud enough for the leader to hear the importance he attached to the words: "Tell him exactly this: that my father knows the Sword."

The Kenyan looked at him, speechless.

Tonio could not recall the name Pierre had mentioned the day before, but he remembered its meaning.

"Go on, tell him! My father knows the Sword!"

The Kenyan translated. The rebel's reaction to the word *banga* was immediate: his eyes under his turban opened wide.

"Bulls eye!" Tonio rejoiced secretly. He took advantage of the man's amazement to lay it on more thickly. "And if Morgan, or the Sword, get to know how you've treated the Merchant's son and his friends…I don't think they'll be very happy…"

There was a long silence when the Kenyan finished. Then the leader moved away from the Land Rover, turned towards his men in the other car and barked out an order. They got out of the vehicle reluctantly and made their way back towards the horses.

Then the leader turned once more to Tonio and said, via the Kenyan, while spitting on the ground, "All right…we won't take the vehicles. But that one, that traitor, thief, son of a Cairo whore, must stay there so that the worms of the desert can dine off him."

He shouted something to his men again, got on his horse and rode off at a trot, followed by his band.

Tonio realised that his breathing had become quick and shallow. His tongue hardly moved in his parched mouth. He forced himself to calm down. He went straight to one of the women and took a bottle of water from her hand and drank a long draught.

He then signalled to Rashid, who followed him into the cave where the Egyptian had been killed. They found him lying face down in the centre of a red stain, which had spread under his body, but had been easily absorbed by the sand. A few flies were crawling over his staring eyes and in his half-open mouth. Tonio thought back to the scorpion he had seen a few hours earlier.

He overcame his desire to vomit.

They could not find any documents on him. Evidently the rebel leader had taken them. It took them ten minutes, helped by the Kenyan, to cover the body with large stones. They then returned to the vehicles.

"Let's get out of here Rashid. Put Yussuf in the back. I'll drive."

The two English women did not have to be asked twice. As quick as a flash, they gathered their things from the ground and got into their Land Rover, followed by the Kenyan.

They settled Yussuf on the rear seat of the vehicle, and after a few minutes they left.

It was only after a few hundred metres that Tonio realised his hands were shaking. He could still see the Egyptian's face in front of his eyes.

He had been involved in two violent deaths in the space of a few days, and a blind rage knotted his stomach. Without realising it, under his breath he began cursing war, arms, Pierre and even himself for having landed in such a situation.

The road was a succession of steep hills, descents and sharp bends for about thirty kilometres. At one stage, they even had to abandon the road because of rocks which had fallen from above. The only consolation they had was that at some points the valley was so narrow, and the walls so high, that the sun was blocked out, giving the group a brief respite from its heat.

After more than an hour, when it was almost five in the afternoon, they came out of that inferno to find themselves once more in the open desert.

To their surprise, they even saw in the distance a train from Wadi Halfa heading south.

They stopped to put water in the vehicle radiators. When Tonio got back in, he felt Yussuf's grateful hand clasping his shoulder.

37

It was already dark when they arrived at Wadi Halfa. A few dim lights showed in houses built of corrugated iron. Yussuf indicated to Tonio that he should carry straight on towards the centre of the town. He pointed out a low building with plaster flaking off it, which he said, was the railway station. There were not many people on the road. One or two scruffy cafés with oil lamps on their tables welcomed a few customers.

Still being guided by Yussuf, Tonio drove through the centre and towards the lakeside. They stopped in front of the entrance to a house, which Yussuf said was a hotel.

On a wooden board hanging on the door of the house, was a sign in Arabic and underneath that was written by hand: *Al-Bahara Motel.*

Everyone got out of the vehicles, tired and covered in dust. Tonio was exhausted and hungry. The temperature had fallen considerably. It seemed almost cold.

The motel was a real surprise. Inside there was a courtyard of beaten earth, divided into two halves by a large curtain tied to a wire, with about twenty beds evenly distributed on both sides. A few clients were already there and were trying to settle down for the night as best they could. Tonio and the two English women stopped at the door, puzzled. A tall young man with long jet-black hair approached them with a broad smile on his lips.

"Hi there, welcome to the Al-Bahara Motel, I'm Ammar El-Mardi, at your service."

Then he noticed Yussuf and Rashid. "Hey Yussuf, hi Rashid;" then continuing in English, "what's happened to you?"

he exclaimed, looking at Yussuf's swollen face and the dried blood. "Have you been hit by a train?" Seeing the two brothers' expressions, he did not ask further questions.

"We need a doctor here. Ali!" he shouted towards the interior of the motel. A barefoot little boy appeared immediately. Ammar said something to him and he ran off.

Ammar showed the group where they could sleep with a bit more privacy. Around the sides of the courtyard there were small rooms made of corrugated iron sheets, each containing three beds, a clothes hook and a small table, all in blue metal. There were stained mattresses on the beds. There were no sheets or blankets.

All settled down as best they could. After a while the doctor arrived on a bicycle, and cleaned Yussuf's mouth and gave him some painkillers. He advised him to go to a dentist when he got back home.

Later, after washing as best they could in an outside bathroom, they all went to eat in one of the cafés which they had seen on the way in.

Tonio arranged to sit between Yussuf and Rashid. He ordered an omelette with goat's cheese and tomatoes. The two women followed suit. The Egyptian beer was excellent, although not chilled.

Their conversation was limited. All were probably thinking about the day's events.

Tonio noticed that the attitude of the others towards him had changed somewhat. They now treated him with a certain respect. Even Yussuf, who was considerably older than Tonio, showed an open admiration for him, mixed with gratitude.

"Yussuf," Tonio asked, while waiting for his omelette, "where's the airport here at Wadi Halfa?"

"Airport? There isn't an airport here."

"An airstrip then? Is there a disused airstrip, do you know?"

"Not as far as I'm aware. But Ammar might know. Hey Ammar!" he said to the man from the motel who had just come in. "Is there an airstrip at Halfa?"

"Yes, about a kilometre from here in the desert. The British built it after the Second World War. It served as a communications base between Egypt and North Sudan. It's rarely used these days because most of the time it's covered in sand."

They ate in silence, Yussuf very slowly. Seeing the state Yussuf was in, Tonio wondered whether he would finish up with three gold teeth in his mouth too.

After dinner, the two English women and the Kenyan went straight to bed. The three men stayed on for another beer.

"Yussuf, could you take me to this airstrip?" Tonio asked.

"At this time? Why?"

"Because I'm waiting for a plane."

Yussuf nodded, smiling. "A plane eh? My friend, you're no priest, you're the son of a merchant, you know the head of the rebels and now you're waiting for a plane in this arsehole of a place known as Wadi Halfa. You're full of surprises!"

They took Rashid's Land Rover and set out on the only road going east. Quite soon, the road disappeared under a thin film of sand.

After less than ten minutes, when they were thinking of turning back, they found a small isolated hut. Part of a side wall had collapsed. They stopped in front of a closed door, lit by the headlights of the car, on which there was a rusty sign: *W.H. Aerodrome – No Fuel – No Security – No Customs*. Somebody had scrawled underneath: *No Nothing*.

Tonio went to inspect the airstrip. It was bare earth covered with a layer of sand but, in his opinion, an aircraft would be able to land there.

They drove back to the motel. Tonio threw himself on to his bed fully clothed, and fell into a restless sleep almost immediately.

He slept badly, partly because of the cold and partly because he was listening out for the sound of an aircraft engine.

Yussuf woke him at eight.

"I think your plane's arrived. I heard it a little while ago."

Tonio sprang out of bed and followed Yussuf out of the motel, while looking for Ammar to pay the three dollars for the room, but Yussuf shook his head and dragged him to the car where Rashid was already waiting.

They saw the plane from afar, sitting on the airstrip, surrounded by a small group of people. The panels which normally covered the port engine were on the ground, and a man standing on a tool-box was busy working on a labyrinth of wires.

Three or four of the people standing around the plane were soldiers. Tonio and Yussuf approached, and stopped at the rear of the group. He saw Bruno beside the man who was repairing the engine. Instinct told him not to approach any further. After a while, Bruno turned around and saw him, but pretended not to recognise him.

Yussuf began to ask, "Is this the plane which…" He did not finish his question, because Tonio had kicked him hard on the shins.

After a few minutes, Tonio heard Bruno speaking in Italian to the mechanic, who must have been the pilot. "You ought to try and go round these people," he said, pointing to part of the engine with his finger, "and get into the plane from the other side." At first Tonio did not understand what he was saying, but then he realised that Bruno was actually speaking to him!

Bruno continued, "Inside, at the back, on the floor there's a trap-door. Get in there and shut it behind you. In a moment, I'll create a diversion." The pilot, clearly an accomplice, nodded.

Tonio squeezed Yussuf's arm and whispered in his ear. "Goodbye, my friend, I have to go now. I'm sure we'll see each other again, one day. Stay here, and don't move."

Little by little, Tonio edged towards the tail of the plane, as if he were admiring it.

All of a sudden, a muffled explosion came from the open engine, followed immediately by a hissing sound and a spurt of warm engine-oil. Bruno and the pilot hurled themselves backwards, falling into the crowd. There was a moment of confusion.

Tonio reached the open door in two strides and hurled himself into the plane. Without getting up, he crawled forwards on his elbows and knees, so as not to be seen through the windows, reached the trap door and lowered himself through it. He closed the trap door behind him, plunging himself into total darkness.

He stayed there for a good twenty minutes, unable to move and sweating from the heat. He imagined that the interior of a coffin pushed into the flames at a cremation would be very similar to this.

He could only make out vague sounds and muffled voices. Finally, he heard footsteps on the floor of the aircraft followed by a couple of attempts to start one of the engines. At the third try it came to life with a deafening and regular roar. A moment later he heard the other engine start up.

The din, in his confined space, became unbearable. The plane began to move, at first slowly, then ever faster, bouncing off the uneven earth. Tonio clearly sensed the moment when it lifted into the air.

The aircraft had not even levelled off when the trap door was opened, and he was confronted by Bruno's smiling face. "That beard suits you. You look like an Arab. I almost didn't recognise you down there."

Tonio came out of his hole and they embraced.

Bruno introduced him to the pilot, a former officer in the Italian Air Force, who now worked for a charter company based in Panama.

Tonio looked around him. The plane was spacious, with seats for about fifteen people and big enough to stand up in. Out of his hiding place, it was less noisy than he had imagined.

Bruno got Tonio to tell him about his recent adventures in the Nubian Desert.

Then it was his turn. "Unfortunately I've got bad news. The ship carrying Pierre's arsenal has been hijacked just after leaving the Port of Biserta. It happened the night before last. I spoke to Pierre early this morning and he had got the news from one of our men who managed to escape. It seems there were about ten of them, Tunisians – or at least North Africans – and Italians. According to our man they were Sicilian."

"Sicilian!"

"That's what he reckoned. He's from Marseilles and he's often worked with Sicilians on cruise-liners. And there's more: Pierre's convinced that not only was everything organised by Rainer, who must have found out where the ship was being loaded with the arms, but that he was also involved in Nadhir's death. Samira, who's still in hospital, must have said something to the police because they've issued a warrant for Rainer's arrest. Pierre is also certain that the arms will be delivered into the hands of Sicilian and Calabrian criminals, especially after what Rainer blurted out in front of you."

Tonio's brain began racing at high speed. He thought back to what Pierre had told him a few days earlier: about the criminal elements being in overdrive because of the imminent arrival of a large shipment of arms. Then to what Rainer had said to him: arms already sold which he *had* to deliver; the arms in Peppino Cantera's cellar; the hidden 'mafioso'...he was sure that the arms were indeed heading for Sicily or Calabria, but where exactly?

He asked Bruno if there some maps or charts on board. Bruno went to ask the pilot and came back with a bundle of papers under his arm. After looking at a few, they found one of Southern Europe which also showed part of North Africa, including Tunisia.

Tonio spread it out on the small table between the two seats, and began studying it. He found Biserta on the map and saw just how close it was to Sicily. More to the point, he noted something which he had not been aware of before: that the northern most part of Tunisia was further north than the southern most tip of Sicily. At the nearest point they were only one hundred and fifty kilometres from each other! He looked at the west coast of Sicily, reading the names of the ports: Trapani, Marsala, Porto Empedocle…all too large and too well monitored. He stopped all of a sudden. Gela! The ship was heading for Gela. He was certain of it.

His friend at the Banco di Sicilia had told him that Peppino Cantera was rebuilding the Port of Gela. The ideal place to hide a large cargo.

He was convinced that those two sons of whores had become partners. He had to stop them.

"Bruno, where are we heading for?" he asked.

"Cairo. From there we'll catch a commercial flight to Paris."

Tonio continued to look at the maps, reflecting. Then he asked, "Where are we now?"

"Well I don't know exactly, we've been flying for half an hour and we're actually following the Nile as far as Cairo…but why, what's on your mind?"

Tonio remained silent for a few minutes, studying the map, and then he said, "Bruno, I know where the ship's going. I'm sure. Look! Here, to Gela!"

He quickly outlined his reasoning. Bruno at first listened to him a little doubtfully but, little by little as Tonio spoke, he began to understand.

"We have to go to Gela right away. We don't have a moment to lose!" Tonio insisted. "What range does this plane have?"

"I don't understand. You want to go direct to Sicily in this plane? But that's pure madness!"

"Bruno, I know it may seem mad to you. But we have to stop those people, otherwise everything we've done so far will be for nothing. Just think of all those arms in the hands of criminals…we must try and get there before the ship does…we have to alert the Italian Police!"

Bruno remained silent for a moment, then said, "Let's go and talk to Pino up front and see what he thinks."

The two men explained the problem to the pilot, showing him the map. The latter looked at the map silently, chewing a toothpick which he had in his mouth.

Finally, after a few minutes he said, "Um, yes! It's possible." Then he added, "If we were to head off north-west now, we would reach the Libyan coast in…let's see…roughly eighteen hundred kilometres, at three hundred kilometres an hour…the plane's empty…let's say in six, maximum seven, hours. There we're going to have to find somewhere to refuel her again. Then another…let's see, five hours and we're at Catania. Twelve hours in all, perhaps thirteen at the most."

"Let's go for it then," Tonio enthused. "Let's try it! Come on Pino, you'll be well rewarded."

"OK lads, but I have to do a few calculations…I need a few minutes."

Tonio and Bruno went and sat down and waited. Less than ten minutes later, Pino called them. "This is the flight plan: from here straight to Al-Bayada, a little town I know, one hundred and eighty kilometres from Benghazi. It's a domestic airport so they could create problems, seeing that we'll be coming in from Egypt.

"However, we only need to ask them for fuel and we'll say that we're taking a short-cut to Italy because of an emergency. They'll probably not allow us into their terminal, even to relieve ourselves. That's fifteen hundred kilometres. At three hundred kilometres per hour, that's five hours' flying-time. With the fuel we've got, we'll have to use half the reserve tanks. I hope we don't run into any storms or strong head winds.

"From Al-Bayada to Catania, is another twelve hundred kilometres, another four hours flying. If all goes well with take-offs, landings and refuelling, I'd say eleven, maximum twelve hours, in all. We could be at Catania around eight or nine o'clock this evening."

Tonio smiled. Bruno had told him that the ship was on old tub which travelled slowly. With a bit of luck they would reach Gela before the ship. But what made him particularly happy at that moment was the thought that soon he would see Irene again, and he would meet his son Nanni for the very first time.

38

At first, the control tower at Al-Bayada refused them permission to land, but on hearing that there was an emergency, and that they were low on fuel, they were forced to allow it.

They had flown over the Sahara Desert for hours. Overcome by the monotony and soothed by the constant droning of the two Pratt & Whitney engines, Tonio slept most of the way.

As soon as the plane stopped on the runway, they were encircled by troops, and a Libyan official got in, demanded their documents and asked numerous questions. They explained that they were tourists who had been sightseeing in Egypt, but had just learned that Tonio's father was at death's door. The officer seemed to be satisfied with this. They offered him cigarettes and drinks while they were waiting for the fuel tanker.

At one point, Tonio asked whether it was possible to get something to eat and to make a couple of phone calls. At first the officer said that it was impossible, but on seeing the wad of dollars in Bruno's hand, he invited him to follow him.

In the terminal, Tonio called Pierre and told him of the plan to go straight to Gela. Pierre did not agree with them exposing themselves to unnecessary risks, and insisted that the police should be involved. Tonio assured him that as soon as they arrived there he would make contact with the police.

"If your theory is right," Pierre concluded, "I wouldn't be surprised if Rainer was on board the ship."

Tonio called Irene. She was close to tears of joy on hearing Tonio's voice. He explained to her their plan to go to Gela. She said that they could meet up that very night at Nunzia's house. He also begged her to call her friend Marta's husband, the Police Inspector, to whom he could give some very interesting information concerning a shipment of arms destined for the mafia.

"Irene, Bruno and I need some weapons. Could you get one or two for us?"

"Well, for a start, good old Nunziatina has her son's shotgun here at home. Giannino hasn't used it for quite a while. He goes hunting every now and then. I can also go to *babbone*'s house and get his gun…but is it really necessary?"

"I hope not, my love, but with types like Peppino and Rainer, if my hunch is right, it'll be best to be well prepared."

They ate some tuna and tomato rolls, before leaving half an hour later.

Tonio was speechless at the sight of the sun setting over the sea, two hours later. When the yellow became orange which, in it's turn, became a blood red reflection on the occasional cloud on the horizon, he could not help thinking about the blood on Awad's face, and on the large Egyptian's, down there in the desert.

Pino's calculations were spot on. They landed at Fontanarossa Airport at Catania at eight-thirty. By now it was night. The landing formalities were swift and, after taking leave of Pino, they hired a Peugeot 306 from Hertz.

Following Irene's instructions, they took the S417 main road and then, at the turn off for Caltagirone, the S124 as far as the country road up to Mazzarino. They arrived a little before eleven. Nunzia's house was in a little street on a slope, in the shadow of the ancient Arabian castle, with a splendid view of the plain below.

Irene was waiting for them at the door. Tonio took her in his arms and kissed her, without saying a word. When they tore themselves apart, Irene pushed him gently away from her, opening her eyes wide. "Tunuzzo, you've got a beard! I don't know whether I like it…"

Tonio introduced Bruno to her, and they went in. Nunzia was waiting for them inside.

"Welcome Signor Tonio. My house is your house."

It was very clean, with freshly painted walls. The entrance immediately gave onto the sitting room. There were a few pieces of dark wooden furniture, and a large kitchen which also doubled up as a dining room.

A man and a woman with glasses of wine in their hands approached.

Irene introduced them. "Marta, Carlo, this is Tonio. And this is Bruno."

Marta was a woman of about twenty-five with short blonde hair with a fringe. Her eyes were large and grey. She moved towards Tonio and kissed him on the cheek, smiling.

Carlo had a firm handshake. He was shorter than Tonio, but under a blue tracksuit, one could make out his well-toned physique.

After the initial greetings, Irene signalled to Tonio to follow her to the floor above. Nanni was sleeping in one of the two small bedrooms. Tonio approached the bed and stopped to look at the child's black hair, his delicate skin and his very long eyelashes. All of a sudden the accumulated tiredness of the past few days disappeared.

Seeing his son for the first time, he felt the need to be elsewhere, far away with him and the woman he loved.

Downstairs again, he began to recount the events of the last few days, but he was interrupted by Nunzia who, guessing that he and Bruno had not eaten much during their journey, dragged them off to the table in the kitchen where baked macaroni was the order of the day. It was only then that Tonio realised just how hungry he was.

It was almost midnight when he finished telling his story.

He turned to Carlo. "I'd like to go to Gela now, tonight, to see whether my theory's correct. According to Bruno's calculations, if they haven't been delayed, the ship should arrive in the next few hours. In fact, it could even be there already. How far is Gela?"

"Not very far," Carlo replied, "but what will you do if the ship has already docked?"

"I don't have a precise plan, but with your help and your men, we could lie in wait for them, and you could arrest Rainer and Peppino for illegal arms trafficking."

"Um, it's not that simple. It's a major operation which has to be well organised. I'll have to alert my superiors in Palermo…the three or four men which I have at my disposal here at Mazzarino aren't enough. And I'll need a search warrant.

"Before coming here, I went to look at the port at Gela. The only place where a ship could tie up and unload goods easily, is near two new warehouses which are almost completed. They've been built near a temporary wooden jetty, about thirty metres in length. The area is completely fenced off and there's a watchman there. I need time."

"I know it'll take you some time," Tonio said. "But there's nothing to stop Bruno and me from going to look at the place. If the ship has arrived, we will let you know straight away by calling you on your phone there." Tonio pointed to the mobile which Carlo had in his hand.

"OK." Carlo said. "If you want to go, then do so. But I beg you, don't *do* anything. Don't take any initiative on your own. No rushes of blood to the head. You must wait for me to arrive with my men. I'll need at least a couple of hours to organise everything. If all goes well, I should be there before dawn. This is my mobile number. There's a petrol station less than a kilometre from the port on the road towards Ragusa which has a public phone from where you can call me. Get some change. Call me from there." He gave his wife a hurried kiss, and left.

"Tonio, I'll come with you," Irene said. "I know the road. I know exactly where the shipyard is. Peppino took me there once. It's dark, and it's difficult to find."

"Well, I don't know…I think it would be better if you stayed at home…with Nunzia and Nanni…"

"No, please let me come. Marta can stay with them. I'm coming!"

Tonio looked at her. She was even more beautiful than he remembered. She had lost weight. Her long hair was gathered up in a neat ponytail. Tonio could not take his eyes off her lips, which did not have any trace of lipstick on them.

"Here," she said. "This is Giannino's shotgun with a box of cartridges, and this is *babbone*'s Beretta 7.65. Do you know how to use it?" Without waiting for a reply she continued, "It's really easy, look. This is the safety catch and the ammo clip goes in here. It has twelve rounds. Here's a spare clip. Let's go."

It took them over half an hour to travel along the S190 which led to the coast.

During the journey, after a few minutes' silence, Irene turned to Tonio, "Oreste called me today. It seems that your friend Pierre has made another donation to Ciao Africa. A much bigger sum than before. And he's promised to send large amounts of money regularly. It seems that he and Oreste will meet up in Rome soon. It's fantastic."

"It certainly is!" Tonio said, nodding slowly with a smile on his lips, "the Merchant really has repented!"

They turned onto the S115, the road which runs along the whole length of southern Sicily, heading for Gela. Less than ten minutes later, they saw the petrol station mentioned by Carlo. They drove another six or seven hundred metres and slowed down. There was very little traffic about.

"There's the shipyard and the two warehouses! They're below us," Irene said.

At that point, the road was about thirty metres above sea level. Tonio reversed and turned the car round. The three of them got out of the car and approached the low wall, which skirted the road. The sound of waves breaking on distant rocks could be heard clearly.

The ship was there!

It was possible to make out a few lights on the deck. On the jetty a few men were walking to and fro.

On their right, they could make out the outline of two large warehouses against the dim lights of the shipyard. In front of the warehouses, the light was brighter. Lorries could be heard in the distance. Tonio could also make out the metal fence, surmounted by barbed wire, which surrounded the whole area of the shipyard. The back of the warehouses, near the road, was in total darkness. The whole complex had a sinister and threatening appearance. 'It seems like a prison', Tonio thought.

"I'll go and take a closer look," he said, to the other two, "you stay here."

"In your dreams," Bruno replied. "Do you want to deprive me of some fun now that things are hotting up? I'm coming with you."

"OK. Irene, you stay here. When Carlo arrives, tell him that we're down there taking stock of the situation. If something should happen, go and call him from the petrol station."

Fifty metres from where they had stopped, a road leading to the shipyard sloped down to the warehouses. The metal fence started from that point.

Tonio and Bruno walked in that direction. The road was blocked off by a barrier, at least three metres high, which had barbed wire on top of it – impossible to enter there.

The two men decided to turn back and climb over the low wall skirting the road, and to slip down the earthy slope which led to the rocks by the sea.

Ten minutes later, they were crouching outside the fenced area, a few metres from the shore. Bruno, with the shotgun in his hand, looked like a soldier in the trenches ready to attack.

At that point the fenced off area, which followed the curve of the shoreline, finished where the wooden jetty began.

From their position Tonio and Bruno had a good view of the large area in front of the warehouses. They were two large buildings about fifteen metres wide and at least double that in length. The shutter door of the furthest warehouse was open, and at that moment, a large forklift truck appeared and moved off in the direction of the ship. Before going onto the jetty, it slowed down to let an identical one pass the other way – it was loaded with an incredible number of cases – and this second one disappeared into the warehouse.

The nearer building seemed to be incomplete. They could see some scaffolding at the sides and a large opening at the top, above the main door, was protected by vertical translucent plastic strips hanging from its upper edge, covering the opening.

Tonio and Bruno were about ten metres from the jetty. They saw two men walk down the ship's gangway and stroll towards the warehouses.

Rainer!

Tonio thought that the other must be Peppino Cantera. They were speaking in loud voices and seemed to be excited about something, but Tonio could not hear what they were saying, although he could guess.

The two men stopped underneath the large floodlight which lit the far warehouse, where the fork-lifts had gone in and out. Tonio observed them; Rainer was the taller and the light reflected off his fair hair. Peppino was quite stocky, his black hair was beginning to recede and he had a prominent paunch. He seemed to be about fifty, but Tonio knew that he was actually a lot younger.

They heard a clang from the fence, fifteen metres from them. Tonio and Bruno fell to the ground hidden by some low shrubs. Raising his head a few centimetres, Tonio noticed two men coming out of a metal gate: part of the metal fencing which he had not noticed before. One of the men had a shotgun over his shoulder. They passed less than three metres from them, in silence. They went off along the shore, examining the narrow beach with a torch.

Tonio noticed that they had left the gate half open. With a nod of his head he indicated to Bruno that he was going in. Bruno nodded that he was ready too.

They moved slowly, keeping their heads down. They reached the gate and opened it gently, without making any noise.

They entered and crouched down near the corner of the warehouse.

Looking up towards the road, Tonio thought he could make out Irene's head watching him.

Tonio peeped round the corner to see what was happening in the area in front of the warehouses. He saw Rainer and Peppino approaching. He flattened himself against the wall.

Now he could hear what the two men were talking about.

"...no sweat," Rainer was saying, "the only problems we've had have been caused by my father at the beginning, and this Tonio bloke that I've told you about. I hope they're giving him a good going over in Sudan, where I left him the other day. Once again, I repeat, I've looked after the merchandise during the journey. At this rate the unloading should be finished in a few hours, and the other half I can transfer without any problem tomorrow. The false manifest about the cargo of printed circuit boards you've already got. See? All as smooth as clockwork."

'Apart from the odd corpse here and there, you son of a whore', Tonio thought.

"Yes," Peppino replied, "you've kept your word. The boys in Palermo and the Calabrians will come from tomorrow to fetch the stuff they've bought."

"Oh yes, the money, don't forget, transfer it through the BNI as stated on the documents, so I can screw Dottor Antonio Brignani, the prick, twice."

There was a moment of silence, then Tonio heard Peppino's voice saying, "Antonio Brignani…Antonio Brignani…I know that name…who is he?"

"He's the manager of the BNI bank in Paris."

"Paris! That's where I've heard it! Antonio Brignani…"

"Do you know him?" Rainer asked.

"I don't, but that whore of a wife of mine…yes. They knew each other a few weeks before our wedding…and…and…"

'…and you're a cuckold', Tonio thought, with a degree of satisfaction he had seldom experienced in his life.

"Hey, what are you doing there, who are you?" a voice shouted behind them, outside the metal barrier.

They had been discovered. The men had returned from their patrol, and had spotted them.

39

They turned round instantly. In one quick movement Bruno flattened himself and levelled his gun in front of him. Peppino's man, the one with the shotgun, fired and peppered the ground a few centimetres from Bruno's head.

Bruno's shot, fired a split second later, also peppered its target, but this time on the man's face, hurling him backwards. The other man had his gun out, and was about to shoot, but Bruno's second shot hit him between the thigh and groin, and he fell backwards onto the ground. Tonio, stunned, had not even thought of taking his gun out of his belt. The wounded man began to shout, "Aahh!! Mother of Mercy, Mother of Mercy, you son of a bitch. Aahh, sweet Jesus, sweet Jesus, what am I to do now, aaahhh!" He was like a pig being led to slaughter.

Bruno had got up on his feet and was pulling Tonio towards a side door in the warehouse a few metres away. Tonio signalled to him that they could escape through the metal gate and return to the car.

"No," Bruno whispered, "we'd be sitting ducks climbing up towards the road!"

They went into the warehouse and crouched against the wall, near the rolling shutter doors. The light which was filtering through from outside was very faint.

Tonio heard movement behind a wooden wall, followed by Rainer's voice whispering close by, "Police?" He could only be a few centimetres away from Tonio, separated only by the thickness of a wooden panel.

"I don't think so," Peppino replied.

"Well then? Who is it?"

"I don't know, but I don't think it's the police. If it was them, they'd have surrounded the place and would have ordered us out by now. It's someone else wanting to stick their nose into our business. I don't like it at all. I think we should move the ship away. We can complete the unloading here later, or somewhere else. Any moment now the police really might come."

"Perhaps you're right. Go and call Tore and the others. Look how those shits are running away. Get them to come here and help us sort this problem out. Then go to the ship, so that we can move her. Ahmed's still on board."

"I wouldn't do that if I were you, Rainer!" Tonio said in a firm and clear voice.

There was a moment's silence, then Rainer's voice could be heard. "Tonio? But what the fuck are you doing here…how the fuck did you manage to…you son of a whore…"

Bruno jumped on Tonio, dragging him to the ground at the same time as a series of shots exploded through the wall, leaving splintered holes in the wood.

Tonio fired a shot back, but it was too high, near the ceiling.

"Look, there," Bruno said getting up again, "another door, there at the end, let's get out! Run! I'll cover you!"

Tonio ran towards the opening which was barely visible in the darkness. He had almost reached it when he heard some footsteps getting closer outside. Beside the door, a wooden stairway led up to another floor in the warehouse. Tonio climbed the first few steps and flattened himself against the wall, with his gun pointing towards the door, a couple of metres from him.

He turned his head to see where Bruno had got to. He was following, while watching the door they had come in by carefully. As Bruno turned his head to see where Tonio was, Peppino burst into the warehouse firing a volley of shots.

Tonio saw Bruno's body shake from the impact of the bullets. He had been hit several times and had fallen heavily to the floor without uttering a word.

Tonio screamed and fired in Peppino's general direction without even taking aim. Peppino, with his head bowed low on his shoulders, rushed back out of the warehouse.

The sound of the shots, amplified in that large empty space, reverberated in Tonio's head, creating a physical pain in his ears.

The sound of footsteps outside the nearby door had ceased.

'Shit, I'm trapped', Tonio thought. This notion paralysed him. Fear – the same fear which he had experienced many times during the previous days – came flooding back to him with such intensity, that he was forced to slide slowly down the wall to a sitting position. He was aware that he was shaking.

He heard a slight sound coming from the furthest door.

Almost without thinking, he fired a shot in that direction. The noise stopped.

He could half make out Bruno's body, motionless on the floor. The same rage, that liberating rage which always overcame his fear, overwhelmed him again, welling up from the depth of his being.

He got up slowly and began to climb the stairs. He had almost reached the top when he heard Rainer's voice.

"Tonio, can you hear me? Put that gun down! I think our friend Bruno's dead. You're on your own. Put the gun down!"

"Go to hell, Rainer! You and your crooked friends should put *your* arms down. The police will be here any minute!"

"Don't talk bollocks Tonio! You know very well that you're alone now. You're on your own. Put that gun down, let's talk."

Tonio had reached the top of the stairs. Only a feeble light came from outside through the plastic strips, which were hanging in the large opening at the front of the upper storey.

He looked around him. It was a terrible mess, typical of a building site: benches, oil-drums, scaffolding and tools were spread everywhere.

At that very moment, the light outside was switched off. Now the darkness was total.

Tonio remained on his feet, in the middle of the floor, motionless. His fear came back in waves.

Then a small light came on in the ceiling of the warehouse. Its solitary bulb cast a ghostly light throughout the whole area.

Rainer's voice could be heard again. "Tonio, listen to me! I think we've still got time to sort things out. There's no need to shoot. Can you hear me? We can talk!"

At last Tonio's brain started to work again. He thought that he needed to gain time until Carlo and his men arrived.

"What do you have to say to me, Rainer? You've really done it now. You've killed people…I haven't anything to say to someone like you."

"Of course we've got things to say to each other, Tonio. I want to explain how we can work things out. Can I come up? Just me. May I come up?"

Tonio reflected. He looked at his watch. Only an hour had gone by since he had arrived there with Bruno. He needed to stall for more time.

"All right then, come up," he said, "but first, send the shit-heads who are with you away." He hoped to be able to pass himself off as a tough guy and give the impression that he was self-confident. "If I see even one solitary head appear at the top of the stairs, apart from yours, I'll begin shooting, and at you first. Have you got that? I'll shoot at you first, have you understood me fully?"

"Loud and clear." Then, to others, "OK lads, get out of here now and go to the ship."

Meanwhile Tonio continued to look around him. He had to find a safe spot. He didn't trust that slime-ball. Not far from the opening covered in the plastic strips, he saw three or four large oil-drums. He quickly went and crouched behind them. The floor at that point was covered in large metal plates, evidently to make it easier to move the oil-drums and other things to and from the opening.

"Tonio, I'm coming up, I'm alone. And I'm not armed, OK?"

"OK, come up, slowly."

First of all, Rainer's head appeared. Tonio could see it through a very narrow gap between two oil-drums. Then Rainer climbed up the last few steps. He was looking around for Tonio. He began to approach.

"Where are you?"

Tonio did not reply.

"Where are you, Tonio? Look, I'm unarmed!" Rainer said, spreading out his hands.

"Stop there, don't move. What have you got to say to me?"

Rainer's head turned towards the oil-drums. "I think we can come to some agreement you and me," he said. "You know better than me there's a hell of a lot of money at stake..."

"So what should I do? What are you suggesting? That I become a partner?"

"And why not? Pierre, who's lost the plot now, is finished. After this operation his reputation as the Merchant will have been well and truly fucked. Now it's my business. You and I can get together and make a mint of money."

As he said this he took a couple of steps nearer the drums.

Tonio, still with his gun in his hand, watched him from his hiding place.

"I told you to stop there, Rainer! Haven't you got it into your head yet, that I don't give a damn about the money? I don't want anything to do with someone like you. I saw you when you killed Awad. You were completely unmoved by it. And Nadhir?

You've eliminated Nadhir too?" It was an assertion rather than a question.

"He was another dead weight, Tonio. Times have changed. There's no room for loyalty, honour and all those crap ideals any more."

"That's where you're wrong, Rainer. I believe in those crap ideals." As he said this he rose to his feet, showing himself to Rainer and pointing the gun at him. "I want to see you marched off to prison for the rest of your natural days. Down below, there's Bruno's body: the Bruno who saved my life at least twice this evening. He won't be able to do that a third time. Do you think I can remain indifferent to all this and let you and your delinquent friends get off totally scot-free?"

"Tonio...Tonio," Rainer interrupted him, raising his eyes to the ceiling as if he were speaking to someone who was stubborn and being deliberately obtuse.

With a lightning movement, Rainer took his right arm from behind his back, pulled out a gun and began firing in Tonio's direction. The latter clearly heard bullets hitting the oil-drums. He fell to his knees after firing a shot in his turn.

He remained in that position for a few moments. Then he looked through the narrow gap between the drums. Rainer was no longer to be seen. Tonio wondered whether he had hit him.

Then he heard a strange gurgling sound. He looked at the floor in front of the drums and saw a black stain, slowly getting larger, on the metal plates as it lazily oozed towards the window at the front of the warehouse. Oil!

He had to find out where Rainer was, to see if he had hit him.

"As if we didn't need any proof, Rainer, you're the filthy son of a whore!"

His only reply was that the latter began firing again at the drums, with the result that even more oil leaked from them.

Tonio, however, was gripped by fear. He raised the gun above the edge of the drum and fired a couple of shots at where he thought Rainer was. He heard Rainer's steps approaching the stairway, running. Tonio fired another shot in that direction. The bullet hit one of the metal columns in the warehouse with a spark, a few centimetres from Rainer's face. Rainer changed direction and turned back towards Tonio, shooting like a madman. Tonio saw him through the narrow gap, crouching forward and running with his gun spitting fire towards the drums.

Then the unexpected happened.

Rainer reached the metal plate, which was covered with oil, and began slipping out of control. He was like someone wearing a pair of ice skates for the first time, pawing the air and flailing their arms and legs in a desperate attempt to find some form of support. He continued sliding towards the window opening.

It happened in a split second.

As he fell backwards towards the opening, the plastic strips opened like the curtains in a theatre before a performance. In a fraction of a second, Rainer was swallowed up into the night.

He did not make any sound, but Tonio clearly heard the thud of the body landing on the cement floor below.

He got up slowly. He approached the opening, taking care where he put his feet, and lifted up one of the plastic strips.

In the faint light coming from the other warehouse, Tonio saw Rainer lying on his side, his legs separated as if he were walking. Blood, which appeared black in that light, was flowing from under his head.

40

Tonio ran down the stairs with his heart beating wildly.

On arriving at the ground floor, he glanced quickly out of the door. There was no one in sight. He went up to Bruno's body, which was lying face upwards in the middle of the warehouse and he closed the eyes with his fingers. His friend was still clutching the shotgun in his hands. Tonio walked down the full length of the warehouse and, having checked and made certain that there was no one outside waiting for him, he crossed the large apron in front of the warehouse, towards Rainer's body. The silence was broken only by the sound of waves breaking rhythmically on the shoreline a short distance away.

He knelt down next to Rainer, put down his gun, and tried to turn him over. As his head moved, Tonio thought he detected a movement in his mouth. He placed two fingers on Rainer's neck, but there was no pulse. Rainer was dead.

He was about to get up when he sensed a movement behind him. He hardly had time to turn round before a foot kicked hit him violently on his shoulder, making him roll over onto Rainer's body and away from his gun.

Peppino was standing over him, the gun in his hand aimed at his head. "And so, you ugly turd, you've come to break our balls here in Sicily too, eh?"

Tonio did not reply. He looked for a way out. From the corner of his eye he could see his gun, on the ground near Peppino's feet. The latter saw his glance and kicked the weapon away. It hit the warehouse door with an unpleasant metallic noise.

"Just look at the strange ironies of life," Peppino went on. "A couple of years ago I wanted to come to Paris to screw you. But then I thought it wouldn't be worth it, since the damage had already been done. Destiny's incredible at times. And lo and behold, here you are, served up to me on a silver platter…incredible."

Tonio looked at him. He was fairly tall and was wearing a crumpled dark striped suit without a tie. His eyes were small and close set. What struck Tonio most about him was the shape of his nose: it was large and hooked. It seemed like the beak of a predatory bird.

"You fucked my girl before I married her. And you're that stupid that you even knocked her up too. Real shit stuff, eh! Then, by an incredible coincidence, you turn up here and try to screw up the biggest deal of my life. I still can't take it in…"

Peppino remained silent for a moment, looking at Tonio. He seemed to be thinking.

"Wait a minute," he continued, " unless…but of course! The whore has kept in touch with you! Only she could have tipped you off about this place! Who else but her. I know she's keen on you. The father of the little bastard…of course, everything fits now!"

"Leave Irene out of it. Keep her out of this mess. Irene hasn't got anything to do with this," Tonio said in a shaky voice.

"Don't you realise just how pathetic you are?" the other began again. "Do you take me for a complete idiot?"

Tonio remained silent for a few moments. Then Peppino began speaking again with a mocking smile on his lips. "Now I'm going to give myself one of the greatest pleasures of my life, telling you a couple of things before planting a bullet in your head; if only to make your stay in hell that bit more pleasant when you get there.

"I fuck that whore how and when I want. The more she resists the more pleasure I get by taking her by force, do you understand? She's my personal whore. It's useless for her to try and get away, because sooner or later, I'll find her again wherever she is. And once the old boy snuffs it, all her family's inheritance will come to me. That's why I married her, the bitch.

"Many years ago my father didn't manage to get rid of old Consalvo; instead her idiot mother got killed. I, on the other hand, have managed things without lifting a finger, do you understand? I'll get the money and I'll keep a beautiful whore at home, free, gratis, for nothing! Fantastic! What do you say to that?"

Peppino became silent and moved one step towards Tonio, pointing the gun at his head. "Now, you piece of shit, go to hell!"

Tonio closed his eyes.

At that very moment, a deafening shot rang out. Tonio opened his eyes in time to see holes punched in Peppino's stomach, and his body lurching backwards. His eyes followed his fall as if he were watching it in slow-motion.

Stupefied, he turned his head towards the corner of the warehouse and saw Irene with the shotgun still at her shoulder.

Later, as the light of dawn illuminated a perfectly calm sea, a series of snapshots became engraved in Tonio's mind for ever: Irene approaching him after letting the shotgun fall; Peppino dying with the word "whore..." on his lips; the sirens of the police cars; Carlo running up to help with his gun in his hand; the shouts of men trying to escape; the actions of the police who were catching them; the long embrace from Irene; and, much later, his own uncontrollable tears on seeing Bruno's body, covered in a plastic sheet, being taken away as the sun shone high in the sky.

The next day, after leaving the offices of Police Headquarters at Caltanisetta, where the magistrate had taken their statements in Carlo's presence, they went to Irene's house. There, Tonio was introduced to Calogero Consalvo, an old gentleman sitting in a large brown leather armchair. On the floor there were numerous newspapers covering the shoot-out at Gela on their front pages.

The deaths of Rainer and Peppino were reported as a settling of old scores between the mafia and arms traffickers. Bruno's death was explained as being accidental. His body would be repatriated to France the very next day. Tonio was not even mentioned. Carlo had done a good job in covering everything up.

The success of the operation which had led to the impounding of a ship full of arms, which would otherwise have fallen into the hands of criminals, was entirely attributed to Inspector Carlo Ranieri. To put even more icing on the cake, he had also arrested, in don Peppino Cantera's house, a dangerous mafia boss who had been on the run for years.

"Irene," the old man said to his daughter at one point. "I want to tell you something which I've been meaning to say for a long time."

Tonio made to move away discreetly, but don Calogero's voice stopped him.

"Please stay Dottor Brignani. I'd be pleased if you hear what I've got to say to my daughter, not least because I've come to realise that there's more than just a simple friendship between the two of you…Irene I want to ask you for your forgiveness…"

"Forgiveness? For what?" Irene replied.

"For the life of hell you've had to put up with because of me. It was me who persuaded you to marry that…that…"

"Don't think about it any more, *babbone*…who could ever have imagined…I don't have to forgive you for anything at all…we were…how shall I put it, taken in, that's it. Forget all about it." They embraced each other tenderly. "Think about getting better from now on."

"And what will you do now, Dottor Brignani, will you go back to Paris?"

"Not straight away, don Calogero. I'd like to stay around here for a few days. I'm sure Irene will need a hand at the moment. I'd also like to get to know Nanni better…and also this beautiful island."

In the car, returning to Mazzarino, Tonio took her by the hand. "You saved my life!" he said simply.

She was looking at the road as it climbed up to Nunzia's house. "You saved mine too!" she said.

They stopped outside the house. Nanni, held by Nunzia, came towards them.

Seeing them approaching, Irene began speaking once more without turning round. "You've been a good banker. You're an absolute disaster as an arms dealer. I'm wondering what you'd be like as a winegrower." Then she turned towards Tonio. "Would you like it?"